# ...it's never too late to fall in love

**an anthology of
romantic short stories**

**Third Age Press**

ISBN 978-1-898576-36-5
First edition

Third Age Press Ltd, 2011
Third Age Press, 6 Parkside Gardens
London SW19 5EY
Managing Editor Dianne Norton

The moral right of the authors has been asserted.

Copyright remains in the hands o the individual authors.

All rights reserved. This book is sold subject to the condition that it shall not, by way of trade or otherwise, be lent, re-sold, hired out or otherwise circulated without the publisher's prior consent in any form of binding or cover other than that in which it is published and without a similar condition including this condition being imposed on the subsequent purchase.

*It's Never Too Late to Fall in Love*
(Sandy Wilson, from *The Boyfriend*)
Cover illustration by Mig
Cover photo by Adam Norton
Cover & layout design by Dianne Norton
Printed and bound in Great Britain by IntypeLibra

*It's never too late to have a fling . . .
for autumn is just as nice as spring . . .*

*. . . it's never too late to fall in love*

an anthology of
romantic short stories

. . . . *Boop-a-Doop Boop-a-Doop Boop-a-Doop*
(Sandy Wilson, *The Boyfriend*)

### The following stories were also short listed for consideration by the final judging panel

| | |
|---|---|
| Howard Cooley | *Caroline and the Widower* |
| John Dimiter-Murray | *No Regrets* |
| Micky Dugan | *Do you smile to tempt a lover Mona Lisa* |
| Margorie Fisher | *A Secret Affair* |
| Jennie Fursland | *Dear Alice* |
| Wendy Gayler | *Never Never Land* |
| Chris Hazelgrove | *Do it Yourself* |
| Barbara Hendrick | *Best of Foes* |
| Anthea Holland | *Deliberation* |
| Cheryl Jeffrey | *In Sunshine and in Shade* |
| Carolina Kenealy | *No Man Land* |
| John Margeryson Lord | *Dear, Oh Dear* |
| Sarah Lovett | *The Lady and the Knight* |
| Denis Marsden | *There's Always Brian* |
| Helen J Park | *Alexander's Choice* |
| Malcolm Peake | *Losing Harriet* |
| Judith Rhodes | *Best Man* |
| Valerie Sabir-Ali | *The Promise* |
| Julie Saunders | *Easy as ABC* |
| Ann Smith | *The Flood* |
| Gordon Thynne | *The Autocrat of the Dinner Table* |
| Jane Walker | *Mysterious Ways* |
| Jane Wells | *Grand Circles and Gowns* |
| Beryl Wilkins | *4:20 from Victoria* |
| Deriel Williams | *A Different Time Frame* |

# Contents

| | | |
|---|---|---|
| Introduction | | 6 |
| *Life Class* | Peter Johnson | 9 |
| *A Cat About the House* | Norma Murray | 15 |
| *Copperplate* | Sue Wilson | 35 |
| *Life Without Grace* | Ed Lane | 44 |
| *Spot On* | Jane Walker | 69 |
| *Dancing Round The Med* | Denise West | 76 |
| *Lightning Never Strikes Twice* | Paul Chiswick | 80 |
| *The Last Verse* | Margaret Foggo | 102 |
| *An Estate of the Heart* | Brenda Jackson | 112 |
| *Collectability* | Denis Marsden | 137 |
| *Predictive Text* | Heather Shaw | 139 |
| *The Secret Life of Madeline Greatorex* | Patricia Stoner | 159 |
| *How Little Time* | Cedric Parcell | 166 |
| *A Good Sense of Humour* | Margaret Kitchen | 183 |
| *Stranger Love* | Carol Homer | 193 |
| *Rendezvous* | Malcolm Peake | 215 |
| *In Sickness and In Health* | Gwen Anderson | 221 |
| *Second Time Around* | Gillian Lazar | 224 |
| *Stardust* | Jean Dorricott | 239 |
| *Ménage à Troisième Age* | Stephanie Richards | 248 |
| Acknowledgements | | 256 |
| The Judges | | 256 |
| The Authors on The Authors | | 258 |
| More About Third Age Press | | 262 |

# Introduction: *The Eyes Have It*

Reading 170 stories by thirdagers about thirdagers gives one a fascinating insight into what appeals, in romantic terms, to the older person. So, ladies and gentlemen, for those of you on the look-out for a bit of excitement or a satisfying relationship, pay attention to what your eyes are saying about you. Colour matters to some – blue seems to be the most attractive – but it's more, it appears, what the eyes reveal about the person within that's important. And that, perhaps, is the clue. In further evidence, I submit the perception that fewer of the women in the stories were given a detailed physical description; more of the men were and it was interesting that apart from a portly vicar who'd been prescribed walking for his health, and a few who were a bit scruffy, most of the men in the stories seemed to be 'fit' in every sense of the word. Oh, and an appealing voice . . . maybe with a regional accent . . . also helps (at least if you're a man!).

The competition rules didn't set out to define romance anymore than they defined 'thirdage'. As a founder of the U3A in the UK, I firmly agree that 'thirdage' should never have a chronological connotation. I apologise if any readers feel cheated by the inclusion in these stories of a few characters who, while being 'mature', are still in 'fulltime gainful employment' – but their ages are germane to their stories.

So, we have romance past, present and, in many cases, future. While not being a 'How To' book, I do hope the stories will encourage people to follow a stray balloon or take that step that may lead them to new adventures. Quite a few of the stories are, not surprisingly, about beginnings, and perhaps readers will enjoy imagining how these fledgling relationships blossom into romance. They do purvey, with the heartfelt emotional truth that I think comes from older people writing about older people, that there is something precious about a new beginning at our time of life – something so vulnerable that you want to cherish it, nurture it, savour it – that the headlong dash of youth into romance may not appreciate.

While the thread of romance knitted every story together, it was the context chosen by the authors that made each one unique and interesting and worthy of publication.

If you needed proof that learning in later life is beneficial, the most popular plot line centred on a U3A (although the competition was not restricted to U3A members) or other types of educational or leisure activity. Running a very close second was the reunion – often accidental – with a long lost love or the kindling of an old flame, usually after the death of one of their spouses. Next came travel – not surprisingly – including cruises on which the travellers were all definitely NOT looking for romance; strange and accidental encounters (including those befalling long established couples – the unusual circumstances causing them to see their relationship in a new light) and then dating agencies or lonely hearts columns or websites.

It probably says something about my own misconceptions that I was taken by surprise that so many (46) of the stories submitted were written by men but, I think, only in a few cases does that seem obvious.

It was pleasing that a number of stories centred on the romance in existing relationships, sometimes in unusual situations; others on finding love in a care home and even death got a look in from time to time.

In fact there was more death in the stories than sex and what sex there was was usually just hinted at. Did the labelling of the competition as one for 'romantic' short stories inhibit

*Introduction*

people from including the more physical elements of relationships? Or was it the thought of fellow U3A members reading the steamier fruits of your imagination that held you back? Only one story centred on same-sex couples.

Judging was difficult and, of course, reflected personal taste as the judges readily admit:

*Those I gave the highest marks used humour, wit, plots not totally related to age or with added information (like the 'troubles' in Ireland, storms in the Scilly Isles, art and Shakespeare), but that's what I mean by personal taste.*

*The quality of writing was high, and as I sat at my kitchen table reading about a slice of their lives, all of the characters came alive. The stories that won me over had believable plot lines, good dialogue, interesting three dimensional characters and the narrative held my attention. But reading all of them was a pleasure.*

*I approached the project in the spirit of someone with a fairly open mind leafing through a magazine (I know short stories appear in books and anthologies, but never mind) and coming across a piece of fiction, more or less unsought among other articles and features. I read each story just once and then marked it straight from the heart: no intellect, just feelings. Stories of this kind are bound to have some inbuilt predictability but any twist has to be plausible, so it's a narrow path. It's just a matter of how that path is trodden.*

If there was one emotion that occurred in a number of stories it was the feeling that 'this' is ridiculous 'at my age' – but I like to think that that feeling arose more from surprise than embarrassment – and then everyone of them went on to prove that 'it' was anything but ridiculous.

*Dianne Norton, Editor*

# Life Class

Peter Johnson

'Hello, Tony, what d'you reckon today – male or female?' Max greets me at the foot of the stairs leading to the studio for our weekly life drawing classes. Lugging our equipment we hobble upwards; both of us are down for knee replacements. Others come clattering up behind and we make room for them. Places round the model are at a premium; the class is popular and it's first come first served.

My wife persuaded me to go. 'You're lazy. You know you like drawing, you're quite good at it' (flattery). 'And it'll get you out of the house' (probably the real reason).

'*"Disegnia Antonio, disegnia Antonio, disegnia e non perder tempo"*,' Max declaims with a smile as we reach the door.

'Come again?' I query.

'Draw Antonio, draw Antonio, draw and do not waste time'. Michelangelo to one of his assistants, I read it last week. Good advice for you and me.'

A superb draughtsman, Max is a retired lecturer from a well-known art college; he comes to keep his hand in. I'm a one-time editor of art books (if you can't do, publish others instead). He's for the traditional, anatomical approach. 'Notice how the deltoid rolls over the collarbone and attaches itself to the scapula, and you'll understand how the arm's held up.' He's lent me an artist's anatomy book and I try to follow what it says.

We're late; the others are already drawing away. 'See you in the coffee break, Tony,' Max mutters, as we separate to find ourselves places between the thicket of easels.

Ready at last I look beyond my blank sheet of paper to study the naked human body we have all come to draw from for the next three hours.

She – for our model this week is female – has her back to me. She stands, legs slightly apart, the right foot pointing outward, the left carrying the weight up through the tilted pelvis through the slight curvature of the spine to the nape of the neck. ('Notice how the deltoid . . . '). I also notice the twin dimples on either side of her sacrum, just above a pale bikini demarcation cutting across the subcutaneous fat that sheathes her gluteii maximii; that she's quite young, perhaps in her twenties – and if the front view matches the back . . . *Disegnia Antonio* . . . I pick up my crayon and start attempting to delineate what I see in front of me.

'Time's up; thanks, Sharon,' says our tutor half an hour later. The model relaxes, shakes out her arms and shoulders and walks away to put on her dressing gown. I look at my drawing. Not enough time to finish, nevertheless I'm reasonably pleased with it; I've got the weight distributed down that left leg, even though the head's a bit small. The model is chatting to the tutor; he's demonstrating what the next pose is to be. By the time I've replaced my drawing with a fresh sheet of paper and cleaned my bifocals, she has disrobed and is composing herself on a chair, sideways on to me, her head in profile. 'This one's until coffee break.'

*It's Never Too Late to Fall in Love*

I wish I could draw like Max, perceive like him; when I look at his work it's so consummately observed ('when the knee drops, the pelvis tilts, and that 's counterbalanced in the shoulder angle'). Draw the chair first, I remind myself, put her on it afterwards. The model's face is expressionless. As I sketch away, her eyelid droops. And why not? If I had to sit motionless in front of a crowd of scribbling, middle-aged and elderly people I'd blank off myself. (*Disegnia Antonio*).

'Five minutes left,' intones our tutor. I've scarcely finished the chair when, 'Time's up, thanks Sharon. Coffee break, folks.'

Instead of going down to the canteen I lumber over to where Max is still seated.

'May I look?' He shows me, a deft sketch in sanguine crayon on rough paper, unfinished but yet complete, the lines and shades flow across his page; it is alive with eloquent movement.

'Almost Michelangelesque,' I compliment him.

Max grunts. 'Hardly. But I try to keep him in mind, just keep on at it, like he said. Knew what it was all about, old M.'

The others come filing in from their coffee break. I go back to my place, clip on a fresh sheet to my drawing board.

'This one's until the end of the session,' says our tutor, pulling out a large foam mattress and some cushions: 'Sharon, I want you to lie down and make yourself comfortable.' She takes off her gown and, almost catlike, arranges her body on them. For the first time I see what the front of her is like. There seems to be a smudge on her lower body. I lower my head the better to see through my bifocals. And what I see is a butterfly, a blue, tattooed butterfly midway between the swelling of her right iliac crest and the hirsute stripe on her mons veneris. I start to draw but my mind is confused. What

*Life Class*                                                                    11

was the tattooist thinking, feeling, when he applied his cyan needle to that tender young flesh? (*Disegnia Antonio!*). As I outline her head I catch her eyes . . .

And with that glance I'm transported, I am on a country lane, and in another time.

I am with a girl. I do not have to describe how, when, or why I was with her, these things transpire. We're walking along a chalk track beside a huge stand of beeches, miles from anywhere, anybody, we have been walking now for over two hours, it is high summer. Her hand is in mine. I do not at this moment know what this girl is thinking, feeling: I am so caught up with my own, they are such that I am bursting with them. I cannot, but I must. They are natural.

She lays her head on my shoulder, looks up at me. And what is natural becomes urgent, immediate.

I lead her off the track into a little thicket, its centre furnished with springy grass and a few fallen dried beech leaves. A release of pigeons clattering away above us tells me we are alone. Now we can only see ourselves; our surroundings do not matter.

I kiss her and we tumble down. 'You're going to seduce me aren't you.' – her vibrant note of affirmation in my ear.

. . . *e non perder tempo.*

We are lying on our backs side by side, our noses just touching. I turn my head, open my eyes and squint up through the lemon haze. Then. And then . . . More delicately than any falling leaf it flutters down, drawn by what pheromone I still know not, and alights upon her stomach. She does not feel or see it, her eyes are closed. Enraptured, I watch it uncoil its tiny proboscis and briefly sample the dampness of our commingled sweat.

With a tremor of its small blue wings it is gone.

'. . . Butterfly,' I mumble.

'. . . What?' She kisses me fiercely; a flurry of her determined limbs. 'Come here, I think I want you again.'


'. . . Five minutes left!' I am juddered back into the present. (*Disegnia Antonio* . . . is this all there is left in life?) I look down through my bifocals onto my sheet and am surprised, astonished, for I must have been drawing all the while. I emphasise her relaxed limbs, enhance the shading of her foreshortened arm. Something still missing. I reach into my pencil box, choose a blue crayon, and put it in.

The model and the others have gone when Max limps over to me and looks over my shoulder. 'That's good, Tony, very good. One might almost say it was done with love. Frame it!'

Mmm.

I give him a lift to his door. He gets out. 'Thanks'. He puts his head in again. 'You know, that one's far too good for mere drawing. If I were fifty years younger . . . ' He grins. I smile back at him, I know what he means.

'See you next week,' I reply. On the way home the car gives out a rhythmical thumping noise and I'm reminded that I must put it into the garage.

'There's a letter for you,' my wife says, handing it to me as I enter. 'Lunch is on the table'.

I open it. It's from the hospital; my knee replacement is fixed three weeks hence. I show it to her. She puts her arm around me. 'Oh Tony, don't worry.' And I'm suddenly filled with a rush of affection for all the hard work she's put into keeping me by her side, so squeeze her back.

*Life Class*

Bedtime. My knee is painful. I'd asked the surgeon candidly, what was involved, make no bones about it, I said.

'Oh, we just saw off the heads of the femur and tibia, put a dab of cement onto the ends, bang a metal hinge into place and sew you up again, no problem. Should last you the rest of your days.'

Huh!

I lie in bed reading, as does she. The words jumble on the page, I cannot concentrate. Lights out, a kiss, the silky down that was on her upper lip is now a bit bristly. I lie on my back staring up into the blackness. I must put the car in. Yes, it's good, I will frame it, give it to her for her eightieth birthday; but I'll be in hospital on the day (bang a metal hinge in. . . ). I turn towards her dear, aged body and gently ease up her nightgown. I put my hand upon her rectus abdominis – Oh, stuff you, Max!

No, my hand moves gently onto that special, secret place where once a small blue butterfly alighted.

She murmurs and I fall asleep.

# A Cat About the House

Norma Murray

Only the flintiest of hearts would turn away the animal now standing in the middle of the kitchen floor, so dejected, with its round yellow eyes staring out of a grey moon face, making such a pitiful noise. Not a meow like her other cats had made, more of a mewling whinny, like a squeaky toy being trodden on accidently.

In her new place Elizabeth was determined everything would be different, and this definitely meant no animals. She would tolerate nothing that needed her care, or love. Once and for all she'd got rid of things to tie her down. From the day she'd moved in she'd promised herself, life would be uncomplicated and simply her own.

So it was unfortunate not to have noticed the cat flap fitted in the door that led onto the communal courtyard – here she made a mental note to call the builder straight away and get the damn thing taken out – there was hardly enough space for her in the new bungalow, let alone a cat.

Steadying herself with one hand on the kitchen table, Elizabeth leant down and passed her hand across the intruding cat's back. What she discovered made her tut with disapproval. Once you got through the thick coat with its pathetic mass of knots, the poor thing was nothing but skin and bone.

'Who's been mistreating you, eh? Well just a drop mind, and then back out you go.' She had to get the cat flap sorted, otherwise the animal would, as like as not, be back the minute she put it out the door.

Taking a cereal bowl from the cupboard, she poured out a little milk and placed it on the floor. 'There, only skimmed I'm afraid.' She watched the cat's head dip straight down into the bowl and smiled, 'Not that you seem to mind.' It lapped furiously, wiped the dish clean with a pink curved tongue, licked its lips and looked up, as if expecting more.

Half a tin of tuna later the grey cat with its coat of matted fur, lay curled up on her hall chair while Elizabeth skimmed the A to Z. Very few of the other bungalows had been occupied yet, so the poor thing was obviously a stray; would Cat Rescue come under C for Cat or R for . . . ? She was half way down the page listing Animal Rescue Services, when the door bell chimed.

Well, she certainly wasn't expecting anyone this hour of the morning, and she wasn't dressed either. Feeling conspicuous in her faded blue dressing gown, she squinted into the spy hole, so conveniently fitted next to the front door.

On her doorstep was a man. He was standing too close for her to see anymore than part of his face, but she could tell at once she was right not to have opened the door. With his straggly grey hair tied back into what looked suspiciously like a pony tail, she wondered what on earth he wanted, but curiosity certainly wasn't enough to tempt her to open the door. Hoping he hadn't yet spotted her outline through the glass, she walked backwards into the kitchen, pulled the door to and waited. When he didn't ring again, she hurried to her vantage point by the side window and looked out. The man, with his threadbare jeans and scruffy plaid jacket was busy knocking on her neighbour's door.

Possibly some sort of doorstep peddler she thought, trying to sell something or other. Well, he'd get short shrift round here. She was surprised he even dared put his hand on the knocker of a door so plastered with warning stickers, *No Hawkers, No Circulars, No Uninvited Callers*. As the man walked away up the shared path, Elizabeth saw the curtain opposite twitch and let her own drop back so quickly she didn't have time to note which way he turned when he reached the street.

Elizabeth dressed hurriedly; she had a busy morning ahead. Although she didn't regret her decision to bring only a few mementoes from the old house – the furniture was far too dark and grand to fit into her purpose built retirement cottage for a start – it did mean she still had so much to do to get her new place fitted out. Luckily, the money made selling off one or two of the better pieces meant she'd about enough spare cash to furnish her tiny new home from scratch.

Silly really, she reflected, shrugging on her good wool jacket and searching around for her handbag, staying on in that gloomy old dump for years after . . . She shook her head – no need to dwell on the past. She'd done it now, got rid of the house and bought a retirement bungalow, just like her daughter suggested.

Pulling her new front door behind her with a satisfying click, she set off up the path. It wasn't until she got as far as the bus stop that she spotted the poster pinned to a tree. It was more of a scribbled notice really. Written in a loopy, rather old fashioned hand it said, *Runaway grey cat, answers to the name of Mr Bumble. Sorry, satisfaction at returning him is your only likely reward.* Underneath was scrawled a mobile number and a small cartoon of a cat carrying a suitcase. Elizabeth raised her eyebrows at the bluntness of the message, and then smiled. Not having a pencil to write down the telephone number, she carefully removed the notice from the tree, folded it in half and put it in her pocket.

When she got home, Mr Bumble, if that was his name, was still curled up where she'd left him on the hall chair. At the sound of the front door closing, one cautious yellow eye opened, before the cat stretched out his paws and jumped to the floor. Then he stalked into the kitchen to stand beside the fridge, as if he'd been doing it every day of his life. Elizabeth, reluctant to make too intimate a contact with such grubby fur, tickled him behind his ears with the end of one well manicured nail. The cat accepted her attention as if it were his right, before retuning his hopeful gaze back towards the fridge.

After tipping the remaining half tin of tuna into a clean bowl, she felt in her pocket for the notice. Leaving the cat to make the most of his supper, she made her way into the hall and dialled the number. It rang for a while before a male voice challenged.

'Hello, if you're flogging anything, I can tell you now you've got the wrong bloke.' Elizabeth couldn't help but smile at this opening line.

'Well, no. I'm not selling anything, but I think I may have found Mr Bumble for you.'

'Mr. Who? Oh! The cat. Right, good. He's nothing but a bloody nuisance, but tell me where you are and I'll come and fetch him . . .' Elizabeth was shocked. So her first instinct had been correct. Should she be returning any animal to a home where he was so blatantly unwanted? Was it any wonder the cat looked so badly neglected.

*It's Never Too Late to Fall in Love*

The voice on the other end of the phone came again, this time a little less challenging. 'You still there? Where's the old bugger got to this time? I'll come and pick him up.'

Elizabeth thought fast. Did she really want a stranger coming to her house when she was on her own, and she didn't know anyone in the area well enough to ask them to pop around and wait with her.

'No, it's quite alright. Give me your address and I'll bring him round myself.' As she said it, she realised it would probably mean a taxi ride, an unnecessary expense, but she might be able to get the bus back.

'If you're sure? Only it's the second time this week the bloody things gone missing. If you could drop him by later that would be great.' She suggested the following morning, scribbled down the address and, feeling a little doubtful that she was doing the right thing, rang off.

It didn't take her long to discover, using the local street map given her by the estate agent, the house was only round the corner. Conveniently opposite the very bus stop where she'd been standing that morning.

By the time she was out of bed next day, Elizabeth had begun to hope the cat had taken himself off home through the cat flap, never to return, but Mr Bumble – as she now knew to call him – was curled up snug on the hall chair. After serving him a fair sized piece of chicken left over from her own supper of the night before, she found a suitable box, made it comfortable by folding up a towel, and popped him in. Before he had time to make much of a protest, she tied the box lid down by means of a piece of packing twine. Then placing her indignant visitor by the front door, she pulled on her coat. It was only a few hundred yards, she reassured herself. If she took her time, she'd manage right enough.

*A Cat About the House*

Southlands, the house where she was to deliver the cat, was grander than most of the others in the street, with a drive wide enough to accommodate several cars if it hadn't been almost totally overgrown with weeds. Resting the box on the gatepost she looked around and took a breather, hoping someone would see her and come hurrying out. With trails of Boston Ivy sprawling as far as the green tiled roof, the whole place had a forlorn, uncared for air. When no one appeared, she started a slow walk up the drive. Leaving Mr Bumble on the lowest step, she made her way up to the front door.

A baying hound, somewhere in the lost recesses of the house, joined in with the persistent yowling coming from the box. From the depth of its mournful tones, Elizabeth decided it was likely to be a very large dog indeed, and felt tempted to leave the cat where it was and make a quick escape. But, duty bound, she pulled on the bell, straining hard to hear if it was working or not. Before she had time to put her hand on the knocker, a snarling right beside her made her jump.

Perched on the bay windowsill, a few feet from her ear, was a frantic little dog. What it lacked in size it certainly made up for in ferocity, as it scrabbled with its claws to get at her through the gap at the bottom of the sash window. So close she could smell its doggy breath, she watched in mute horror as its pointed muzzle, complete with full set of yellow teeth, snarled barely an arm's length from where she was standing.

By the time she'd retreated to the bottom step, the dog, giving up on the gap, had taken to throwing itself in full fury at the glass. Deep inside the cardboard box Mr Bumble gave an answering wail that seemed to match exactly her own opinion. This was no house to leave a poor defenceless cat. She would rather look after Mr Bumble herself than abandon him in such a place.

Hurrying as best she could across the weed covered drive, with poor Mr Bumble yowling and scrabbling inside his box, she imagined the whole window crashing to the ground behind her. Rather breathless, Elizabeth made it out onto the street, not daring to look over her shoulder until she had her key safely into her own front door.

The minute the box was opened, Mr Bumble shot past her legs to take refuge under the bed. And there he stayed, his two yellow eyes glaring at her from the depths. Locking the cat flap as a precaution, she did her best to lure him out with a bowl of milk, but it took several spoonfuls of moist tinned tuna spread out on a saucer, to tempt him to emerge.

Getting to her feet with some difficulty, Elizabeth looked again at the shabby cat beside her. 'But what am I going to do with you? Eh Puss? I can't keep you here.' Ignoring her completely, he gave a suspicious glance towards the cardboard box, before returning his snub nose back to finish off the tuna. She'd hardly served him his second helping when the phone rang.

'Excuse me,' a vaguely familiar male voice said, 'only you said you'd be bringing the cat back this morning. I'm afraid I was working in the yard and may have missed you.'

Elizabeth stared at the receiver for one small beat, but her reply was firm, her resolve unshakable, 'With all those dogs . . . if you think I'm going to give up a poor animal . . . ' she didn't bother to finish what she was saying, she merely pursed her lips and replaced the receiver in the cradle. She knew exactly what she would do. This man may have retrieved her phone number, she could cope with that, secure in the knowledge he had no idea where she lived. She would contact her old vet, the very person to help her find a home for the poor cat.

*A Cat About the House*

But as it turned out the vet was less of a solution than Elizabeth anticipated. The one she knew, and had trusted with her own cats for years, seemed to have inconveniently retired only months before. After dashing out and buying a new cat basket, Elizabeth found herself explaining to a very disapproving young man, who could have hardly been much more than a teenager, that the cat wasn't hers. 'He's sort of lost and rescued,' she started to explain.

'In that case,' the half-fledged replacement insisted, 'he'll need to be scanned. There may be an owner out there desperate to find him.'

Elizabeth hid her disquiet well; it had never occurred to her that Mr Bumble might be chipped. If the vet phoned the man from Southlands, what she saw as essentially a rescue might appear, to this supercilious young man, not to mention the cat's supposed owner, quite different. But surely, the cat was so obviously neglected. No one would ever think she'd taken him on purpose. Would they? Nevertheless, when the vet continued, 'You do realise this cat is a pedigree Persian blue and quite valuable,' she decided to go on the offensive.

'Well he's still a stray; you've only got to look at the state of his fur.'

'Yes, his coat is very neglected.' The vet felt around the top of the cat's neck and shook his head, 'Hmm! No sign of a chip under the skin. If we can't get hold of his real owner what I suggest, if you are willing of course,' he looked up at Elizabeth and smiled for the very first time, 'is that I check this boy over and get my assistant to give him a thorough cleaning up. He'll have to be shaved down both sides of course.'

A vision of Mr Bumble looking for all the world like a skinny grey lion, flitted though her mind. 'Do you think that's really necessary, can't you just . . . bath him and trim him up a bit?'

But the vet wouldn't think of such a thing. He was adamant. Thorough removal of the matted fur was the kindest thing to do, and Elizabeth was left with the vague feeling of having committed some enormous crime just by the very act of suggesting otherwise.

Before she had truly thought out the implications of what she was letting herself in for, not to mention the cost, she'd left Mr Bumble behind for an overnight check up and promised to be in when the vet phoned the following morning to give her the news.

As it turned out, the cat was fine, he said, a little under weight to be sure, but they'd descaled his teeth, updated his jabs, made the necessary adaptations to his coat and if she continued to feed him on a special – and Elizabeth predicted, punitively expensive – diet, he would be as good as new in a few weeks.

That afternoon Elizabeth found herself in the back of a taxi, next to her newly shorn companion in his brand new cat basket, picking long grey cat hairs off her skirt and wishing she'd not sat on the hall chair to put her shoes on before she came out.

'At least,' she confided, doing her best to tickle his odd little face through the mesh. 'Our worries about problem cat hair have been solved for a while.'

Three messages were flashing on her answer phone when she came in. Two from her daughter, the first asking if she was alright, the second demanding why didn't she switch on her mobile like any normal human being, the third Elizabeth recognised as coming from the cat's supposed owner. He came straight to the point sure enough. 'Look, what's going on? I want my cat back. Please phone this number.' She checked; it was the same as the one on the sheet of paper she'd taken from the tree.

*A Cat About the House*

By the end of the evening the man had phoned so many times, she'd grown quite used to hearing his voice on the answer phone. It was a pleasant voice, she decided; not in the least bit cross at all. Certainly not as angry as she would be in the circumstances. As she played his last message for the second time, she couldn't help feeling a bit sorry, if it wasn't for those awful dogs . . . But then she remembered the mess the house was in and felt reassured. No matter what, the cat's welfare must come first. Mr Bumble would be much happier with her until she could find him a permanent home able to give him the care the vet had impressed upon her, such a high maintenance cat needed.

'So sorry, Mr Southlands,' (as she'd taken to calling the voice on her answer phone) 'I'm afraid I'm now going to delete all your calls.' And with that she pressed the button. Then, after checking on Mr Bumble, who was soundly asleep on the hall chair, she went to bed with a satisfied conscience.

It was three days later, after Mr Bumble had settled in really well and was quite used to a litter tray – certainly more than Elizabeth had grown used to having to empty it – that she saw the man with the pony tail again. She was getting off the bus and he was standing on the other side of the road, a white carrier bag in one hand and holding one of the most geriatric Dalmatian dogs she'd ever seen, close beside him on a short piece of rope.

Poor man, most likely one of those rough sleepers, she was just thinking, when he yelled across in her direction. Several other passengers turned their heads, but Elizabeth knew better. Vaguely pleased to have her instinct not to open the door to him fully justified, and determined not to make eye contact, she hurried off as swiftly as she could, round the corner to her own front door.

She'd hardly got as far as taking her coat off, when the doorbell chimed. Expecting the delivery of a rather cosy cat bed, a bargain won on eBay, Elizabeth was completely taken by surprise when she opened the front door to be confronted by the very man with the pony tail, complete with dog.

Doing her best not to look as discomposed as she felt, she glanced first at him, then at his bag of what appeared to be perfectly ordinary shopping, then finally down at the dog. Noting with concern that the dog wasn't only very elderly, but blind as well, she enquired, 'Yes?' in a light but not particularly friendly tone, while taking care to close the door until the gap was only a few inches wide.

Half expecting a request for money, it came as a complete shock when the conversation started out on a completely different tack.

'So you're the lady who nicks cats?'

'What?' For just a moment Elizabeth's customary calm was ruffled, before she managed to claw back most of her composure. With an appearance of unhurried poise, she gave the coolest of smiles. 'I think you have the wrong address.'

But the man on her door step wasn't to be so easily fobbed off. 'Look love, I recognise you. You had my notice off the tree, so I'm guessing it's you who's got my cat.'

Elizabeth was tempted to finish the conversation there and then by closing the door in his face, and may have done so if the dog hadn't perked up with sudden interest. Lifting its blind eyes upwards, it sniffed towards the crack in the door, and woofed. Before she knew what was happening, Mr Bumble was off his chair. Just at the point she was saying she didn't own a cat, a cat appeared miraculously, to wind itself around her ankles.

*A Cat About the House*

Before she had time to say anything at all, the man on the step beat her to it. 'Bloody hell woman, what have you done to that cat?'

Elizabeth glanced down and it was as if she saw Mr Bumble for the very first time. His gloriously fluffy tail, which now fanned over his body like a fat grey ostrich feather, was much as it had always been, only a lot cleaner and well brushed. However his scrawny, shaven sides, with the narrow ridge of silken fur still left unclipped all down the centre of his back, gave him a punkish, Mohican look, made stranger still by the tufts of fur left like moon boots, all around his feet.

Before she could prevent it, Mr Bumble was through the door and sniffing noses with the blind Dalmatian. It was obvious, not least because of the way the dog's tail was pounding back and forwards, the two animals were old friends.

Elizabeth stood her ground, defiant. 'You know, people like you don't deserve to own cats,' she said, determined to get her defence in first. 'He turned up here starving, and filthy. It's cost me an absolute fortune in vet's bills.' She stopped when it became obvious the man just wasn't listening. He was squatting down, staring, holding his hand out towards the cat. Mr Bumble, his yellow eyes peering out of a grey fur bonnet, sniffed the man's fingers and gave his most distinctive cry.

The man's face creased into smiles. 'Well old Bum-face; it is you, only I wouldn't have guessed it if it hadn't been for Lulu.' At the sound of her name, the old dog responded by wagging her whole body, right from nose to tail. Then with a sigh the man stood up and looked Elizabeth in the eye,

'Well, perhaps you'd like to explain what this is all about then.'

Elizabeth pressed her lips together, finding it hard to reign in her displeasure. 'As I was saying, it's criminal neglect. You should be ashamed, such a lovely animal.'

The man stared at her, his half amused expression turning to one of incredulity. 'Don't make judgements on things you know nothing about.'

'Judgements . . . pardon . . .' Elizabeth allowed her voice to rise above her usually reserved and cultured tones. 'I'll have you know, we were about to be attacked by the most ferocious dog. Only a fool would have dreamt of leaving . . .'

'So you scalped the poor bugger instead.' The man snorted. 'Look, okay. I can see now what's happened. You think Bumface was in a state because I wasn't looking after him properly. That's rubbish, and as for 'attack', let me tell you, Dandy is no more ferocious that old Lulu here.'

'If you are referring to that maniac Jack Russell? It did its best to get at . . .' hardly able to swallow down her indignation, she pointed towards Mr Bumble, who was now sitting between them on the door step washing what was left of his facial fur with a paw, '. . . through the window.'

The man with the pony tail smiled. 'Look, let me explain, Mr Bumble isn't my cat.' At this point, Elizabeth attempted to interrupt, but was waved silent. 'Hang on, hear me out. He belongs, well belonged, to my late aunt, as did the two dogs. Unknown to me, she'd been unwell for some time. Well, to cut it short, a neighbour took in the dogs. In the panic, Bumface was forgotten.' Elizabeth longed to tell him to use the cat's proper name, but thought better of it when the man continued. 'I found him half starved, still locked in the house. It's only thanks to me and a few careless mice I suspect, that the poor bugger survived.'

'Ah!' Elizabeth could think of nothing else to say.

*A Cat About the House*

'He's always been a bit of a wanderer, that's why my aunt never let him out.'

Needing time to collect her thoughts, Elizabeth leant down and stroked the cat's pathetically thin back, 'I see. Perhaps in the circumstances . . .'

'. . . you owe me an apology and I accept. And a cup of tea while we sort this out won't go amiss.' Elizabeth looked at the man again. Although his long hair and tatty jeans were certainly disconcerting, she couldn't help but think that she'd probably misjudged him. Not being one to hang on slavishly to first impressions, she led him and the dog through into the kitchen. Where, after taking the precaution of opening the back door onto the communal courtyard area, she filled the kettle and turned it on.

An ever hopeful Mr Bumble took up his usual stance by the fridge door, the blind dog alongside him, wagging her tail. Smiling, the man with the pony tail offered Elizabeth his hand.

'The name's Frank by the way, Frank Bellamy.'

Elizabeth's fingers stretched out, intending to encounter his only briefly. 'Elizabeth Brown,' she replied, a thrill of unexpected pleasure shooting through her body as he clasped her hand warmly. Such a firm and masculine hand – it was a long while since she'd touched a man's hand – other than professional types like estate agents and solicitors, which she felt she could discount.

'Pleased to meet you . . . Elizabeth? Not Liz then?'

She found herself smiling, 'Well, when I was a girl, perhaps, but I haven't been called that for years.'

Frank grinned, 'Liz suits you better. You don't look much like an Elizabeth to me.' When she raised an enquiring eyebrow, he continued, 'Not half prim enough. Okay if I call you Liz, then?'

Where would be the harm she thought, and nodded.

'The problem is,' Frank explained, stirring sugar into a second mug of tea, before reaching out for another biscuit, one of a special packet kept in the cupboard for visitors, and up till now unopened. 'I've left my small-holding down in Devon to come up here and sort things out. My aunt left a will.' Here he laughed, 'I'm her only living relative, so I get Mr Bumble, bless him, and the dogs of course – along with the contents of the house, such as it is – and the animal rescue centre gets the rest.'

Elizabeth nodded in sympathy, 'Ah! Bit eccentric your aunt?'

'You might say that. Look, I'm going to have to ask a favour. I've friends keeping the small holding going for the time being. And I can take the dogs down there, no problem. But what the hell am I going to do with old Bumble here? I mean, much as I love him,' Elizabeth looked at him sharply, unsure if he was serious or not, 'Look at him, now he's starkers, he'll freeze, not to mention there's no one to look after him while I'm dashing back and forwards. Will you hang on to him, eh! Lizzie?'

Elizabeth was taken aback, as much by being called Lizzie as by the realization he wanted her to keep the cat after all. She looked down at Mr Bumble asleep, curled up in between Lulu's paws. 'It seems a shame to split those two up.' Her face flushed as she continued, 'I never intended to hang on to him, only find him a suitable home.'

'Well, the very least you can do is look after him for a bit, until I get the totters in to clear out the place? He's likely to go missing again otherwise.'

*A Cat About the House*

It was almost dark when she stood in her doorway and waved goodbye. Elizabeth couldn't help but notice the curtain opposite twitch. 'Tomorrow, it's a deal then,' Frank called over his shoulder, before he, with Lulu staggering along beside him, turned the corner.

As she washed up their two mugs and plates, she couldn't help but wonder what she was letting herself in for. 'Frank,' she smiled as she said his name out loud, had been all for getting in any old house clearance people, without even checking though his late aunt's things. It had been Elizabeth's suggestion that some of the bits and pieces might be valuable.

He'd shaken his head at first,and said, 'No way, just a load of tat. The old girl was never one for jewellery or anything like that.' It was only when Elizabeth, in a cautious, roundabout way suggested some of the furniture at least, might be worth looking at, that he'd asked for her help. Would she do him the favour of going round there tomorrow morning, he said, and help him have a root through? Then afterwards, perhaps they could have a pub lunch.

It took a ridiculous amount of time for Elizabeth to choose what to wear the following morning. Old clothes he'd said, the house was in a real mess, but still she didn't want to look dowdy, and there was the prospect of a pub lunch too. In the end she went for her faded denim trousers, not jeans exactly, but certainly very casual and the red fleece, a favourite from her gardening days.

Frank was waiting at the window and, with the blind dalmation keeping mutely to his side and the wriggling Dandy pinioned under one arm, he ushered her in through the hall. Treading carefully, Elizabeth followed man and dogs into the front room. To her relief, the Jack Russell ignored her completely, choosing to jump straight back to his stance on the window sill.

*It's Never Too Late to Fall in Love*

'On guard for squirrels,' Frank explained.

The room was large and gloomy, with a permeating smell of damp and animals. And from the look of the sofa and chairs Elizabeth could see the aunt had shared her life closely with her beloved pets. An ancient television, a scratched occasional table and a glass fronted mahogany bookcase finished off the room. Elizabeth pointed out the bookcase as being possibly a candidate for auction and, Frank duly attached a large blue post it note, 'So I won't forget which one,' he said ruefully.

'Better put another on the books inside,' she suggested. 'They might interest a dealer too.'

Together they made their way through each downstairs room and it wasn't until she tripped on the steps leading to the back kitchen that Elizabeth realized how weary she was. When an anxious Frank offered her his arm, she did her best to laugh the stumble off, 'I'm fine, a little problem with my knee, that's all, it's nothing,' but was relieved when he decided they'd done enough for the day.

'How about we go and have that bite to eat?'

Elizabeth shook her head. Her leg was throbbing. 'Some other time perhaps. I think I'd better . . .' Not wanting to say she needed some time with her foot up, she held out her filthy hands for him to see.

He grinned, 'Yeh! Woman, you need a wash. Tell you what, how about I walk you home, give the dogs a run and then fetch us some fish and chips. Bring them round to your place, in about an hour.' And that is exactly what he did.


It was some weeks later that her daughter, during her weekly telephone call, remarked on her mother's increasingly buoyant moods.

*A Cat About the House*

'Oh! I'm looking after a cat for a friend and generally making myself useful,' Elizabeth explained, running her hand over Mr Bumble's now thick, velvety fur coat and deciding not to mention Frank as an individual, at least not yet. It had been such fun helping him sort everything out, and she felt real pleasure over the noteworthy sums the furniture had only recently fetched at auction.

But as she put the phone down, it dawned. She could no longer hide from the truth. Within days, the house would be on the market. Frank was down at his place in Devon, settling Lulu and Dandy; once he'd signed all the papers, what reason would there be for him to stay around anymore?

And now Mr Bumble's fur was nearly grown back, he'd be off to Devon too. She buried her face into the cat's soft fur and held him tight, while trying not to think of how soon all the bathing and brushing he needed would be Frank's responsibility, not hers. In truth she couldn't bear to think of the pair of them, cat and man, disappearing out of her life forever. Yet there was little she could do about it.

Three months ago she'd sworn never to have another cat, but then three months ago she'd not wanted to open her front door to Frank either. Why had she been so stupid as to get involved? Where was the uncomplicated life she'd promised herself?

The doorbell chimed. Tipping Mr Bumble gently onto the floor she made her way into the hall. She wasn't sure what surprised her most, the enormous bunch of red and gold sunflowers, or Frank grinning over the top of them, wearing a jacket and tie. Thrusting the roughly tied bouquet into her arms he said, 'I thought I'd better bring you some before they're all gone.'

Elizabeth let out a gasp. 'They're lovely. Are they ones you've grown yourself?' She couldn't help but remember her own garden, back in the old house; she'd grown sunflowers there too, but nothing like these. 'The colours are . . . amazing.' She turned away, determined not to let Frank see the tears welling unexpectedly in her eyes; so silly to be upset.

'I thought we might, if you haven't eaten that is, nip out for something.' Self-conscious, knowing she was covered in cat hairs, Elizabeth ran her free hand across her skirt. 'There's no hurry,' he continued, 'I mean, you look fine as you are, but there's plenty of time to change if you want to.'

'You've booked a table already?'

Frank gave a grin, 'Do you think I'd have got all togged up like this to have a fish and chip supper?'

'That would have been fine with me,' Elizabeth said quietly.

Half an hour later, after she'd put on her newest blue dress and Frank had used every container he could find (including a bucket from under the sink) to accommodate the flowers, they sat opposite each other in a restaurant Elizabeth had never been to before. The novelty made her feel rather shy. Yet it was pleasant feeling she decided – if strangely unsettling – as if she was meeting him for the very first time. She'd grown used to having him around in his plaid working jacket and threadbare jeans, yet there was no denying, Frank looked very attractive all dressed up. Yes, very nice indeed, even if his hair was still long and tied back by a rubber band.

Realising the ends of his fingers were only a few inches from hers across the tablecloth, she smiled. What would happen, she wondered, if she reached out and just touched . . .

'Elizabeth.' She jumped. How serious he sounded, using her full name. 'I've something to ask you, but I'm not sure how you'll take it.'

*A Cat About the House*

Elizabeth clenched her knees tight together under the table. Doing her best to look composed and unmoved she smiled. 'Ask away.'

His words seemed to rush at her from nowhere. 'We need to talk about the future.' As he paused the very pit of her stomach turned over. So he felt the same; he'd miss her too. And then reality followed like a hard punch in the guts.

'I'll never be able to manage old Bumble. Will you keep him?'

All of a sudden she felt ridiculous and very, very old. Of course, he wanted her to have the cat. Mr Bumble was high maintenance. What had she been thinking he was about to say? Some sort of declaration of undying love. Who was she kidding, at her age? With her wrinkled face, old lady legs and sensible shoes. Who was she trying to fool, having blonde tints put in her hair to hide the grey? How absurd.

She thought of the new dressing gown and pale cream silk nightdress she'd bought only recently and cringed – so humiliating – she wanted to get up and leave with what remained of her dignity still intact, but was unsure if her leg might give away. Frank was staring straight at her. He wasn't smiling.

'You see Elizabeth, he was saying. 'No way can I look after him like you do. And I wondered, if perhaps, if you kept him, and you had time . . . I know it's a lot to ask . . . but maybe you'd like to come and stay with me, just for a while of course, to see if you might like . . . It's not much of a house, but there's plenty of space, too much for just one in fact . . . and bring old Bum-face as well.'

*It's Never Too Late to Fall in Love*

# *Copperplate*

Sue Wilson

After putting Mother to bed Jean Portman enjoyed quietly sitting with the newspaper. It was her special time when she could relax at last, sip a cup of tea and be undisturbed by the prattle of the inane television which entertained her aged parent. On Fridays her particular pleasure was to peruse 'Soul Mates', the lonely hearts column in the local paper. She treated herself to an Earl Grey and read the news in detail, starting with the headlines and slowly working her way through to page eight. There must be no cheating. Everything must be read in orderly sequence so that the ultimate arrival at her favourite feature was put off in exquisite anticipation.

She was uncomfortably aware of why she enjoyed 'Soul Mates' so much. It gave her a brief voyeuristic view into the lives of other lonely people. Sometimes there was a humorous entry. 'Short fat ugly bloke in his 40s wishes to meet female. Any female!'

Several hinted at previous misfortune. 'Must be sober'. 'Must like children'. 'Must be sincere'. Miss Portman amused herself by pairing up advertisers and imagining scenarios for them. She slowly devoured the columns of desperation until she reached the last item. She re-read it and frowned. The last two words irritated her. They said 'Mum's welcome.'

'How ignorant,' she fumed. 'There should be no apostrophe. One assumes that he intends to convey a tolerance for other people's children. But he's actually said that Mum is welcome. He'd certainly have a surprise if I arranged to meet him and brought Mother.'

Jean Portman had no intention of answering any of the advertisements she read every week. Since her mother's illness she had relinquished almost all of the meagre social life she had enjoyed. She contented herself with solitary pastimes and the inappropriate apostrophe unsettled her. Any hope of concentrating on the crossword had disappeared. That night her mind kept returning to the illiterate advertisement.

In the morning she was too busy to worry about trivial things like ungrammatical strangers. Mother had to be toiletted, washed and dressed. The unchanging daily routine took over in the dutiful tasks. Change Mother's draw sheet, make the bed, do the washing, make lunch, feed Mother, wipe the dribble from her chin, smell the gut wrenching odour.

'Oh my God', Jean thought, as she spooned broth into her mother. 'She's soiled herself again. Couldn't she wait until after lunch? What is she now but an old nuisance? Mum's welcome? He's welcome to my Mum right now. He'd feel differently if he had to change her like a baby every day.'

An hour later, after cleaning her mother up for the third time, Jean's savage anger was unabated. She sat at the dining table and began to write a bitter tirade to the originator of the offending advertisement. 'How would you like to have a mother like mine? She is 92 years old, incontinent and suffering from severe Alzheimer's Disease. She has to be taken to the toilet. She has to be fed. She has to have her dribble wiped, her bottom wiped, her teeth cleaned, her bed changed. There is not a crevice of my mother's body with which I am not all too familiar.' She was getting into her stride now, letting the words, the resentments, the bitterness of all her wasted years flow onto the page along with the tears.

When she reached the bottom of the paper her anguish was spent. She stared in surprise at the untidy scrawl that crazily wriggled its way down the sheet. 'This is not good enough Jean Portman', she admonished herself. 'This handwriting is a disgrace.'

She had always taken pride in presentation and even now, in her chaotic existence, clung to the standards by which she had been raised. She took a clean piece of writing paper and began again. While her mother snored in the armchair, she wrote out a proper letter to the Stranger of the Apostrophe. She began by explaining that his advertisement had been grammatically incorrect and described in explicit detail why he would not find her mother welcome. At the end she paused. The very idea of signing her name to such a catalogue of misery shamed her.

This was merely a handwriting exercise and therefore a salutation and signature were not necessary. She gazed at her handiwork with satisfaction and folded the sheet of paper. There was no harm in actually writing the address on an envelope in her beautiful copperplate – just to see what it looked like.

Her mother woke with a jolt and began prattling for a drink. Jean forgot her letter and went to put the kettle on.

On Tuesday and Thursday mornings the Home Help arrived and Jean looked forward to the opportunity to get out of the house. Tuesdays were reserved for shopping. She tried to

*Copperplate*

think of everything she would need for the coming week. When one had a dependent relative there could be no popping out for a forgotten loaf of bread. Shirley had offered to do the shopping but Jean clung to her treasured hours of escape like a shipwrecked mariner clutching at a mast. She sailed through the supermarket and wallowed in the self indulgence of peace.

Thursdays were even better. Thursday was the major treat of the week. Thursday mornings made the other wretchedly monotonous days bearable. On alternate Thursday mornings Jean went to the U3A Book Group at ten o'clock in the library. It gave her an opportunity to meet other people and discuss the set book. She could not actually call her fellow members friends. She never invited them back home for obvious reasons, but they were like minded women whose company Jean enjoyed. U3A was her only opportunity to communicate with the outside world and she relished every minute of it. Since having to take early retirement to care for her mother, Jean had not been in contact with any of her ex-colleagues. They were all much younger than her and they had little in common. She knew full well that the whole office had regarded her as highbrow and old fashioned. At least the U3A members were on the same wavelength and they all shared a love of good literature.

Alternating with the Book Group was the U3A Art Appreciation Group. Jean had only been attending for two years. The group used to be held at William's house in the next village. Jean could not drive and there was no bus available at the end of the meetings that arrived back home in time to let Shirley get away. Eventually the numbers grew too much for William's house and the group moved to the public hall behind the library. As some members were in the book group, the facilitators came to the alternate week arrangement which

*It's Never Too Late to Fall in Love*

was ideal for Jean. Both meetings were now held at Jean's end of the town and so she had the opportunity to renew her reading material and enjoy cheerful company for two precious hours each week.

A new gentleman had joined Art Appreciation last week and Jean had watched in amusement as Maureen and Anne had fawned over him. To be fair, they were only making him feel welcome but they had seemed a little too gushing in Jean's opinion. As for herself, she had hardly spoken to him and could not remember his name. They had had a guest speaker on Modern Expressionism and so there had been little chance to socialise during the meeting. Afterwards, Jean had hurried around the corner to the library to renew her Dickens and had strolled home contentedly past the spring daffodils. Shirley reported that Mrs Portman had been no trouble. 'Oh by the way,' she added as she buttoned her coat, 'I posted that letter you left on the table. I saw the envelope ready so I put it in. I had a stamp handy so I popped it in the box on Tuesday.'

'Thank you'.

'Oh. That's all right. It's the little favours that count, eh?'

As Shirley closed the front gate behind her, Jean gasped with panic. Her hands flew to her face in horror as she imagined the stranger reading her beautifully penned ravings. At least it was anonymous. She calmed down as she remembered that it was untraceable. 'It's probably in his waste bin by now,' she told herself.

Nevertheless, a small part of her wished for a reply. It was a full week later before she admitted to herself that a reaction would have been interesting. She glanced at the neatly folded newspaper more frequently than usual. Would eight o'clock never come? Mother seemed to be particularly slow

*Copperplate*

at undressing that evening. She grabbed her daughter's arm and prevented her from rolling the thick grey stockings down her vein-crazed legs.

'You forgot the blackout. Quench that light at once or I'll have to report you.'

'Yes Warden. I'll see to it as soon as you're in bed.' It was best to humour her. Jean watched her mother curl her frail body into the foetus position and quietly closed the bedroom door behind her.

She made her cup of tea, settled in the armchair and turned immediately to page eight to see if GJ, Box 4097 had re-advertised. He had not. With a wry smile at her own frivolity Miss Portman turned to the headlines and settled down to read her newspaper properly. She completed two thirds of the crossword, finished the last chapter of Nicholas Nickleby and went to bed.

By the end of the summer she had completed her schedule of Victorian novels. It was time to turn her attention to twenti-eth century authors. She stopped at the corner of Bank Street and smiled appreciatively at the colourful rose beds. 'I'll sit Mother in the garden this afternoon,' she thought. 'I can start my new book after I have mown the lawn.'

She walked in the autumn sunshine to Mafeking Hall where the U3A Art Appreciation Group was held. There were fewer members than usual. Four of their number were away on holiday. Jean quietly envied them. Holidays were an unat-tainable luxury to her. Thursday mornings were her great weekly treat. The new member, George, had settled in well and had even given a talk himself on watercolour painting which wasn't quite art appreciation but had been very enter-taining. George was quite a wit in a subtle way. The latest meeting had been on Reubens with much animated discussion. Talk flowed on to the modern concept of beauty with the emphasis on being very thin. The three men in the group all agreed that they preferred a bit of meat on their women – Marilyn Monroe rather than Twiggy. 'It's no use clashing bones when you have a cuddle', George added. Maureen pointed at his rotund figure and, to gales of laughter from everyone, declared that it certainly wasn't a problem he need worry about.

After the meeting Jean heard the others deciding where to go for coffee. There was always a trip to one of the local cafes after the meetings. The men went their own ways but the women always gathered somewhere for a chat. Jean had gone once, when she had first joined the U3A group, but had not enjoyed it. The other members took this opportunity to gossip about people Jean did not know, or show photographs of their children and grandchildren; a joy Jean was unable to share. Carol, Margaret, Wendy and Irene had monopolised the conversation with the latest minutiae about their grandchildren so Jean had declined all invitations to join them for coffee since then. She had never mentioned her mother to anyone in either U3A group that she attended. She wanted intellectual stimulation in friendly company, not sympathy, and after the weekly meetings she preferred a peaceful hour in the library. She walked round the corner and into the library with her usual eager anticipation and scanned the bookshelves for Steinbeck, but there was none. Suddenly the sunlight shafting through the high window seemed to fade. Her disappointment clouded the day. She selected Solzhenitsyn instead and approached the desk.

'I wish to reserve a book please, 'she announced to the librarian and was handed a request card and pencil. Jean produced her fountain pen from her handbag and answered the questions in her beautiful copperplate handwriting.

*Copperplate*

'Excuse me.'

The words came from behind her and were almost inaudible. Jean continued to write.

'Ahem. Excuse me.' It was a little louder this time and she looked round.

'Yes?' George was staring hard at her request card.

'Er, I couldn't help noticing your beautiful handwriting. It's not usual you see. Er, one doesn't see a decent hand much these days. Not now everyone has computers. Dreadful things. And so I was wondering . . .' His voice tailed away under Jean's gaze.

'Yes?'

'I was wondering if you would care to take a cup of coffee with me?'

Jean was taken aback but managed to retain her outward composure. 'I'm being picked up,' she though. 'At my age.' She looked at the clock above the desk.

'I'm sorry', she said. 'I have an aged relative at home and I must get back to her. Another time perhaps.'

To her surprise he looked triumphant. 'I knew it. The minute I saw that handwriting I knew it had to be you. You have a senile, incontinent mother who needs constant attendance. You hate your life but you love to discuss Art.'

Jean clung to the desk for support. 'The letter,' she thought. 'He's Mr Apostrophe.' Her cheeks were ashen.

'I can sympathise', he continued. 'I too had to care for an Aged P. My dear mother died of cancer last year. I miss her so very much. So I decided to seek someone in a similar situation. I really did mean Mum is welcome. And you were the only one who noticed. But you didn't sign your name.

*It's Never Too Late to Fall in Love*

I gave up hope of ever meeting you. I've been coming to the Art Group every fortnight for months and never realised that Jean, the slender lady with the glasses was Miss Copperplate.'

The shaft of sunlight deepened to a golden glow. Jean felt a girlish smile creep over her face.

'Is that what you called me?' she laughed. 'I called you Mr Apostrophe. I'll meet you here at 10 o'clock next Thursday,' and she turned towards the door.

'And maybe,' she thought, 'I'll invite you home to meet Mother.'

# Life Without Grace

### Ed Lane

Jan picked up my empty glass and studied the twisted remains of the lemon slice that was turning brown in the dregs of ice melt. 'Why are you wasting your life, Michael?'

That was Jan, as direct as a bare-knuckle boxer. I gave her a look that tried hard to say, 'it's my life, I'll waste it as I please'. She didn't appear to get the message so I mouthed, 'what d'you mean?'

Jan waggled the glass, as if inviting me to another vodka and tonic; but wasn't. She raised an eyebrow, pursed her lips and looked at her husband across the table. *Conspiracy.*

David had the shaven-headed look of a football hooligan, minus the tattoos, but was as soft as the soil he tilled. He gave a wry grin. I knew he was going to say . . . Jan thinks . . .

'Jan thinks it's time you got about a bit more. You're almost a recluse in that big house of yours. And you're going to seed, if you don't mind me saying so.'

I did mind. Not that it wasn't true, I just didn't like hearing it, even from a friend.

'Broccoli or carrots? If I'm going to be a vegetable I'd like to be able to choose my own variety. Maybe cabbage would be best though, if you insist I'm turning into one.'

David started another grin but it faded under Jan's message-laden stare. He ducked his head between his hands as if dodging an incoming missile. As I was watching the right jab, Jan came in with a killer left hook.

'He means you could shave every once in a while and get your hair cut occasionally. What self-respecting woman would go out with a tramp?'

Ahhh, the nub, the crux . . . the knockout point. 'What self-respecting woman do you have in mind?'

'We've invited Sally Wordsworth to dinner next week . . . '

Sally Wordsworth. An apt name. And really not my type. I preferred a companion of fewer words and a stronger sense of fidelity; at least I had, at another time, when a woman held my heart in a grip of pure gold. The thought raised a phantom image. I looked at my hands. They were always clean; the Pilate complex. I still blamed myself for Grace's death even though I knew the fault was not mine. Silly, stupid games one plays when young and in love.

We were both correspondents. Me a war dog for *The Times*, she a columnist for *The Independent*, both sent to cover the Troubles in Ulster. Grace was good, better than me, and I loved her all the more for it. I let her win the race to be first on the scene at a major riot and she walked into the path of a car bomb. It should have been me, would have been me if I'd played a harder game.

Grace's 'Death in Service' payout cleared the mortgage on a Victorian town house in London. With my life there extinct, I sold up and moved back to my roots in Leicestershire; hoping for rebirth. The 'big house' had been a Georgian landowner's

*Life Without Grace*

45

folly; now mine. Jan and David lived on Home Farm, smaller and cosier and within fifty yards of my garden gate.

Jan rattled the remaining ice in my redundant tumbler. 'Well . . . ?'

I swam back to the surface of my sea of complex misery. 'Well what?'

'Will you come? Make up a foursome. You'll be company for David.'

David punched my shoulder, a light tap, as if he feared I'd crumble. 'C'mon, Michael. Sally's not that bad. Quite dishy in fact.'

He was right, Sally was an attractive woman. I guessed less than my sixty years but a large divorce settlement and an inbred sense of style took a decade off her looks.

What was I afraid of?

*Commitment!*

I could lie so easily to myself.

I pointed at the glass in Jan's hand. 'Any danger of a top-up?'

*Coward.*

A victory grin crossed Jan's otherwise sweet face, one that sat comfortably beneath an urchin blond hairdo. 'On condition . . .'

Why not? I owed her, big time, for being the world's best neighbour. 'You win!'

Simper. Flirty smile; but not at me. 'I know.'

It had been a bet and I knew what the prize would be. 'Just keep the noise down, you two. I may be vegetating but I still have all my faculties.'

David blushed but Jan just smiled a see-what-you're-missing smile.

Misgivings by the legion. Why had I agreed, given in so easily, to be hung on the village meat rack? *'Can't be too choosy when you get to your age.'* I'd heard it a few times but why corrupt the standards of a lifetime? Few candidates in a small farming village such as Little Lustby – just a smattering of widows and middle-aged divorcees. The name, inherited from Viking settlers, contained more than a nip of contemporary truth.

The face that stared back from the speckled old mirror still had a vague resemblance to Robert Redford. Puffier, older, a few tramlines and a fine pair of matching crow's feet. The hair, thinning but all my own, cut too short for a brain still shackled to the fashions of the 1980s. I'd shaved with care, the elderly Gillette nicking my chin just once. A small cut which bled far more than it should have and needed two applications from the styptic pencil found oozing in the bottom of the bathroom cabinet.

The witching hour was drawing near. A good choice of adjective. Fortification required. Two measures of Smirnoff Blue Label and a dash of tonic should suffice – for now.

Why *had* I agreed? Deep down I knew Jan was right. I'd been alone too long with my memories and self-loathing. It was time for change, to keep Grace close but in a separate compartment, not part of my everyday existence, living with a ghost in every room, seated at every table, at every meal. In bed every night; cold comfort.

And that was another problem. It had been five years since I last dated a woman and that was a disaster, the memories of Grace still fresh, the guilt too strong. I had no clue how to go

*Life Without Grace*

about the art of seduction. Not in this age. How many dates before the bedroom door loomed large? I wasn't prepared for that scenario. My sex drive had dropped to last place on the starting grid. Could I take the humiliation?

I checked my Rolex; a wedding present from Grace. Like me, running slow but its familiar face held the cheerful offer of enough time to down another double.

Jan gave me the big build-up. 'Michael used to work for *The Times* you know, before he retired. Now he writes for the local paper, freelance, wildlife and things, you must have read him.'

She left out the important bits. The freelance job on the local paper was honorary; unpaid. My early retirement a request from on high. Too many lunchtime drinks in an industry where alcohol fuelled the presses. The boat I was pushing out had the dimensions of the QEII. Kill the brain, kill the pain. It was a prop, a habit I had no incentive to break, though I was rarely drunk, keeping just to the right side of sober. It kept me numb, staved off the past; kept me alive.

Sally smiled too much, even when I bored her with the mating rituals of Black Grouse; the lek. The smile was a fixture, her cheeks pulled back and too smooth. Cosmetic enhancements hadn't only been to an impressive bust. She made interested noises but her eyes glazed over and she ceased rubbing her leg against mine. Too desperate by half but knowing when to give up.

She tried not to hog the conversation but discipline deserted her as she started to finish my sentences for me, accompanied by an overloud laugh. David's free-flowing Chablis and boredom had gone to her head. A wicked combination.

He offered to drive her home and I offered to help with the dishes, carrying them into the kitchen for Jan to stack in the dishwasher.

'That went well,' I said. Smug.

Jan gave me a look that could curdle cheese. 'You were awful. The mating rituals of black grouse? You have a sublime talent for making sex sound like a potted history of Byzantine grave diggers.'

Still smug. 'Sorry. Did my best to entertain.'

'Try harder.' She rattled a pair of plates into a dishwasher rack. 'I went to a lot of trouble to get you two together. You really should make more of an effort.'

Irritation surged. 'You needn't have bothered.'

She swung round so fast I almost collected a plate between the eyes.

'Michael . . . !' A warning. The plate waved in dangerous fashion.

I surrendered; both hands in the air. 'Please don't match-make for me, Jan. I know you mean well but . . . '

'You need someone, Michael. You're rotting away. I can see it, so can David. Even the kids think you're fading. Grey by name, grey by nature.'

'That bad?'

She put the plate in the rack and touched my hand. 'Yes, Michael. That bad.'


So I was on my own. Jan had promised to leave me to my own devices but I knew she would keep a protective eye on me. Twenty years my junior but so much more mature. My churlish ingratitude brought home just how deep she had buried her thumb in my pie. Mission accomplished, but I was not pleased with myself, a triumph shallow, made more so by the brutal acceptance that my life was floating towards the nearest storm drain.

I wandered into my study, slid open a drawer and pulled out a crumpled newspaper cutting dated a year before. Was it a year? Already?

It was one of my pieces for the local paper, about an escaped owl named Oscar. The publicity was good. His owner found him and me. Amy, of the sparkling brown eyes and open invitation to visit. Would she remember? Of course. Would she welcome a visit after all this time? Uncertain.

I had her details, written in the margin. She lived on the outskirts of a nearby market town. Should I just turn up? Or should I phone? I left the cutting on my desk and went for the vodka bottle. Dutch courage. I hadn't needed it when accompanying the Paras into Goose Green on my first real assignment, or when embedded with the American 82nd Airborne Division at Salman in the 1991 Gulf War.

I pick up the phone. I put it down. I walk round in circles composing lines in my head. '*Hello, Amy? This is Michael Grey, do you remember me? Oh! Not there? She's on her honeymoon/out with her husband/boyfriend/fiancé. Sorry to have bothered you. No, no message.*'

Escape! Oh, for god's sake, pick up the phone, man. Don't be such a bloody wimp.

'Amy?'

She knew my voice. The pickled vocal cords. 'It's Michael Grey, isn't it? It's so nice of you to call.' Real pleasure? Not even a hint of reproof . . . '*after all this time*'.

'I thought I might drive over to visit you . . . and your owls. How's Oscar?'

'He's well. He'll be delighted to see you.'

Reporter's cynicism. 'Really?'

A hint of amusement. 'You needn't sound so disbelieving. He's like an elephant, he never forgets a friend.'

'When . . . ?'

'Oh, please do come tomorrow. You can help clean out the flights.'

'Sounds . . . unmissable.'

'We'll give you lunch. Come early.'

'We . . . ?'

'Frankie, my daughter.'

A twinge of disappointment. Daughter?

I washed the car. It was as vintage as my Rolex and just as slow; just as much an old friend, infused with an image of Grace in the front seat, hair flying in the wind from an open window. Kept idle in its garage most days but I couldn't bear to part with it although I now preferred to walk. Hunched over, hands in pockets, daring anyone to wish me good day. Why would anyone want to take on another angry old man?

Give up. Cop out. Don't bother going.

*Coward.*

The car was clean and so was I. For the first time in years, I'd taken pleasure in dressing. I replaced my normal Rigsby-style cardigan and corduroy trousers with a smart sweater and

*Life Without Grace*

slacks that still fitted my waistline. Walking and surviving on liquid rations had left me lean. I tossed an old green Barbour into the boot with a pair of wellingtons still bearing the mud of years. The boy scout in me; always prepared for the worst. I left the vodka alone. I was hobbling without a crutch.


Amy hadn't changed. Portraits and attics. The years had barely laid siege. Natural; not enhanced by a surgeon's art like Sally Wordsworth. Highlighted well-cut hair, a mouth with a cute lift at one corner, and determined chin. She was wearing a candy striped gilet, tight-fitting blue jeans and stable boots; workmanlike and feminine all at the same time. She was slender; whip-like, and strong, her grip tight and meaningful as I shook her hand.

She held onto my fingers longer than needed and looked me over. 'Much better!'

'Than . . . ?'

'The last time we met. I recall you looked rather dishevelled.'

> *Her amusement bubbled; water tinkling over stones. Her eyes were brown, flecked with gold and bronze and set in a lovely face.*
>
> *She had her hand out. 'Amy, Amy Armstrong.'*
>
> *That voice, a lilt of brogue, just a note.*
>
> *She tilted her head. 'You're the man who wrote for 'The Times', aren't you? I just loved your reports on the Troubles.'*
>
> *Brain cranked but didn't fire. 'Long time ago, Mrs Armstrong,' was all I could think to say.*

*Amy smiled; breeze-tossed corn; as hypnotic as sunset.*

Flashbacks. I lived with them. I pulled a grimace. 'More like looking a mess. Almost a year and you remember that?'

She smiled, brightening her face and highlighting a brown smudge on her cheek.

I wanted to wipe the smudge away; but didn't.

Amy smeared it herself with a sleeve. 'I'm like Oscar . . . '

'An elephant . . . ?'

She was walking away but turned and arched her neck, swan-like. '. . . I never forget a friend. Come on.'

I followed.

'This is Francesca. Come and meet Michael, Frankie.'

The image of her mother. She could have been Amy's younger sister; mid to late twenties.

'Well now, Oscar's saviour. Good to meet you.' Another firm grip. 'You've come to help muck out, then?' The same brown eyes, narrowed in amusement. Her mother's offspring but with a more pronounced Ulster accent. Who was the father? Where was the father?

Amy gave her an affectionate pat. 'Frankie's a zoologist and English graduate. She had an offer from Paignton Zoo but prefers to work here.' Mock shrug and sideways look. 'The young, who understands them? She's working on a thesis about nocturnal predators for her doctorate.' A note of pride, not even an attempt at concealment.

Frankie handed me a yard brush and looked me over. 'Shame to get your nice clothes all messed up.'

*Life Without Grace*

'I have kit in the car.'

'Huh, huh! The work'll still be here.'

'Come and get reacquainted with Oscar first.' Amy tugged at my sleeve. 'He knows you're coming, he's been jumping up and down all morning.'

Oscar was an American Great Horned Owl. Top predator in the wild; would even take on baby alligators. Amy gave me a leather gauntlet and I held out my arm. The last time I tried it, when he was decorating my gazebo a year before, he had ignored me. Now he came zooming straight across the flight. I could feel the power as talons gripped through thick leather and was thankful he'd taken umbrage at the ski glove I'd offered him then. He turned his head right round in owl fashion, looked at Amy and then back at me, his big yellow eyes unblinking.

'Here!' Amy held something out.

I backed off a pace. 'What's that?'

'Give Oscar his breakfast.'

A dead mouse. It went in three gulps, but for the tail which Oscar sucked down spaghetti-like. He fluffed up soft feathers, shook and flew back to his favourite perch, the floor marked by his droppings and pellets.

'That's you two bonded then. He'll let you feed him from now on.' Amy smiled and pulled the gauntlet from my arm.

'From now on . . . ?'

'I've work to do and lunch to prepare. You'd better get going, Frankie's a hard taskmaster.'

And she was. Five flights in two hours brushed and disinfected. The sixth flight looked empty but she pointed to a dark corner under the roof. 'Know what that is?'

I peered. Saw movement and looked harder. 'Striated Scops Owl. Tiny, just seven inches tall. Great camouflage.'

'And the other?'

Testing me? The wildlife writer; did he know his stuff or did he Google it? Ornithology was the comfort blanket I huddled beneath when the hours proved too uncongenial. I studied the opposite corner. 'Indian Scops Owl. It looks similar but has a broader face and flatter head.' I leered. Couldn't help it. Mr Big of the twitchers.

Frankie was cool, in the real sense of the word, unimpressed. It was something everyone should know. 'This flight'll need swabbing out.'

'Aye, aye, shipmate.' My Long John Silver impersonation was as ancient as Pieces of Eight but still raised a glimmer of a smile. Had we also bonded? The half-forgotten, warmth of companionship; just a small glow but as satisfying as bringing a grin to the face of an undertaker's mute. My turn now. Impish. 'What do you know about Black Grouse, Frankie?'


Lunch was scaring me. Social intercourse with two attractive women. Would I retreat under fire?

Frankie looked across at me, chewing and serious. She swallowed. 'He's real cute, Mum. Where'd you find him?'

The story reeled out but it was obvious that Frankie already knew it. *Cute? Me?*

Frankie was talking again. It was the most voluble she'd been all morning.

'He knows his stuff about birds, don't you, Michael?' She didn't wait for an answer. 'He told me about the mating habits of Black Grouse.'

*Life Without Grace*

Amy raised a delicate eyebrow. 'Oh?'

'Did you know that the females live miles away and only fly in to be shagged by the lekking males, then fly away again, sometimes miles away, to hatch and raise their young? That's one of the reasons there's so few of them. Sometimes they don't find each other.' The emphasis thickly laid. An allegory?

Amy swung two glistening eyes my way. 'Teaching my daughter about the birds and bees?'

I hunched forward. I hadn't looked at it like that. I hadn't mentioned 'shagging' but I could see how it might be misinterpreted. Bluff it out? Stammer an apology? Dig a bigger hole?

'Laid more chicks than I can count with that line.'

Both laughed. Genuine. Sweet music. Another test and I'd passed. I could feel it.

Frankie looked at her watch. 'Hmm. Time to go. Jake's picking me up in an hour and I've got to wash this bird crap out of my hair. Ciao, babies.'

She left in a swirl of paper napkin.

'She's a nice . . .'

'Not leching, are you?'

Now I did blush. Amy was watching me closely, an amused smile playing around her lips. Leg-pull time.

'Frankie's too old for me. She has the aura of approaching Nirvana. On her sixth plane of existence, I'd say.'

'You continue to surprise me, Michael Grey.' She picked up both our plates and walked to the sink. 'You wash, I'll wipe and put away.'

It was an eighteenth-century farmhouse, no room or place for modern kitchen conveniences. Even the Aga looked ancient but was well cared for.

'Sounds like a plan.' I rolled up my sleeves. Did I need to explain? It came out anyway. 'I flirted with Sikhism, Hinduism, otherworldly-ism for a while. Reincarnation, that sort of thing.'

'After your wife was killed?'

I stopped rubbing the sponge around a cup. Mouth dried like one of Amy's dishes. But I needed the release. 'Yes!'

'You were wondering about Frankie's father.'

I swallowed, trying to get the saliva glands back in action. 'Was I?'

'You wouldn't be human if you didn't.'

'And . . . ?'

'He worked in Ulster and died when Frankie was six. That was why I found your articles on the Troubles so comforting. It was the honesty and passion that you put into them. I could tell you felt every word. I truly admired you for that.'

Honesty. I didn't want to look at her; stared into the soap suds that were dying in the Belfast sink. 'I went into hibernation, liquid anaesthetic-type hibernation. I have old baggage.'

'So do I.'

'There's been no one since Grace.' I rinsed the last cup and wanted a sharp jolt of Blue Label.

Amy threw the tea towel over dishes that still remained on the draining board. 'Shall we get comfortable? We can sit at the table or in the living room.'

*Life Without Grace*

The Irish lilt came and went with mood. Grace had been Irish. All lush auburn hair, sparkling blue eyes, high intelligence and stiletto-sharp wit.

'Table's fine.' I sat at one corner, she at right angles, legs crossed; tight, controlled.

'Frankie still has quite a distinct accent . . . ' I was asking a question, without the punctuation mark.

Amy nodded. 'She is her father's daughter. It's her way of keeping him close. That and his medals in a frame on her bedroom wall. She was so young but still remembers the way he was with her; caring and protective. She was born there and often visits her Gran in Belfast.'

'You haven't been back.' A guess; reading the runes.

'No.' Her eyes went distant, searching a long-disappeared horizon. 'I said I had old baggage too. Jeff worked for E4A, the Ulster Constabulary undercover unit. He died in the Mull heli crash. In '94. After he was killed, I went off the rails. Slept around with anyone who would have me. It taught me a lesson.'

'That not all men are wise, kind or trustworthy,' I ventured.

'It's made me . . . wary. Ulster can be an unforgiving place. That's when I decided to move back here with my parents for a clean break with the past. They both died some years ago and left this place to Frankie and me. I was working then, as a solicitor, but now the owl sanctuary takes up a lot of my time. It helps to keep the ghosts at bay.'

Honesty, raw and compelling. There was no need to rattle skeletons but I was glad there were to be no secrets.

That's where the slight accent came from. Married to a Northern Irishman it was difficult not to pick up the verbal nuances. A policeman too, working closely with lawyers. It fitted like a well-cut jigsaw. A drawer squealed open in my mental filing cabinet. 'Jeff Armstrong? Killed along with his boss, Ian . . . ?'

'Ian Phoenix . . . yes. Did you know him?'

'Knew of him. Great policeman, one of the best. I wrote a piece on E4A for *The Times* but it was never printed. 'D' Notice, I think. E4A were very secretive in those days.'

Amy put her hand on my arm. 'My, we do have a lot in common.'

Pain. We just dealt with it in different ways. The past was closing in. 'I have to be going.'

Amy uncrossed her legs but stayed seated. 'Would you like to come again?'

It should have been so easy to answer but I stuttered. 'Sure . . . if you want.'

Now she stood. The top of her head came up to my mouth and I wanted to kiss her; but didn't.

Her hand was on my chest light as a butterfly. 'I'd like that. You could feed Oscar again.'

'Lovely table manners.' I took her hand, shook it, and felt foolish.

The vodka bottle was calling.


It was my fourth visit in five weeks. The three of us had developed a relationship, albeit still fragile. Toes and eggshells avoided with all kinds of pas de trois. Amy had not mentioned Jeff again, nor I Grace. It had been said and was laid to one side. As was any apparent notion of romance. Friends.

Frankie watched us both, like one of her owls. Hooting with glee when one or other of us drew back from a sudden unexpected touch; as if wired to the mains.

We were in with the Scops owls, just Frankie and me. She stopped scrubbing and looked across, head on one side. 'When are you two wrinklies going to stop sodding around and go on a date?'

I developed a sudden admiration for the shovel. 'You think I should ask?'

Two more rasping sweeps of the broom. 'I would. She has other strings, you know.'

I didn't. 'Really?'

'You should ask her about Paul.'

I looked across. I must have seemed like a startled rabbit. 'I should?'

She gave me one of her mother's looks. 'What do you think?'

I thought Frankie was telling me more than I needed to know. 'Perhaps she prefers Paul.'

'Ever read '*Cato*' by Joseph Addison?'

I nodded. Addison, who first penned the much plagiarised line 'He who hesitates is lost'. It was all the answer I got. Clever. Frankie was giving me a nudge in her own English grad fashion.

'Would you mind . . .?' I wanted her approval.


I couldn't eat lunch.

Amy eyed my fork-toyed food. 'Something wrong?'

60     *It's Never Too Late to Fall in Love*

I blurted it. 'Would you like to go out sometime? With me . . . just the two of us. Dinner maybe?'

Stout heart aflutter.

Amy appeared to give it a second's thought and me an indecipherable look. 'I've another idea. There's a weekend coming up with the ornithological group. We have a meeting here tomorrow. Why don't you come, join, and then we'll make room for you on the trip. It's an overnighter at the bird observatory at Gibraltar Point in Lincolnshire. It's roughing it, can you cope?'

Nights in wet, fear-haunted, foxholes in the Falklands. Could I hack it?

'I think so.'

'You'll need a sleeping bag and a pair of binoculars. A telescope if you have one, otherwise I can lend you anything you don't have. What do you say?'

Amy was fired up. I'd never seen her exude so much nervous energy. Frankie was eyeing her from across the table her bottom lip caught between her teeth. Another test?

'Why not? Sounds fun.' I thought I heard Frankie groan.


Paul was half a head taller than my 5'-10'. Rangy, good-looking in a soft kind of way. His hair was shoulder length, pulled into a ponytail and held with an elastic band. He must have been sixty-five and grey flecked with it. He wore western style cowboy boots, a battered black Stetson and matching denim shirt and jeans under a waterproof jacket. Too confident, too overbearing, too loud. And he had a heavy arm around Amy's shoulder in proprietary fashion. She didn't seem to mind. A kick in the gut.

The weekend had just started and already it was a disaster. I'd come kitted like a drop-out from the students union with my sleeping bag rolled and slung beneath the rucksack. I'd opted for my corduroys, a polo neck sweater, the old Barbour and walking boots. I felt as underdressed as a plucked turkey. The other five in the group wore uniform khaki-green waterproofs and seemed a genuine bunch of enthusiastic amateur birdwatchers from 'Ever Decreasing Circles'.

Paul was holding forth at the front of the bus. He was sitting next to Amy and pointing out birds as we passed. He got Stock Dove and Wood Pigeon confused but no one else seemed to notice and I kept silent. Amy turned around just then and raised her eyebrows. I grinned but it was as false as a clown's nose.

Gibraltar Point was desolate; beautiful. Distant calls of Oystercatchers far out across the sands where the tide line was a mere silver sliver against the graphite of the Wash. Accommodation was basic and the observatory a good walk from a visitor centre and café. It was bunk beds and all in together. Not much in the way of privacy which to my mind was a good thing and a bad thing. Good because of the way Paul was leering at Amy. Bad because I couldn't hide with my vodka bottle.

It was a long day spotting and counting wading birds. Bird watching can be a lonely occupation but the group were friendly and eager to learn. I dropped a few pearls to help them along. I said little to Amy, she was velcroed to Paul's side as he spewed forth with what now appeared to be only basic knowledge. We had a raft of Common Scoter seaborne in the scopes which he insisted were Velvet Scoter and everyone took his word for it. I stayed mute. If he was Amy's choice, I did not want to fog his lenses. The small hope I had of romancing her had dwindled, as improbable as finding that one of the soaring gulls was a white-tailed tropicbird.

Why had she asked me to come? Did she want to demonstrate that my chances, if ever they existed, were gone? Did she lack the courage to tell me face to face? I could not believe that of her. Lack of courage was the last thing she possessed. I was at a loss and my misery took another lurch on a downward spiral.

The realisation was sudden. Oh, dear god. I was in love. Madly, stupidly, jealously . . . in love. It had crept up on me. Hopeless, doomed to be unrequited, love. A seed planted on the first day we'd met had germinated over past weeks but I too myopic and scared to admit it.

It was a tiring walk to Skegness station carrying the scope, tripod and rucksack but it was flat going all the way. Trains were few, especially on a Saturday evening in winter, and there was a long cold wait in prospect. I found a bench and contemplated the pit that was my life; all hope sucked down like matter into a black hole.

My mobile trilled. Only three people had the number and I ignored it at first before caving in.

'How's it going?' No preamble, but there was muted excitement in Jan's voice. Maybe I'd over-egged my expectations.

I tried to sound more cheerful than I felt. 'It's not.'

I could hear David's voice in the background, asking rapid-fire questions. He seemed more excited than Jan.

Jan stopped him with a brusque, 'shut up, David.' Then to me, 'what happened?'

'Paul happened. I was playing out of my league.'

'I'm sorry, Michael.'

*Life Without Grace*

So was I, more sorry than I ever thought possible. 'That's life.' Philosophism; I don't know how I managed it.

'What are you going to do now?'

Good question. 'I'm on my way home by train. Would you meet me at the station, I'm just about walked out for today?'

'I'll send David and I'll put a bottle of Blue Label in the fridge. We can all drown our sorrows together.'

'I don't know whether I've ever told you this, Jan, but you're an angel.'

'Now I know you're feeling bad. Chin up, big boy.' She cut the connection before she sobbed. I could hear it in her voice.

The phone then chirruped an incoming text. I thumbed buttons.

The screen lit up. *'Michael, where R U?'*

Buttons thumbed again. *'thought you needed some space . . .'*

Another chirrup. *'tell me where U R. Pls'*

My thumbs rattled on a whim of their own. *'getting drunk'*

*'WHERE?'* Short, sharp. I couldn't ignore it and switched to voice.


'Amy?'

A long pause and soft reply. 'Why did you leave?'

'Broken heart.' Words drawn like wisdom teeth. All pain, loss and regret.

Another long pause and gentle flutter of breath. 'Where are you?'

It seemed too late to matter. 'Skegness station. Train's due in a few minutes.'

'Don't you dare get on it. I'll be there soon.'

'Why bother . . . ?' But the connection had gone dead.

It was barely ten minutes and she came across the concourse like a Tornado fighter, low and fast. I stood. She cannoned into me and drummed my chest with both her fists.

'Buy me a ticket.'

'Why?'

'Because I left my purse in my rucksack back at the observatory.'

'Why do you need a ticket?'

'You can be really dense at times.'

'Part of my charm.'

'We need to talk, Michael.'

'What? About Paul?'

'Paul's my shield . . . and my friend but he's more interested in the driver than me. They brought me in the bus, that's how I got here so quickly.'

I sat. Equilibrium gone. Amy sat next to me and took my hand. Her fingers were cold. *Warm heart.*

A slow dawning. 'Another test?'

She pulled a sorrowful face. 'I shouldn't have. Frankie warned me not to. I was already sure but . . .'

'Wary's a hard habit to break?'

'Yes. Am I forgiven?'

'If I was another kind of man . . . ?'

*Life Without Grace*

'But you're not. That's why I love you.'

The time for words was over. I was twenty-two again and I remembered what I needed to do.

It was the most delicious of kisses.


Sunday morning in bed. I could hear the single bell of the small village church clanging its monotonous clamour a mile away. I turned my head to check my watch and came face to face with a lopsided grin. The cute mouth opened.

'Good morning.'

'Yes it is.'

Amy snuggled closer and I let her slide under my arm. She was warm and perfumed. Her hair tickled my nose. I felt at ease. For the first time in years my demons were absent. 'I'm sorry ... you know ... about not ...'

Amy giggled. 'We'll work on it. Good things come to those who know which erotic trigger points to stimulate.'

Room to manoeuvre; an old habit. 'You know Paul's not a very good birdwatcher, don't you?'

Amy gave out an explosive snort and poked my ribs. 'Where did that come from?'

'It niggled.'

Her chuckle was pure schadenfreude. 'Paul is a volunteer for the RSPB. He's also a psychologist. He no longer practices but all that Jungian stuff is still gumming up his thought processes. He wanted to see how you'd react when he got identifications wrong, deliberately, whether you would try to get macho and show him up in front of the others. It was very naughty but he was trying to make sure I wasn't taking on a monster under that ragged old Barbour.'

'Lack of white wing markings made them Stock Dove and Common Scoter, not Wood Pigeon and . . . '

'You knew the difference but you said nothing.' A lawyer's unasked question.

Emotion nipped with the sharpness of a carpet tack. 'If he was your choice of boyfriend, I didn't want to make him look foolish. I just want you to be happy.'

'You wouldn't fight for me . . . ?'

Shattered bodies in the street; brainwashed killers fed on raw hate. 'I've seen too much violence both mental and physical to want to go down that route.'

'Michael, you're a softy . . . and a sweetie.'

'But not perfect. You know I'm prone to the most awful verbal analogies . . . '

'And you drink too much . . . '

'I'm thinking of mounting an operation to rescue my liver from the evil clutches of alcohol.'

Amy rolled onto my chest. 'Any particular reason?'

A second, that was all the time it took for certainty to stab. 'I don't need it anymore.'

She teased at my chest hair. 'Are you up to telling me all about the sex life of the Black Grouse?'

I was on the starting grid, engine revving.

'I'm in pole position . . .'


It was a small country churchyard outside Portrush on the Northern Irish coast where sea air cut clean. Grace's headstone was one of the largest, the money having been donated by her colleagues on *The Independent*. The clouds were lifting and the early morning rain blowing off the Atlantic was giving way to thin streamers of watery sunshine.

Amy held my hand tighter and grasped my bicep with her free hand, her fingers biting deep. We had prepared some words between us; similar words to those spoken over Jeff's grave the day before.

'My darling Grace. This is Amy, my new wife. We have brought you a gift of flowers; Pink Carnations, Lilac, Lily of the Valley and Jasmine as a token of our respect. Please accept them in the spirit in which they are intended. There is a message in the flowers that says you will never be forgotten. And we will come again as often as we can. Rest in peace.'

Amy took the flowers from my hand as I could no longer see. She laid them carefully on the grave and stood back. 'Do you think Grace approves?'

I wiped my eyes as sunlight sparkled the headstone.

'It certainly looks like she does. She's smiling.'

Amy cocked an eyebrow. 'Is that the cynical old hack talking?'

'You've given me hope to believe in a future and the courage to let go of the past.' I held her close. Now all four of us could move on.

# Spot On

## Jane Walker

Joe Bradley was a happy man. The construction, care and study of clocks constituted both his hobby and his profession. He was a small man, which was fortunate as he spent most of his life in dusty towers climbing up ladders and through trap doors, inching his way past sets of bells, adding a spot of oil here an extra penny-weight there, cleaning, re-gilding and revelling in the precision of time measurement. In the little Yorkshire town of Market Weedon, where Joe had lived all his life, he looked after the Town Hall clock, which had four faces and chimed the quarters; the Park clock which Joe had made himself (it had ducks which bobbed round on a platform and laid eggs on the hour); and the Parish Church clock which overlooked the market place. Caring for clocks was a solitary occupation which suited Joe since he was profoundly deaf.

The church clock was unreliable not because of any incurable fault in its mechanism but because the wooden beam on which it was supported was old and rotten. Joe had decided to replace the beam with a steel bar.

In his brown corduroys and tweed cap, Joe arrived early at the church on Friday morning, unloaded his bag of tools and the heavy steel bar from his van and then drove it round to Beales Yard where the stallholders parked. Friday was market day and he didn't want a ticket for parking on the square. The church door was open and Arthur Young, the churchwarden, was waiting for him in the porch.

'Lock up when you've finished and 'ang on to the key, Joe. I'll collect it from you when I get back tomorrow night'.

Joe nodded and gave a 'thumbs up' to indicate that he had understood.

The tower had three chambers one above the other. A spiral staircase led to the first, the ringing chamber, where six bell ropes, with their red and yellow sallies, were looped up to a metal 'spider' near the ceiling. From here, a ladder and a trap door led to the bell chamber where the great weight of the bells, supported on huge baulks of timber, made the silence, the stillness, almost tangible. A narrow walkway round the edge of the chamber led to another ladder and a second trap door. The clock was housed in the highest chamber.

Although he could not hear the cries of the stallholders and the noise of traffic, Joe was aware of the bustle of the market place. Through the narrow, slit windows of the tower he could see people moving around the stalls and smell the hamburgers cooking in Jack Albright's van. He knew most of the people in the market. Although his deafness had always kept him a little apart, he was well known and well liked in the town. There was the large, comfortable figure of Bessie Dancy with her pails of flowers making a bright splash of colour around the market cross. She was a good sort, Bessie, used to dance with him at the Town Hall Hop years ago. Joe stood for a moment remembering the beat of the music and the soft feel of Bessie's hair against his cheek. Most of

70          *It's Never Too Late to Fall in Love*

the girls had been wary of his strange speech but Bessie had always understood him.

' 'E's alright is Joe', she told them as she clasped him to her ample bosom and quick-stepped him round the floor. She'd married Ted Dancy and brought up four children since then. Now Bessie and Joe each had a bungalow in Park Close and kept a friendly eye on each other.

Joe disconnected the clock hands so that they hung downwards showing half-past-six, then he arranged a cradle of webbing to support the clock from one of the roof timbers so that he could remove the old support and replace it with the steel bar.

Down in the market place the operation went almost unnoticed. The clock had been unreliable for some time and people had stopped paying attention to it. Jim and Margaret Barclay noticed it; they were enjoying a few days holiday motoring in the area and had stopped for a coffee. They would remember Market Weedon as 'that place where we saw the hands of the clock move', but nobody else was looking upwards.

By midday, Joe was satisfied with his progress and climbed down to eat his sandwiches in the churchyard. The sun was warm; he'd have a stroll round the market before going back to the tower.

'Eh up then, Joe. Cup o' tea?' Bob Albright held up one of his big white mugs.

'Aye' Joe fished a pound coin out of his pocket.

'You working up there?' Bob pointed to the church tower and Joe nodded.

'Clock', he said.

'Aye, she's been wrong for a bit'.

Joe retuned the mug, pointed to the tower and gave a 'thumbs up'.

'Right you are, Joe.' Bob turned to another customer.

The beetles which had been champing their way through the woodwork of the tower for fifty years, had moved on from the clock support and made a start on recycling the bell tower ladder in January of the previous year and so could reasonably be expected to finish the job in time for Harvest Festival. Joe noticed the progress they had made as he climbed the ladder again and made a mental note to mention it to Arthur Young when he called for the key.

By five o'clock, the market was over, the stallholders were packing every thing back into their vans. Fred Clark was sweeping up the last of the cabbage leaves before the market place became a car park again. He glanced up as he heard the clock strike one and then two.

'Is Joe up there then?', he asked Bessie.

'Oh aye, you know 'im. Won't leave till e's got the thing right.'

Bessie lifted the last bucket into the back of her van and slammed the door. 'That's me done for today. I'll be glad to get mi' feet up.'

Bessie had bought a pie from one of the stalls for her supper and was looking forward to popping it in the microwave and getting settled down in time to watch the snooker on television.

Joe packed up his tools then waïted, watch in hand, for the clock to strike six.

'Spot on'. He closed and locked the clock door then, with his tool bag over his shoulder, he started to climb down the ladder into the bell chamber, closing the trap door above him.

The beetles had been chewing away all afternoon and were ahead of schedule on the third rung. As Joe put his weight on it the rung collapsed, the tool bag slipped from his shoulder, and he fell with a crash hitting his head on the bell frame. The crash disturbed the air sending sound waves beating against the walls and ceiling, then the dust settled, stillness returned to the bell chamber and the beetles started on the next rung.

The clock struck nine as Bessie Dancy got up from her chair and went to make a cup of tea. Before switching on the kitchen light, she looked across to Joe's house. She liked to know he was there, just over the road. There was no light in his kitchen which was a bit surprising, it wasn't his bowls night and he never went to the pub on Fridays. Of course he might have gone for a bite to eat somewhere, she took her cup of tea back to the television, she'd see if there was anything worth watching until the news and then bed. As usual, Bessie slept through most of the news and it was after eleven when she looked for Joe's light again before getting into bed.

She could tell he was still out because his van wasn't in the drive, Joe's garage was his workshop there was never room for the van. Well, at least she knew he was not in the house and needing help, Bessie settled down to sleep.

The church clock was striking three when she looked out again. Joe's drive was still empty. She'd never get back to sleep now.

Joe was regular – regular as clockwork – if he was going away he'd have let her know . . .

He'd be really mad with her if she called the police and he was perfectly alright . . .

What on earth could be taking all this time, the clock was chiming properly . . .

*Spot On*

Well, Joe was Joe. Once he got absorbed in a problem he wouldn't leave it; she'd known him work all night in his garage.

At half past three Bessie put her coat on over her nightie, got her car out of the garage and drove off to the town centre. Feeling rather foolish, she stopped at Beale's Yard, and got out to look over the wall . . . and there was Joe's van. Thoroughly worried now, she parked in the market place, took a torch from the car and walked over to the church.

Surprisingly the heavy door opened when she pushed it. Bessie was not a church goer – she'd hardly been back since Ted's funeral – but she remembered that the little door behind the font led to the tower. Bessie's skin prickled with fear, fear of the dark, the eerie, holy quiet, the great cavernous spaces where the torch couldn't reach. There must be lights but she couldn't find a switch. Slowly she made her way to the tower door, an open padlock hung from an iron ring, Joe must be still up there. Trying to ignore the terrors behind her, she pushed the door open, shone the torch ahead and was dismayed to see the narrow, curving steps leading up into total darkness. Bessie would not willingly have climbed those stairs in daylight but it was no use trying to call Joe. She flashed the torch on and off a few times hoping he might see it and save her the climb but the stillness was absolute. Afraid of the sound of her own footsteps and terrified of what she might find, Bessie began to climb the staircase being careful to place her feet on the widest part of the step, easing her hips round the curves and stopping every few steps to listen for a sound from Joe. With the torch in one hand, she scrabbled for support on the rough cast stones of the wall with the other. She kept the torch pointed downward finding each step and deciding where to put her foot so she didn't know that she had reached the top until she stumbled over the threshold of a small, empty room. In panic, she flashed the torch around and saw the ropes looped up to the ceiling but no sign of Joe. Then she saw the ladder and above it – Joe's leg with his shoe and his corduroy trousers dangling from the trap door.

Bessie's scream echoed round the room before fading into the stones of the tower leaving only the muffled ticking of the clock and the wild, thump of her heart. She never climbed ladders, but obviously Joe needed help – her help. She never prayed either but 'Please, God, don't let him be dead' was all she could think of as she put her foot on the first rung and began to heave herself up the ladder.

With head and shoulders through the hatch she could see Joe lying on his back with his head in a pool of blood. Bessie shone the torch on his face but he didn't respond. With a final heave, she dragged herself through the hatch and crawled round to his head.

In the strange, dark world where Joe had been wandering he felt something brush his face. Then a light swept across his eyes and he knew where he was, it was the Town Hall Hop he could feel Bessie's hair on his cheek and the strength of her arms as she tried to swing him off his feet.

Then the floor vibrated as the clock struck four.

'Spot on', whispered Joe, and Bessie started pulling off her nightie to bandage his head.

*Spot On*

# Dancing Round The Med

### Denise West

If it was loneliness that had made James Golightly fill in that application form then, he hadn't admitted it even to himself. He had taken shelter from the rain in the public library and flipping through a Cunard Cruises brochure saw the advert in the back. He wrote down the details on the flap of the envelope containing his gas bill and probably that would have been that, except for lunch with Susan.

At her request Jim had met his daughter at the 'Green Edge'. He knew he was in for a lecture when he saw her place both elbows on the table and link her fingers together in a prayer-like gesture. She had always done this even as a small child, when she had to get something 'off her chest' as the saying goes. Jim was struggling with the menu board and wondered if ciabatta was the kind of bread that caused an avalanche of crumbs down your front, but he got the gist of her message.

'I'm worried about you Dad. It's time to move on. Go out and enjoy yourself. Why didn't you take up any of the classes on the leaflet I got you?' But it was the her last remark that resonated in his head and coincidently linked with his find in the library.

'Why don't you start to dance again. You and Mum enjoyed it so? I'm sure you'd find a partner easily enough. All those single women at tea dances itching for a great mover like you.'

That evening he retrieved the crumpled envelope from his pocket and sent off for details. The application form duly arrived and it sat on the dresser for nearly a week by the side of his dental appointment card, and that probably would have been that, except for dinner at Hilary and Phil's.

The Watsons had been his neighbours for years so to be asked to eat with them did not set off any alarm bells in his head. He sat on their moquette sofa with his half of beer when he suddenly noticed the table had been set for four. Then the fourth arrived.

'Call me Maggie,' she trumpeted on being introduced.

He had to admit she was elegantly dressed, but her hair was too blonde for someone that age and in a 'bouffant' style that was perhaps popular fifty years ago. She also had a whitened smile that beamed like a super-trouper spotlight at an Abba concert. Jim's first reaction had been surprise, and then bewilderment, then over the tiramisu came the realisation that he was being fixed up. They thought he needed a woman in his life. His excuse to leave was lame but by the 'After Eight' mints he couldn't stand her another moment, touching his arm constantly, talking non-stop about liposuction and the size of her extension. She may have been called Maggie but he was no Dennis.

The first thing he did when he got home was rummage out the application form and fill it in. He even slipped out to the

*Dancing Round The Med*

post-box on the corner in his pyjamas. Jim knew if he slept on the idea he might change his mind. He knew they meant well, but he was disappointed with their judgement and meddling in his affairs.

The next few weeks, when he had time to look back, were conducted on autopilot and in a daze. First the interview in Southampton; the trial out; the acceptance of the job on his part; the buying and fitting of clothes; the jabs; and finally, telling Susan of his plans. She was both amazed and shocked. Amazed enough to render her speechless and shocked at his daring. Hilary and Phil laughed – disbelief of course – then they sort of avoided him so they didn't have to talk about it. But they did talk about it to everyone else. Mr. Saini mentioned it when Jim called in the newsagent for his daily paper and Mrs.Granger at number nine asked to borrow the hedge-trimmer before he went away.

But away he went. And here he is now. Jim Golightly, widower aged 66, retired plumber, aboard the S.S. Ocean Village sailing towards Gibraltar. Only now he looks different, feels different. In a black tuxedo, white starched shirt, dickie bow and polished patent pumps, we have James Golightly a 'gentleman host', a partner for single lady passengers, dancing his way around the Mediterranean Sea.

He was amazed how easily he fell into the new routine. Mornings were their own to do as they pleased. He lounged about his cabin or topped up his tan and as he felt rusty especially on the Tango and Samba, the head 'Host' Ken gave him brush up lessons in the afternoon. They were present at cocktail parties smart in white flannels and a blazer, drifting amongst passengers courteous and unseen. On-shore days were great. He headed off with the other hosts, five they were in all. They did all the usual touristy things like gazing in awe at Palma Cathedral, walking the old walls of Dubrovnik,

*It's Never Too Late to Fall in Love*

writing postcards, buying tat, wearing silly hats that really didn't suit them to keep off the sun. But it was nights when the ship came alive and his job really began.

With dinner over passengers would drift towards the ball-room where a large orchestra was in full swing. Under the glittering, mirror ball they glided around the floor, dancing every dance making every woman believe she was Cinderella for a night. Then as the last waltz faded he would fall into bed exhausted, his tired feet still pulsating from the beat. It was hard work with strict rules. No drinking, or fraternising. But, it suited him right now gave him a focus and a sense of being useful.

When he looked back over all the hours he spent in that hushed kitchen, with the cat asleep amongst the pot plants on the windowsill and the rays of the sun moving slowly over the plastic tablecloth, he knew where he would rather be. And when eventually the adventure was over and home beckoned, as it surely must, it would be bearable knowing he could set sail again whenever the call came.

If it was loneliness that had made James Golightly fill in the application form then it worked for he isn't lonely now. If he did it to shock them, then all those angry feelings of resent-ment dissolved on the morning tide out of Monte Carlo. It was one of those bright blue days when the sea shimmered in the silver light and the steady thud of the engines sud-denly fell in with the rhythm of his heart. Just for a moment it was if they were one great heaving whole pushing on with the journey and finding a passage through the waves. That morning James Golightly threw his grief overboard and for the first time in an age felt the day held promise.

*Dancing Round The Med*

## Lightning Never Strikes Twice

### Paul Chiswick

My first husband had always loved the Isles of Scilly, ever since he was a boy. At one time his father owned a cottage on the edge of Carn Morval Down, so Oliver was as familiar with St Mary's as he was with his own face. We honeymooned here, two love-struck young newlyweds filled with hope for our future together.

For someone brought up in the industrial griminess of Wolverhampton he had an intense passion for the sea. Perhaps it was an ancestral spirit reminding him his past was rooted deep in some far-off Scandinavian land.

When God knitted my DNA in its unique double helix he dropped that particular stitch. I was never taken by the sea, certainly not the grey and angry sea dashing against the rock-strewn St Mary's coastline. That ineluctable sea, with its power to destroy, terrifies me. One day, I stumbled across a book, *Ships, Shipwrecks and Maritime Incidents around the Isles of Scilly*, and bought it for Oliver, thinking it was a fiction full of romantic maritime tales. Only when I came to write a dedication in it did I realise it was a catalogue of poor souls who had lost their lives in these boiling waters.

Oliver laughed at my pusillanimity, saying Neptune would only turn his attention to you if you took him for granted. I would not be convinced, so he never pressured me if an opportunity arose to jump aboard a boat and cross the water to the nearby islands of Tresco and St Martin's. Instead, we contented ourselves with exploring the coastline and looping round Old Town, Higher Moors, Maypole and Porthloo. He never complained, but if his nostrils caught a salty tang he would look out to sea as if a Siren's enchanting song had wafted in on the breeze.

Now here I am again, gazing at my reflection in the window of my B&B room, turning back the years in my mind.

Remember this place, Oliver? Of course you do. This is where we made love, laughed, and learned about each other. This is where you laid out your plans for our future in words that painted such a brilliant picture on the blank canvas of my adoring mind.

This is the place I never wanted to see again.

You were always good with words, even your last ones. You could make arsenic sound as appetizing as strawberries and cream.

*Don't worry, Eleanor. Yacht racing offshore is no more dangerous than skiing. In fact, it's not as dangerous as skiing.*

That was a lie and we both knew it. You might have broken your leg on the slopes but you would never have . . . never have . . .

*Take care of Lucy while I'm away.*

You had to go. Danger was your drug of choice at a time when that expression had yet to be coined. I knew that, although I could not accept it. You had a family, Oliver; a family you left rudderless.

*Wish me luck.*

Luck? You had it in spades – a thriving business, a beautiful house, a doting wife, a delightful young daughter, and enough money never to have to worry about it.

*I love you.*

And I love you so much it still hurts. Thirty-one years, Oliver. Thirty-one years since that horrendous day. I have tried and failed to put your death behind me, to reconstruct my shattered life. Yes, I have found another man. You know I could never have lived my life like a nun. He's kind, generous and thoughtful and thinks the world of Lucy and Hughie. My fondness for him grew slowly, year by year, like the rings of a tree trunk.

But Oliver, dear Oliver, he doesn't come within a country mile of you. Not a single day passes without my heart somersaulting when I think of you; my daring, devil-may-care, beautiful man. I keep my memories private; hide them away in my grief-filled locker. Secrete them even from Lucy, now more than halfway through her fourth decade of life.

I don't want to be here, Oliver. I want to be a million miles away from these islands that stole you away from me. Islands they say appeal to the human spirit, yet leave mine cold. Perhaps it is because life here is governed by the sea and tides and mine is governed by an eternal emptiness that I cannot reconcile myself to forgive them.

Or forgive you.

'Are you all right, Eleanor? You look a little peaky.'

Immersed in my own thoughts, I forget Robbie is with me in the room.

'Sorry, darling, it's the helicopter. That whup-whup-whupping noise has given me a headache.'

Culpability does not sit on the helicopter's shoulders. Ever since Lucy booked this trip for us my nerves have been as taut as piano wires, my poor nails chewed almost to the quick. That was three months ago. Three months, during which I should have stood my ground and told her no, I am not yet ready to face my demons, will never be ready.

'Perhaps you should lie down for a while.' Robbie's face creases in that concerned way he has when treating me as if I were a child. I shouldn't complain. He is the one who does my shopping and maintains my house and garden ever since I had the cancer scare two years ago, days short of my sixty-first birthday. Fortunately, that was all it was, a scare, but it shook me badly.

It frightened the pants off Robbie.

This year, Lucy took it upon herself to suggest where Robbie and I should spend our late summer holiday.

*How about St Mary's, Mother? It holds happy memories for you, doesn't it? You would both love it there.*

Oh, Lucy; so cunning yet so transparent. How conveniently you forget my one memory that taints them all.

And why suggest it now after all this time?

I cannot bring myself to ask her, not outright just like that. There has always been a pressured edge to our relationship, like two tectonic plates riding against each other until a dramatic displacement takes place and all hell breaks loose. Sometimes I wonder if she blames me for the loss of her father, as if I have been clumsy or careless. I doubt she remembers Oliver. It could be she has constructed flesh and bones from the many public images there are of him, although the photographs I possess are locked away, deliberately out of mind in a tea chest stowed in the darkest recesses of my attic.

*Lightning Never Strikes Twice*

I do recall she spent one entire week – she would have been fifteen or sixteen – in Southampton Central Library, gluing herself to the microfiche reader and hunting through rows of old newspapers.

*What are you doing in there, Lucy?*

*I'm looking for Daddy.*

*Why?*

*Do you have to ask?*

My mouth flapped up and down like a ventriloquist's dummy, but the ventriloquist wasn't there to throw the words. Her eyes held mine, challenging, and I knew then Oliver would always be with her; an unseen presence, as real to her as if she were holding his hand.

A mother should never say this about her child, but I was relieved – actually relieved – when she went away to university. I had begun to spend more time with Robbie who was stoking up the courage to ask his estranged wife for a divorce. Lucy treated me as if I were Jezebel, as if I had betrayed Oliver, made a cuckold of him. Conversation had to be dragged out of her, the words backed up, clogging her throat. She overheard Robbie say he wished he had a wife like me. She flew into a fury and raked her nails across his face, leaving bloody trails. Robbie and I didn't see each other for some time after that, not until after she left university.

After graduating, the bright lights of London beckoned her and she slipped effortlessly into the glittering world of advertising, marrying her boss and bearing his child along the way. For years I never saw her, receiving only a monthly telephone call that she must have felt duty bound to make.

Then her life spiralled out of control. The business failed, her husband committed suicide, and she was left, penniless and homeless, with a ten-year-old child to care for.

Guilt climbed all over me. I had been blind to my child when she needed me most. How selfish to have put my own interests before hers. So when she dug her heels in and insisted we make this journey, I gave up resisting and thought it better to say, yes, it is about time, before I am too old.

Now it is too late. Now Robbie and I are here and tomorrow we will be there.

On the one hand, my natural curiosity begs to be satisfied. 'There' is where Oliver met such a tragic end. On the other, it scares me half to death wondering what I will encounter when we are there.

While Robbie unpacks my case, I continue to stare out of the rain-splattered sash window, the wind whistling eerily through its ill-fitting frame. A small flotilla of boats bobs wildly on the choppy waters of St Mary's Pool and in the near distance Samson rises up, barely visible in the squall. The few people on the street are bent forward from the waist, leaning into the wind, hands holding hoods, multicoloured anoraks glistening wet. Maybe my memory is selective, choosing only to pick out days of uninterrupted sunshine, but I swear that when Oliver and I used to come here we never experienced such a downpour as this.

Should I kneel down here and now and thank God for such foul weather? Pray it continues so I have a perfect excuse for keeping my feet on terra firma? If only I could, but I cannot. God has abandoned me and Robbie is watching me like a hawk.

'Lucy asked me to give you this,' he says, taking a folded sheet of paper out of his inside jacket pocket.

'What is it?'

'It's a newspaper cutting.'

*Lightning Never Strikes Twice*

'A newspaper cutting?'

'Yes. She found it years ago in the library. She says you should read it.' He unfolds the sheet and holds it out. I can see it is an old photocopy.

'Would you mind reading it? My eyes feel like they're being pierced with hot needles.'

He opens his spectacles case, takes out his reading glasses and hooks them over his ears.

'It's from *The Times,* dated 15th August 1979.'

Blood turns to ice in my veins. Why Lucy? Why are you doing this to me?

He begins to read. 'The Fastnet race has been held every year since 1925, except during the war. It is a classic amongst offshore races. Starting at Cowes on the south coast, it goes around the Fastnet Rock off the coast of Ireland and finishes at Plymouth, a distance of 605 miles.

'The race has an excellent safety record, only one crewman being lost overboard in 1931. On 11th August a record 303 entries got underway in fine weather. The following day, weather conditions in the Atlantic became increasingly unsettled with wind speeds reaching 30 knots. The bad weather moved towards the race area. The BBC shipping forecast did not report the approaching gale until it was too late. By the time the official gale warnings were broadcast the wind speed was nearly 50 knots and many yachts were out of control and in great danger. Last night the situation worsened rapidly, the coastguard receiving numerous May Day reports —'

'Robbie, please, no more!'

He peers over the top of his glasses and I see collusion in his eyes. Lucy and he, once adversaries, have become allies.

I press my fingers to my temples and suck in a lungful of air. An original cutting from the same newspaper gathers dust in my writing bureau, out of sight, but not out of mind.

He draws himself up to his full height, towering over me. Arms crossed over his chest, mouth stretched in a tight line, I recognise the signs of an impending row.

'You two were in on this together weren't you?' I say.

'I happen to agree with Lucy, Eleanor. It's about time you laid Oliver's ghost to rest.'

'I . . . I will, one day. I promise.'

'When? Tomorrow? Next week? Next year?'

'Please, Robbie, my head . . .'

'You're a coward, Eleanor. All we're asking you to do is take a boat trip to see where he lost his life. Is that so much to ask?'

'Darling, I can't . . . I can't . . .'

'You can. That's why we're here. You promised her, remember?'

Did I? Did I really? I suppose I must have done. Lucy is not given to fabrication.

I reach into my handbag, pull out a tissue and ball it up in my fist. 'Must I do this, Robbie? Can't we just turn around and go home?'

'No, we can't. You're not the only one who carries this particular monkey on your back, you know.'

'But I don't see how Oliver's . . .' the word doesn't want to come out, '. . . death affected her quite so much. She was only five at the time.'

'Hughie found the photocopy on her bedside table. He couldn't understand why you hadn't been to see where Oliver died. She really didn't know what to tell him.'

'Ah.'

Hughie is my grandson; sixteen, strapping, and sailing mad. He hopes to represent Great Britain in the men's one person dinghy in the 2012 Olympics. Very proud of his grandfather Lucy says, although he has never mentioned Oliver to me. I suppose she has told him to tiptoe carefully around his grandmother's emotions.

'Hughie's more mature than his years, Eleanor. He's very good at looking at things from more than just one viewpoint. He says the sea can be forgiving as well as cruel.'

Forgiving? The only image I can conjure up is an angry maelstrom dashing itself against razor-sharp rocks; jagged, black and smelling of sulphur, Oliver's yacht pitching and rolling, its fragile backbone snapping in two.

Thoughtless words rush out before I can stop them. 'Does he? And he would know would he? I wouldn't be surprised if he ends up like Oliver!'

Robbie's cheeks flush crimson. With embarrassment or anger? His emotional barometer has never been easy for me to read. I take a step toward him needing to apologise, wanting him to enfold me in this arms.

He raises his hands, palms outwards as if to push me away. 'I'll put that outburst down to your headache. I'm going out for a cigarette and then a stroll to the Star Castle to book a table for dinner. We can discuss this again later.'

'The Last Supper?' I say, only half-joking.

'Oh, for pity's sake!'

He stuffs the photocopy in his pocket and marches through the open door.

Last night's dinner with Robbie at the Star Castle should have been a joyous occasion, reliving the one time Oliver and I had dined there. Then, we had been overawed by the opulence of the place and the ostentatious displays of our fellow diners. We were half their age, underdressed, and much too frivolous. We laughed about it for days afterwards, Oliver mimicking the stuffy old colonel (or so he imagined) on the neighbouring table.

It has all changed now. Paintings by local artists hang on pastel walls. The dining room is more akin to a French café; scrubbed wooden tables, each decorated with a slim glass vase containing a single red rose, its efflorescing fragrance mingling with the aroma of garlic and onions drifting in from the kitchen. It is a setting where Robbie and I could have talked amicably about things of little consequence: next door's cherry tree's thick roots disfiguring our lawn; Betty Kennedy's torrid affair with the butcher; plans for the village hall restoration. Instead, hardly a word passed between us, Robbie still angry with me, methodically and determinedly working his way through the courses, drinking far too much Pinot Noir. He did link my arm on our way back to our lodgings, though whether it was in forgiveness or out of a desire to maintain his equilibrium is debatable.

Poor Robbie, I don't know why he hasn't left me before now. It can't be easy trying to fill another man's shoes. His was the first shoulder I cried on after Oliver's accident; burying my face in the warmth of the Arran pullovers he is so fond of wearing. After that, well, he was always there to comfort me, to wrap me in his arms and stroke my hair with his long artist's fingers. Before long, he became my constant com-

*Lightning Never Strikes Twice*

panion, accompanying me on my many visits to Lucy as she attempted to repair the broken pieces of her life. I don't know what I would have done without him. I had never learned to drive when Oliver was alive, had never needed to.

Selfless, faithful Robbie. Always there for me.

Try as I could, I found sleep elusive, fighting a nightmare determined to impose itself; a swirling wraith, impossibly tall, limbless, with a grinning mouth full of huge, gleaming white teeth. It towered over the hazy figure of Oliver who was shouting, *Don't worry, Eleanor. Yacht racing offshore is no more dangerous than fighting this devil,* before the wraith drew a glinting knife and sliced it viciously across his mouth. Blood spurted everywhere in a fine crimson mist, but Oliver's mouth went on shouting, louder and louder and louder until everything began to spin, faster and faster and faster until I jerked awake, sweat pouring out of every pore in my body.

In the end I gave up, resorting to my old ally Mister Zolpidem, his chemical charms coaxing me into the welcome blackness of sleep.

I awake to find sunlight lancing through the gap in the curtains. Bright red figures on the bedside clock declare the time is 8:52. The smell of bacon frying hangs in the air. At first, I am a little disorientated and cannot recall why the window is on the left side of the bed and why there should be the sound of laughter outside it. Then it dawns on me where I am.

I hear a light tapping on the door.

'Are you awake, Eleanor?'

Robbie. Can he hear me breathing? I jam my fist in my mouth, squeeze my eyes tight shut.

Go away.

His knuckles attack the door like an angry woodpecker. 'Eleanor! Are you there?'

'Is something the matter?' another voice, more distant, concerned, unsure.

'No, it's nothing. My friend is . . . a little hard of hearing, that's all.'

'Well, if you wouldn't mind hurrying her along. We finish serving breakfast at nine-thirty.'

'Yes, sorry.'

The whisper floats through the keyhole like poison gas. 'Don't be so childish, Eleanor. The boat's at eleven and there's no way you won't be on it.'


When I enter the cramped dining room, Robbie is sitting at a table in conversation with a woman who is the spitting image of Anne Widdecombe. He scowls and points at the chair next to his. Now I feel like an errant child as I edge around the tables, forcing a smile for the seated guests.

'Thish is your other half, I gather,' says the Widdecombe lookalike, giving me a smile that reveals a perfect set of dentures, much too large for her mouth. As I take my place, she holds out her hand and clacks, 'Ruby Shpredbury. Pleashed to meet you.'

I nod, but leave her hand suspended. 'Eleanor. Eleanor Magnusson. I'm not his other half, I'm his . . . we're just good friends.'

Sharing a table with a stranger is not my idea of fun. Any minute now this woman will tell me what an unusual name I have; she is sure she has heard it before; it seems to ring a bell.

*Lightning Never Strikes Twice*

'Magnusson? What an unushual name. I'm sure . . .'

'Full English?' A teenage girl slouches at the edge of the table, weight on one leg, face blank with boredom. A black skirt barely covers her backside and there is an egg stain on the front of her white blouse.

I could not digest food even if my stomach reached out of my mouth and dragged it in.

'No, thank you. I'm not hungry.'

'Tea? Coffee? Juice?'

'A glass of water would be fine.'

The girl looks at me as if I might be ET, and yes, I am tempted to ask if I can phone home, because at this precise moment that is exactly where I want to be.

'Beautiful day.' Ruby's face beams at me. 'Robbie tellsh me you're taking a little trip out to the Weshtern Isles.'

A tic triggers in my right eyelid.

'I've never been there myshelf, but I do hear they are so wondroushly myshterious. Mind you, you don't want to get too closhe to that nasty Bishop Rock.'

A cold finger traces the curve of my spine.

'The forecast is for fair weather,' says Robbie quickly, giving me a sideways glance. 'Probably be as calm as a millpond.'

'Ain't never calm, never,' snaps the girl, banging the glass down on the table as if somehow it is to blame for her working in this place. She holds out her hand, shows an ugly red scar that runs from the base of her little finger to the fleshy mound of her thumb. 'Got that on The Bishop. Could have been much worse. Dead lucky I was.'

'Heavensh.' Ruby's face turns puce.

I experience a moment of nausea.

Robbie glances at his watch. 'Time to go, Eleanor.'

'Last Supper done with, now the crucifixion?'

Ruby and the girl stare at me, their eyebrows knotted like spaghetti.

A crowd is gathered outside the Harbourside Hotel on the tarmac road running parallel to the quayside. A dozen or so feet below the roadway, a line of boats wait patiently, diesel engines putt-putting. An overweight woman with a clipboard holds her hand in the air and barks instructions. The crowd splinters as chattering people line up in orderly queues for their designated destinations: St Agnes, Bryher, Tresco, St Martin's.

Oliver once told me tourists rarely venture as far as the Western Isles and the local boatmen are careful to pick the calmest of days before setting out. Needle-sharp rocks lie in wait for those who stray from the narrow safe passages. Only the insane would insist on making such a journey if the weather shows the faintest signs of turning foul.

Foul weather has hammered the islands for the past week.

Why, oh, why is it so good today?

'There's our boat,' says Robbie. 'Let's go.'

He clamps his hand on my forearm and hauls me to where a green and cream boat nestles between much more solid neighbours. Its wheelhouse is set aft, barely big enough to hold one person. The deck is uncovered, affording no protection from the elements.

I shrug off his hand. 'You can't be serious. If you think I'm setting foot on that, you've another think coming.'

For a split second, I see uncertainty in his eyes and then it passes.

*Lightning Never Strikes Twice*

'The chap comes highly recommended. There's nothing to worry about.'

'But look at it! If a big wave hits that thing, it's bound to end up upside down!'

The familiar look rolls on to his face. 'Oh, so you know all about boat building now? Come on, mind the steps.'

As I tread gingerly on the weathered concrete steps, holding on to a filthy rope that passes through iron eyelets driven into the harbour wall, I notice how low the tide is. A fringe of dark seaweed, smelling of roasted nuts and iodine, runs in an uninterrupted horizontal line below which the wall is scabrous with barnacles.

'Careful, missus, the step's a mite slippery.' A hand grasps mine, warm, reassuring. Taking my eyes off the steps, I look into the face of the boatman, a face etched with fine tracery like a spider's web. Penetrating blue eyes peer from under brows the colour of cigarette ash. It is impossible to say how old he is; he could be anything from fifty to seventy. He is certainly dressed the part. Blood-red Dutch Fisherman's cap, faded black sweatshirt with white letters – Captain's Rules. Rule 1: The Captain is always right. Rule 2: See Rule 1 – heavy corduroys and roped-soled shoes. As I hover above the gunwale I feel the boat rock, and for a brief moment the gap between the wall and the boat draws me like a magnet.

The boatman's free hand firmly cups my elbow. 'Steady, there. We don't want any accidents.'

I really cannot believe how small this boat is. The last time I was on water was a Nile Cruise. Three decks up, I could have been in a five star hotel, there was so little movement. It never occurred to me how the ship would behave in rough weather. Why would it? There was no possibility of breakers crashing on the Nile.

'I really don't want to do this,' I whisper to Robbie, every muscle in my body tightening. 'Please take me back.'

'Sit down, or you'll hurt yourself.'

He settles himself next to me, jaw tightening.

In less time than it takes to cook a casserole, we'll be there.

The boatman pushes the throttle forward and the boat jerks into life, its bow rising. From where I sit I can see the sickle sweep of Town Beach, the white-walled and grey-roofed houses of Hugh Town crowding the water's edge. Robbie takes a book out of his rucksack – *Isles of Scilly Guidebook* – flicks through it and stops at a page titled 'Getting your bearings on Scilly' that portray a stylised map. I try not to look, but I can't resist. My eyes flit westwards past St Mary's, The Gugh, St Agnes, Annet, finally coming to rest where the print almost bleeds off the page.

I gasp. There it is; tiny, the size of a full stop. Insignificant in the white space that surrounds it.

The Bishop Rock.

'Name's Gabriel, like the angel.' The boatman doffs his cap and takes a bow.

Robbie points at me, then himself. 'Eleanor. Robbie,' he calls above the thrumming of the diesel engine.

'Welcome aboard the Pride of Bryher. Be with you in 'alf a mo. 'ave to run through the safety stuff, see?'

We are now heading out to open sea. To my left, high above me on the harbour wall, two small children wave at us. Without thinking, I wave back and continue to watch them as they grow smaller and smaller.

*Lightning Never Strikes Twice*

Gabriel trims the throttle and the engine settles into a steady beat. He bends down and then steps out of the wheelhouse, clasping an orange life jacket in each hand.

'Best if you wear these,' he says. 'Case you go overboard.'

Beads of sweat bubble on my forehead. 'But the forecast is for good weather, isn't it?'

'So 'tis, missus, but these waters can change mood faster than a chameleon. My advice would be to put this on. If you don't want to, you don't have to. It's your choice.'

Robbie takes one lifejacket from his hand, stands up, slips his arms through the holes, loops the straps around his waist and ties them. He does it in a practised, familiar way. The way he used to do it when Oliver took him out on his boat, leaving me biting my lip as they tacked away. Then he takes the other, holds it out, waiting for me to push my arms into it.

'Accidents can happen very quickly on the water, Eleanor. I think you should put it on.'

The jacket is bulky, uncomfortable, chafing my neck. I feel as if I have been forced into a dress that is two sizes too small.

My eyes glue themselves to the boat's planking deck, not wanting to see the empty sea stretching ahead us. I try to blank my mind, but a lonesome seagull trails our wake, its harsh mewing setting my teeth on edge.

I almost shed my skin when Gabriel's voice booms in my ear. 'Ain't nothing as beautiful as the Western Rocks on a calm day. If you look to your over there, that's Annet we're passing.'

Robbie takes my hand in his, pats it. 'Won't be long now.'

'Seals at nine o'clock.' Gabriel points to where the disembodied head of a Grey seal breaks through the sea's translucent skin. As I watch, more heads pop up. There is a whole crash of them – bulls, cows and calves, eyeing us as we chug past. It strikes me they are the watchers, not us.

'Aren't they beautiful?' Robbie takes his camera out of its case and trains it on the curious animals. As he does so, two oily backs silently part the water not ten yards away.

'Porpoises,' says Gabriel. 'And look there – you don't often see that – a pair of Shearwaters.'

I look to where he points. Two black and white birds glide past and settle on a finger of rock. Behind them, larger birds, green as dark seaweed, stand in a row like sentinels.

'What are those?' I say.

'Cormorants, last year's young. By next year they'll be jet black.'

For the first time since we arrived I feel the tension ease as the peaceful scene draws me in. Only the occasional plopping sounds of the seals emerging and submerging break the silence. The seagull gives a final cry then wheels off towards the rocks.

The boat is now seesawing gently, a whipping wind tugging at the sea, sending flecks of white foam like spit over the water. Rain begins to pitter-patter on the rippling surface, hardly noticeable at first. Then fat drops hurtle down, pockmarking the sea.

Gabriel shrugs. 'Probably just a passing storm.'

*Probably?*

Then I spot it and a fist clamps my throat. Impossibly tall and limbless: the Bishop Rock lighthouse.

Gabriel moves closer and I smell tobacco mixed with engine oil. 'Magnificent, isn't she? Unmanned now, of course.'

The sea here is agitated, waves licking at the rock. I crane my neck to see the lantern high above.

'Neptune's sleeping today,' he says. 'The old lighthouse, she'll try her best to make sure he don't wake up and take anyone unawares. Mind you, sometimes the old beggar catches her out.'

I gasp, my lung stabbed by an invisible lance.

'My brother lost his life here.' Robbie's hands grip the side of the boat, knuckles white as bleached shells, as he stares fixedly at the giant finger. 'In the Fastnet.'

Gabriel's eyes spring open. 'You talkin' about the Grimaldi, mate?'

I clamp my hand over my mouth. The name haunts me. Too close to grim, grimace, Grim Reaper.

'A bad do, that. Neptune was mighty angry that day.'

I cannot help it. 'Angry?' I say.

He nods. 'I was right here in seventy-nine. When it happened.'

'Surely not? You said the lighthouse was unmanned.'

'Oh, aye, 'twas. But I weren't in the lighthouse. I were in an 'elicopter.'

'A helicopter?'

'Aye. At the time I were in the RNAS, based at Culdrose. We were mobilised as part of the rescue effort and directed to assist a yacht in trouble close by The Bishop.'

'The Grimaldi.' The name slips out before I can catch it.

'The very same.'

'Did you . . . did you see what happened?'

98        *It's Never Too Late to Fall in Love*

He tugs his chin, as if the memory lies beneath its skin. 'As much as I could, given the conditions.'

'Tell me.'

'We received a report from a vessel of a yacht bein' tossed like a cork by a gigantic storm. The crew were tryin' to out-run it, but it kept knockin' the poor boat flat time after time, like it were swattin' a fly, hurlin' the sailors into the sea and to the end of their safety-line harnesses. The next we heard, a huge wave had flipped the yacht over and on to its back, dismastin' it.'

'And then it broke up on the Bishop Rock?'

'Not until later, after we'd rescued as many of the crew as we could.'

'Off the rock?'

'Lift them off the rock? Listen, we couldn't get nowhere near The Bishop. The crew had inflated their life raft and aban-doned the boat before she capsized. That's where we found the six of them – in their life boat.'

Robbie's brow furrows deeply as he asks the question. 'What happened to the captain? My brother?'

'We asked them that after we winched them into the chopper. They said he had been swept overboard by a breaker and car-ried away before they saw The Bishop. The boat was crippled so it was impossible for them to try and rescue him.'

'So he didn't die on the rock?' I say.

'No, missus, he didn't.'

My knees give way and I begin to slip to the floor. Gabriel's hands catch me, and help me on to the seat. Robbie's arms are now around me, hugging me, tears streaming down his face.

*Lightning Never Strikes Twice*

I don't know if I should feel angry or relieved. How cruel that poor Oliver was the only casualty on that fateful day. Yet, truth is, it was not the Bishop Rock, the object of fear I have carried with me all these years, which took his life from him.

Gabriel's words run around inside my head.

*The old lighthouse, she'll try her best to make sure he don't wake up and take anyone unawares. Mind you, sometimes the old beggar catches her out.*

I stare at the lighthouse and see it in a different light: a white and towering splendour; protective, commanding, indefatigable.

The mariner's friend.

'It's over, Eleanor,' says Robbie, squeezing me tightly. 'Time to move on.'


Robbie and I sit on the low quay wall that skirts Porthcressa Beach. The light is leaking away and the only sound is of a pewter sea sucking gently at the sand.

We're eating fish and chips with our fingers, something I haven't done for years. Not far away a huge gull stands motionless, its beady eye staring unblinkingly at the grease-proof paper in my hand.

Robbie's gaze is fixed on the lights of a tramper, a dark silhouette gliding along the line of the horizon. 'I'm sorry for getting angry with you earlier,' he says. 'It's just that . . . well, I was hoping you would rediscover some of the happiness you found here with Oliver.' He turns his head and looks into my eyes. 'Only this time, it would be with me.'

Seven years were all I had with Oliver. Seven years of intense passion that had my heart pounding and my head spinning.

The image I hold of him is frozen in time. What kind of father would he have been to Lucy had he lived? Would we still love each other? Robbie had been my constant companion for almost forty years. He had guided me through my highs and lows, never complaining, never faltering.

There can be no greater love for a person than that.

Oliver loved me, but Robbie is in love with me.

I feel his hand settle on mine and my heart flutters. I lean against his shoulder and press my cheek against the softness of his Arran pullover.

'I'm sorry you had to wait for such a long time.'

'I would have waited forev

'I know you would, darling. I know you would.'

They say lightning never strikes twice. They're wrong.

Oliver is gone, finally laid to rest, but Robbie remains.

Tonight I will sleep without the comforting presence of Mister Zolpidem.

# The Last Verse

### Margaret Foggo

She stood foolishly holding the balloon and wishing it was all over. Yesterday she was fifty-nine and today she was sixty. So what? She had survived Tom's death by five years. Was that an achievement? If not what else was? The comfortable bland existence she had found herself inhabiting? No, she thought not. Her family thought otherwise however. There was a marquee on the lawn, albeit a small one and a sumptuous lunch, a birthday cake of embarrassing proportions and a pile of presents. And now this! But 'this' was the children's idea and as they crowded excitedly around her she could not help but enter into their enthusiasm.

The balloon straining on its silver cord floated about a yard above her head, magnificent in its blue and silver livery, with the words 'Happy Birthday' inscribed on its heart-shaped face. It bore a little label which on one side read 'Barbara Wood. Heatherset, May Road, Flenbury', and on the other, 'Found by', with a space for a name and address. More champagne was called for and the children gathered round.

'Where will it go Granny?'

'I don't know James. Perhaps not very far.'

'Oh yes', he said, 'it will. China or Africa. You'll see.'

There was a burst of foolish clapping and she released the balloon. Freed, it drifted towards a large rose bush and there was a momentary gasp of horror but then, as if making up its mind it engaged with some eddy of air and sailed up into the cloudless summer sky. They all stood immobile, heads tilted back until the tiny speck, on its long journey, was no longer visible.

Then, at last, they began to leave. Farewells were shouted, car doors banged, wheels crunched on the gravel drive and at last she was alone save for the blackbird in the willow singing its heart out to the fading sky. She went into the house and through to the kitchen.

'Mavis, you must go home. You look tired to death. The catering people will clear up everything tomorrow. You've done wonders so, come on, off you go.'

'What a lovely party you had, Mrs Wood. All the family here and so many friends. A day to remember. I've put the leftovers in the fridge and it's tidy here so I'll see you tomorrow. You should go and have a rest now too – you must be very tired.'

After she had waved Mavis goodbye she stood for a while in the doorway. The bird had stopped singing and save for the faintest rustle of leaves the silence deepened in the twilight. It was a time for reflection and instead of returning indoors she sat down on the steps. Sixty, she thought, and another ten years to seventy and further to eighty. She shivered. And then what? What would she do with it all? The same old things? Gardening, the charity shop, bridge. Forever? And then of course there was the family – two sons and one daughter, all married with children and living quite near and all vying

*The Last Verse*

with each other to express their concern, to offer advice, to impose their wishes on their widowed mother. She moved fretfully on the uncomfortable step. It was all so predictable. Not what she wanted although exactly what she did want continued to elude her. Later that night, getting ready for her bath she looked critically at her naked body in the mirror. Time had laid its finger upon her but the touch had been light. Nothing to worry about there yet. Luxuriating in the warm perfumed water she found herself humming the Flower Song from *Carmen.*

Over the weeks the party had faded from her mind and so for a moment she was confused by the contents of the cheap brown envelope that arrived by the morning's post. It was the label from the balloon she had sent on its travels on her birthday and the 'found by' part was filled out with the name and address of one Alfredo Campanelli, 75 The High Street Ledford. It had not gone far then. Ledford was a market town a mere twenty miles away. For a moment she was childishly disappointed but then laughing at herself she put the label under an eggcup on the dresser and forgot about it. But some days later when a tedious afternoon's bridge had been cancelled she remembered it and thought she would go and search for Alfredo Campanelli so that she would have something to tell her grandchildren.

On arriving in Ledbury she very soon realised that 75 The High Street must be a shop and despite the absence of numbers on the premises she eventually found it. Above the shop window in bold gold letters was the name Campanelli. It was a greengrocer's and what a greengrocer's. Under a green and white striped awning lay the produce. Hot pyramids of orange and lemon citrus fruits stood beside cool green grapes and melons while not far away was the ruby glow of red onions, the misty white of mushrooms. And the smell! The sweet heavy scent of strawberries underpinned the astringency of the Granny Smiths. She stood intoxicated with its allure and then became aware that a man had appeared in the shop doorway. Predictably he said, 'May I get you something?'

He was a big man, not fat but large in bone and muscle, his skin, warm olive. Beneath the brim of a straw hat his eyes twinkled on the world in a kind of amused benevolence. He was about her age she thought and his presence confused her – she'd come without any idea of what to say. Fumbling in her bag she produced the label from her balloon and mutely held it up to him. He looked at it and burst into a peal of laughter.

'But I thought you would be a little girl', he said.

'Well it was a little girl's idea. Where did you find it?'

'It was in the rubbish I swept up at the end of the day. It must have blown in from the pavement. I am afraid the little girl will be very disappointed that is has not travelled very far. That is a great shame.' She smiled at his dejection.

'I can tell her it was found by an Italian and perhaps she will draw her own conclusions and not ask any more.' He shook his head in disbelief.

'But let me give you something for her. My raspberries are very fine this year.'

But as he turned away to get them he was suddenly distracted by a small man who rushed into the shop. He grasped Mr Campanelli by the arm and drowned him in a flood of excited Italian. Apparently his news was not welcome for Mr Campanelli appeared quite distracted. He gesticulated wildly around the shop but the little man only pulled harder at his sleeve.

*The Last Verse*

'You must forgive me,' he said to her, 'I have had bad news. My mother – she has become ill. They wish me to go to her at once. But what am I to do? How can I leave my shop?

To her total disbelief she heard herself say, 'I'll look after your shop for you.'

He stared at her in astonishment. 'You! How can you?'

'I'm quite used to shop work. I work in a charity shop. I know all about tills and giving the right change and that sort of thing. And I'm quite honest.'

'Even so.'

The little man began to tug more urgently at his arm. 'Pronto, pronto', he begged. Mr Campanelli found himself dragged on to the street.

'In one hour I will return', he called back desperately.

He did not return for over two hours. She had sold all the strawberries and courgettes and was down to the last melon when he came rushing back, apologies tumbling from his lips.

'How was your mother?' she asked.

'They have taken her to the hospital. She has had a small stroke but it is not so bad. Soon she will be complete again. But you, what can I say? Such kindness to a complete stranger.'

'Don't worry. I enjoyed every minute of it', she said. 'Really I did.'

'But what can I do in return?' he said. 'You are not a lady I can offer money to.'

She smiled at him. 'I'm very hungry.'

106      *It's Never Too Late to Fall in Love*

He took her through a maze of little streets to an Italian restaurant. It was charmingly old fashioned with red and white checked tablecloths and candles in wax encrusted wine bottles. They ate saltimbocca and drank a rich fruity wine that had somehow incorporated sunshine in the bottling and they talked easily, relaxed, with time forgotten. He told her of his childhood home, of the high brown hills drowsing in the heat, of the groves of olive trees and the colourful village where he was born. He spoke of it with a love that she thought had survived many things. It was nearly dark when he walked with her to her car.

'And so' he said, 'shall I ever see you again?'

'Of course' she answered. 'I would like to spend another day working in your shop if you'll have me.'

He stared at her in amazement.

'You wish to spend your time serving people with vegetables? Surely that is not possible.'

'Oh yes it is. At least in your shop. I've really enjoyed today, every bit of it.'

'But I cannot afford to have an assistant.'

'Oh you don't have to pay me. Just dinner afterwards, like tonight.'

He stood thoughtful. 'There will be many regulations that forbid it I am sure.' Then as if sensing her disappointment he said, 'Very well then, we will try it. You will come and see me in the prison. On what day will you come?'

'Thursday, if that suits you. I shall really look forward to it'.

*The Last Verse*

It was on the third Thursday that he kissed her as they said goodnight by her car. It was not the urgent, demanding kiss of a much younger man but deep and slow with the assurance of growing love. It penetrated the core of her being like the spreading warmth of brandy. For the next Thursday she packed an overnight bag. He made no comment when she left the bag in the small untidy room behind the shop but when they went to retrieve it after closing time he stood quietly looking intently into her face.

'You are quite sure?' he asked.

'Yes', she answered. 'And you?'

'Oh yes. Quite sure.'

Together they went up the iron staircase outside the building that led to his flat above the shop and he showed her around with pride. A living room vibrant with colour, the kitchen full of lingering unfamiliar scents and finally the bedroom with its huge brass bedstead covered with a dazzling white duvet. He put down her bag and gently turned her towards him – a question still on his face. For an answer she put her hand up and reassuringly touched his cheek. In the early hours she woke feeling cold and wondering where she was, then with a smile of pleasure she remembered and reaching down pulled the duvet up to settle it close around them.


And so the summer passed on its quiet way into autumn. It was an uneventful time. They worked together every Thursday and dined at the same small restaurant. Sometimes they went to the cinema or into the country where they walked hand in hand along the peaceful lanes. They talked of their families and their friends, of the past and the present but not of the future for they knew they had none together. There was no way she could see him happy in the confined strictures of her home in Flenbury and she had been too long used to comfort and easy living to think that she could settle into an urban life in a flat above a shop. But it simply did not matter. He had told her that for him every life was like a poem and like a poem was separated into verses, all part of the overall structure but beautiful in their individual way. Together they were sharing a verse in their lives, maybe the last and with that they were content.

Then one day she emerged from the back of the shop to serve a customer and stood confronted by her daughter. Jane stared at her for a moment in silent astonishment but soon found her voice.

'Mother, what on earth are you doing here?'

'I work here' she said, 'on a Thursday.'

'You work here every Thursday! What in God's name for? Are you short of money or something?'

They became aware that someone had entered the shop and was looking at them curiously. With a curt, 'I'll be in touch', Jane left.

They all came two days later as she was sure they would. All three of her children with faces set like mourners at a funeral. She offered them drinks but they shook their heads so she poured herself a large gin and sat down and waited. They looked at each other awkwardly and then Tom, the eldest, began to speak.

'Jane tells me that you are working in a greengrocer's in Ledford. We are all concerned that you are in some financial difficulty. It doesn't seem possible but is that so?'

*The Last Verse*

'Of course not', she replied. 'I do it because I enjoy it.'

'Working in a greengrocer's?'

'Yes. Why not?'

'We would understand it better if it were an antique shop or something like that', her youngest son put in.

'Well I suppose it would look better if any of your friends happened to see me.'

'Oh come on Mum, you know I don't mean that.'

They sat silently for a moment and then Jane said, 'People say that you are never here on a Thursday night. Do you stay in Ledford?'

She wanted to say, what business was it of theirs but she only said, 'Yes.'

'Well, where do you stay?'

She felt her anger rising but realised it was not yet time for it. She remained silent,

'Well', her daughter persisted, 'where do you stay? Not with the greengrocer, surely?'

Still she held her tongue.

'God', said Tom. 'Are you actually saying that you spend the night with the greengrocer? I really can't believe it. It's so unlike you – so disgusting.'

Disgusting? She thought of his big gentle hands, the shyly whispered words of endearment, the happy morning awakenings. Disgusting? Oh no. Not ever. She felt their dirty words besmirching something fragile and precious. It was now time for anger. She got to her feet, she was shaking but her voice was steady.

'I have listened to you and now I would like you to go. Because I love you all dearly I will do my best to forget this evening but I will continue my life as I think fit and God, not you, shall be my judge.' Then quietly she left the room.

Later that night she wondered if they would abandon her but thinking of her spacious house and grounds she thought wryly that they would not. They had too much to lose. Not much comfort perhaps but it would have to do and she put it out of her mind. Tomorrow was Thursday and all would be well again!

# An Estate of the Heart

### Brenda Jackson

The balcony was in partial shade as the evening sun slid toward the horizon. Annette placed his drink next to the day-late English newspaper. Sitting back in her rattan chair she scanned the distant hills as if looking for answers. Ice cubes chinked as she swirled her drink around the glass before swigging it back in one. Turning to gaze wistfully at his empty chair she felt a surge of anger course through her body. 'Damn the man for dying!' she spat as she reached over for his tumbler. 'Well old girl, you've certainly doubled your alcohol intake. Cheers.'

'Señora Philips. Señora. Are you there?'

Annette leant forward and peered over the balcony.

'Oh, it's you Rico. Is everything all right?'

'Yes, señora, everything very good. How you say? Everything tickety boo.'

Annette laughed. Alec had spent many an hour in the shrubberies teaching Enrico the finer points of English. Some of the not so fine ones too.

'I just come to say next week I go to Barcelona. I be back by Thursday. Is okay with you I come work your garden on Sunday?'

'Yes, of course Rico. Anytime to suit you. Are you doing anything special in Barcelona?'

'Oh, Mrs P. I have interview to go work botanical gardens. I tell you, one day I be big time. Like your Mrs Jeekol and Mr Titchymarsh. One day I be Spain's most famous gardener.'

'What on earth will I do then? The place will go to rack and ruin without your magic green fingers. I'll never be able to afford you once you're rich and famous.'

'Mrs P, you will always be my number one customer and I never will charge you top dollar. I learn so much from Mr Alec. One day, if I create my own flower I call it Mr Alec Philips. You think he like that?'

'Rico, I think he would love that. I am sure he is looking down on you, keeping a beady eye on what you are doing in the garden. Would you like a drink?'

'No, thank you Mrs P. I go collect my grandmother from town with her shopping. Will I see you Sunday or you going to beach?'

'Yes, I'm going to the beach as usual, so I'll be gone before you arrive. There will be some lunch in the fridge. Just help yourself to anything.'

'Okey dokey Mrs P. I see you Thursday then.'

Annette stood listening to the sound of Rico's motorbike and sidecar fading into the distance. How he fit his grandmother and her shopping in it was one of the mysteries of the village. The grandmother had raised Rico alone. Señora Garcia was a small, round, crow-like woman, always dressed in black. She spoke no English. Annette had tried to converse with the old woman. Boy, had she tried. Admittedly, her smattering of Spanish left a lot to be desired, yet the old woman stubbornly refused to respond. Thankfully she didn't resent Rico spending most of his time working in her gardens. My gardens, she spoke aloud to herself. My gardens. My house. It felt odd. Leaning on the balcony, she surveyed the countryside around her. It was perfect. Correction! It had been perfect when she'd had someone to share it with.

Alec had cut a swathe through life. A hurricane of a man. Quite exhausting at times. In the early days she had thought herself too boring. Half expected he would wake up one day and realize he could do better. Eventually she came to recognize that she was his rock. He needed her quiet stability. At night, with the moonlight streaming into their bedroom, they had slept, a tangle of arms and legs. Then he would relax. Come morning, batteries recharged, he was off again attacking life with gusto. They had never had children. It caused her some heartache early on, but gradually the pain had eased.

Alec picked up the lingo in super fast time and enjoyed haggling with the locals. They loved it, slapping his back and guffawing at jokes she did not understand. Alec had the vision to see what could be made of the rambling old place and had made them a dream home. That had been when Rico had come into their lives. He had wandered up from the village to offer his help. The scrawny teenager had surprised them with his enthusiasm and work ethic. After the house was completed Alec and Rico started on the garden immediately around the property. Alec followed much of the original design – a pool and patio area being an extra indulgence. Beyond the gardens the land gradually fell away into a flat-bottomed valley. A path zigzagged its way down to orange groves that still produced plentiful offerings, despite years of neglect. Alec had let Rico take whatever he wanted and his grandmother sold on or bartered most of the crop. They had worked downwards towards the valley and were just beginning to clear the undergrowth from around the orchard when Alec had his heart attack.

'I'm sorry Alec. I'm so, so sorry I wasn't there for you. Here I go again, talking to myself. Whatever would you make of me?' Annette had always supposed that when one of them died they would be together. She felt occasional waves of anger that she had not been with him. Whoever would have expected Alec, perfectly healthy Alec with never so much as a cold, to just keel over like that. Again and again she analysed the day he died. She had been weeding around the patio, the muffled voices of Alec and Rico wafting up to her like waves on a sandy beach. Then Rico had screamed out. They met each other, she and Rico, he running up the slope and her hurrying down.

'Mrs P. Mrs P. Alec, he fall down.'

'Call the doctor Rico. You do have your mobile don't you?'

'Yes Mrs P. I do. I call now.' Rico's hands shook as he fumbled with the mobile trying to find the number of the local doctor.

When she reached Alec he was flat out on his back, arms and legs spread, like a child playing dead in some war game. Get up, she wanted to shout. Just get up and stop messing about. But as she knelt beside him she knew. Alec was not there. This was just a shell. His eyes were open. They stared but did not see. His mouth too. Open, as if he was just about to speak. 'Get me a cold beer, Nettie. We've worked up a fair old thirst, Rico and I.' She stroked his face. It was still wet with sweat. She thought silly things, like, what's the point, he is not here – but perhaps his spirit is hovering. Perhaps

*An Estate of the Heart*          115

he can see me from another dimension. So she stroked his face so he might see she cared.

That was how her nearest neighbours found her. The Mendozas had heard all the shouting and rushed down the hillside.

Señora Mendoza made the figure of a cross as she repeated over and over, 'Dios mio'. Her husband knelt down beside Annette. Putting a hand gently on her shoulder he said, 'I sorry Señora Philips. Señor Alec a good man. A very, very good man. I sorry.'

The rest of the day was a blur. So many people coming and going.

A week later the doctor came up to the house to see her. He had the results of the autopsy. He assured her that Alec would have felt no pain. He would have been dead before he hit the ground. So he was trying to say something, she thought, caught mid sentence. He had a massive heart attack. Could have happened anytime. He may or may not have had a few warnings, like a feeling of indigestion. Annette said, yes, he did mention that sometimes, but thought nothing of it.

After the funeral Rico would turn up for work and just stand and look. He never ventured down the valley. Just stood on the patio. Like a ship becalmed, deflated, unable to function. He had been too young to remember his mother's death and he had no father to speak of. This wonderful Mr Alec, his mentor, was gone. Rico had never felt pain like it. Mrs P, she looked like a zombie but he did not know what to say to her. Then, one morning he woke and things felt different.

Annette heard his motorbike arrive at the usual time and she went out to join him on the patio, but he was not there. The door was open to the shed where they kept the tools. Rico came out, the wheelbarrow filled with garden equipment.

'Good-a-morning Mrs P.'

'Good morning Rico. You do not have to do that you know.'

'Ah, but Mrs P. What Mr Alec say? He say, sitting around on fat backside never get job done. Mrs P, I, Rico, will get Mr Alec's job done.'

Annette smiled as she walked down mid morning to see where Rico was working. She handed him a mug of coffee and he sat on a tree stump.

'Rico, what was Mr Alec saying when he died? What were you talking about?'

'He say, what we need for this job is small tractor. He wanted to clear the old track at bottom of valley to road. When he die I think he saying, "Keep your ears", and then he gone. What he mean, keep my ears? Maybe I hear wrong words.'

'No, Rico. I think you heard right. He would be saying, keep your ears peeled if you hear about a tractor. That would have been it. Well, I guess you'd better do that then.'

'Do what, Mrs P?'

'Keep your ears peeled for an old tractor that would do the job. If that's what Alec wanted, then that's what we'll get.'

'Okey dokey, Mrs P. My ears all peeled.'

From then on Annette and Rico fell into the habit of living life just as it had been when Alec was alive. They did not know what else to do, so they followed Alec's routine.

Annette felt half asleep as the bus turned into the depot. A strong cup of Pete's coffee will wake me up, she thought. Pete and Katrina's cafe was just off the busy seafront. They had been good friends to Annette and Alec for some years.

*An Estate of the Heart*

'She's here Pete,' Katrina shouted as she gave Annette a peck on the cheek. They both settled at their usual table where they could watch passers-by.

'Got your favourite croissants. The ones with an apricot in the middle.' Pete said, as he put the tray down in front of them.

'Oh goody. I'm ready for this. Plus a good old gossip of course. You wouldn't believe how I miss being able to converse in English.'

'Well, you start first because we were wondering if you had heard from the solicitor yet?'

'Yes, last week. I've brought his letter with me. Rather hoped you would read it in case I have misinterpreted anything. You know what I am like. I left all this kind of stuff to Alec.'

Pete took the paperwork and started to read through. Katrina poured them all a coffee and passed out the croissants.

'Well. All seems straight forward on the money side of things. The planning permission aspect is null and void though. Because of Alec's death you would have to resubmit. He's saying that you still have time to get the paperwork in but you'll have to hurry. Plus you still have not made a new will.' Pete tutted. 'Annette it's crucial you get that done.'

'Are you sure you want to go through all of this? Why not just sell up and move here? Much more going on here at the coast. There are some good bargains going. I know of several rather nice apartments. You'd surely make quite a bit on the estate. That would set you up without any money worries.' Katrina had rehearsed a good old armoury of reasons for Annette to move.

'I don't think it would be that easy. With the economic climate as it is and being so far inland, I think I'd have quite a bit of trouble selling. The locals would be interested, but they don't have the money, and the foreigners are all hedging their bets at the moment. Plus, I am very happy there and I'd feel I was letting Alec down.'

'Alec wouldn't expect you to take on all that responsibility Annette. He'd want you to do what was best for you. I know its a cliché, but life goes on. Your life does not stop with his death. Sorry, I think that may have come out sounding rather callous, but you know what I mean,' Katrina apologised.

'Yes, I know. I've just been a bit shell shocked, you know, but I think I'm coming out of it. Rico has been worth his weight in gold. Don't know how I would have coped without him.'

'Yes, but Annette, you're paying his wages and to what end? If you don't sort out the planning permission it will all be a bit of a waste. I mean, Alec's vision was quite expansive wasn't it. How on earth can you deal with setting up irrigation, production of crops and deal with the local co-operatives? Alec was from a farming background, you're not. It's mind boggling Annette.' Pete looked to Katrina for back up.

'Pete's right Annette. This is all too hard. It was okay Alec doing it. He spoke the language and got on really well with the local farmers and villagers. Let's face it, you were just in the back seat. They're not going to feel the same about dealing with you, especially dealing with a woman.'

'I know. You're both right and I do have to start sorting things out. I was vaguely thinking about selling off the bottom tract of land. The bit with the orange groves. It has a track that leads out at the other side of the village. I could sell that off and it would make no difference to my property at all.'

'Now you're talking.' Pete sat back and slapped his thighs. 'That sounds like a plan. Do you know anyone who could come and give you a fair valuation?'

*An Estate of the Heart*

'Not really. There's the agent who sold us the property. He may have an idea.'

'Well, I'll ask around for you. Now you go and enjoy the beach and we'll all go out for a meal at about six o'clock. I was thinking the new place in town? It's not far from the bus station,' said Pete as he rose to greet some early morning customers.


On Thursday Annette had slept in. She walked bare foot onto the patio with a glass of orange juice. She had taken several sips before she realized that she could hear two voices down in the valley. Two! It took her a few seconds to click that no, it was not Alec. Alec was dead. She put down the glass and hurried indoors to slip on a pair of sandals. As she walked down the track she noticed a hat bobbing about in the undergrowth. It looked like one of those big Australian bush hats.

'Ah, Mrs P. You wake.' Rico stood, garden fork in hand.

The hat rose to reveal a lined, sun tanned face and sparkling blue eyes. Annette had never noticed the colour of anyone's eyes before and she could not take her eyes off these.

'Mrs P, this Greg. He from Australia.'

Greg took off his hat and stretched out his hand to Annette.

'Hello there Mrs P,' Greg nodded to her.

'It's Mrs Philips.' she said, automatically putting her right hand into his. 'It's Mrs Philips.' His grip was firm, warm and comforting.

Annette pulled her hand away, flustered.

'Hope you don't mind me giving Rico a hand? I am staying in the village and was out for an early morning walk. We got chatting.'

'Staying? In the village? Where?'

'He stay in room at back of Filipe Gomez. Señora Gomez, she like money.' Rico explained rubbing his fingers together for emphasis.

Filipe Gomez was the local barber. Annette reasoned that this Greg must have asked if there was anywhere local to stay and Señor Gomez would have been quick to jump in with an offer.

'You're a bit off the beaten track aren't you Greg? Sorry I didn't catch your surname?'

'Robinson. It's Greg Robinson. I like to see a bit of a country off the tourist trails. Have all the time in the world these days so I just meander about. Getting a bit bored now so I was delighted to meet up with Rico. Sounds like you have a fairly ambitious project going here Mrs Philips?'

'Yes. Well, it was my husband's project. I don't really feel part of it.'

'Rico says he was quite a man that husband of yours. You must miss him.'

'I do Mr Robinson. I do.'

'Call me Greg. You don't mind if I give Rico a hand for a few days do you?'

'I can't afford to pay you Greg.'

'I don't want money. Just something to get my teeth into for a bit. If you don't mind me saying I think . . . No, sorry it really is none of my business.'

*An Estate of the Heart*

'What? What are you thinking?'

'Well, perhaps it would be a good idea if you became more involved down here. I mean if you don't feel part of it perhaps you need to . . . to own it. Make it yours. Take possession so to speak. The best way to do that is to put a few hours in every day. Not all day obviously. Just a couple of hours in the morning before the sun gets high.'

Annette stood for a moment wondering whether this stranger was simply impertinent or offering genuine suggestion. She decided to give him the benefit of the doubt.

'Perhaps you're right. I may dig out my old walking boots and do just that.' Annette turned to walk towards the house. After a few paces she stopped.

'You'd better come up to the house later with Rico. The very least I can do is give you lunch Greg.'

Greg nodded his thanks.

Greg's arrival brought the place to life. The three of them fell into a happy routine. Annette would go down and join them in the mornings and became wheelbarrow woman, responsible for taking roots and twisted logs and dumping them in a pile near the old gate. Every day Annette dumped the scrub and every evening someone took it. It amused Annette. Recycling at its best. Well, at least it would save them the job of burning. Mid morning she would go up to the house, shower and make them all lunch. Greg entertained them with tales of his treks around the world. Rico was happy having someone to work beside him and Annette found herself walking with a spring in her step.

One morning, instead of going straight down the valley to start work, they came to the house.

*It's Never Too Late to Fall in Love*

'Mrs P. We heard about tractor. Is okay if we go look now?' Rico asked.

'Oh, jolly good. Do you know how much it'll be?'

'No worries. I can bargain like the best of them,' Greg grinned, obviously looking forward to a bit of wheeler dealing.

'Don't be running off with my fortune you two,' joked Annette as she gave them a signed, blank cheque from the small account she and Alec had set up for the project.

Just after midday Annette saw a plume of smoke making its way up the track and voices giving the worst rendition of Waltzing Matilda she had ever heard. Rico was getting an Australian education now. The two of them arrived at the property beaming from ear to ear, both talking at once about how they had examined the old Pegasus tractor, shaking their heads and tutting until they had brought the price down.

They were all in high spirits and Annette found herself asking Greg if he would like to come up to the house and have a meal that night.

'We can perhaps have a game of scrabble or something. Not played that for ages. You can fill me in on your story. I'm sure you have heard plenty about me but I know nothing about you.'

'Thanks Annette. I'd love to. What time?'

'About six thirty, will that be okay?'


'I'm an engineer Annette. I worked out in the bush in mining communities all my life. My wife, Jean, was with me the first six years or so, up until the girls needed to get settled in a school. Then we bought a place just outside Adelaide in the hills and Jean and the girls moved there. Just got used

*An Estate of the Heart*        123

to that kind of life, me working away most of the time and getting back about one week in six. Jean was a tough old bird and the girls accepted it because they never knew any different. In the end I set up my own business and it was a bit easier. Both my sons-in-law came to work for me. Rory married Patty. He's a refrigeration engineer and they have two girls. David married Rhona and they're just expecting their first. Late starters. They've put me out to grass. The girls do the books and pay me my pocket money. Occasionally Rory or David will get in touch wanting a bit of advice, but I think it's just so the old man doesn't feel pushed out, you know.'

'Don't you miss them?'

'Sometimes, but I just ring or email. I use Skype where I find it available. As I say, we're used to being apart. Space doesn't mean as much to us Australians. Easy enough to hop on a plane.'

'What set you off around the world then?'

'My daughter Rhona. After Jean's death I rattled round in the house for a few years and then let them talk me into selling it and moving to a beach area just east of Adelaide. I bought a condo where I had a view of the ocean, but how long can you just sit and read and stare at the ocean? It began to feel more like a prison up there on the seventh floor. It was not me. Trouble was I did not know what was me.'

'No. I know that feeling.'

'Eventually Rhona said there was no point in selling the condo and moving until I really knew where I wanted to be. She said I needed to take time out and think about things. Said I needed a gap year. I told her that was just for students and hippies but she insisted. So, here I am. Wandering the world aged sixty-six, looking for me.'

They both laughed. Greg was sitting in Alec's chair. Annette surprised herself by not being upset by it. She poured them both another glass of chilled white wine and they sat quietly admiring the view from the balcony.

'Where do you go each Sunday?'

'Visit friends. Pete and Katrina on the coast. They own a little cafe called, oddly enough, Katrina's. Alec and I would go every Sunday on the local bus. It made it a bit of a novelty and meant we could enjoy a few drinks. We'd leave our valuables at the cafe and sit on the sunbeds on the beach. Later, when custom at Katrina's died down, we'd go and shower. Then we'd all go out for a meal before Alec and I took the bus back. Would you like to join me this Sunday?'

'Yes, that'd be good. Not had a swim for a while. Well Mrs P, I think I'd better meander my way back to the village. Mustn't be late for work in the morning or the boss might sack me,' joked Greg.

Annette walked Greg to the door. He started to walk out and then stopped. Turning, he took her in his arms, drew her toward him and kissed her. His body felt hard and warm. Annette felt herself melt, his breath mingling with hers as he whispered, 'Goodnight Annette. Thank you for the most wonderful evening.'

Leaning back on the shut door, she closed her eyes as she tried to control her breathing. She felt ecstatic, dizzy. At the same time, deep within her, a small voice was telling her she did not deserve happiness when poor Alec was dead.


'They seem good people, Pete and Katrina.' Greg settled back on the sunbed and opened up the John Grisham novel Pete had given him. 'How'd you meet?'

*An Estate of the Heart*

'Alec and I just wandered into their cafe. Must've been about eight years ago now. We all hit it off immediately.'

They settled back in a comfortable silence, reading and dozing.

'Look! Surf!' yelled Greg. 'From those container vessels that passed about fifteen minutes ago.'

'It looks a bit wild to me. The kind of sea you'll drown in.'

'No. It's perfect for beginners. I'll teach you to body surf. Come on. Quick before it's gone.' Greg grabbed her hand and pulled her towards the sea.

Annette was immediately swept off her feet but Greg kept good hold and got her through the crashing waves.

'Right. Now you start by swimming and then, when you feel the wave take you, arch your back slightly so your feet feel higher than your head. Then just go with it.'

Annette did as she was told, primarily because she wanted to get back to the beach and the safety of dry land as soon as possible. She did not like this at all. She felt the wave lift her. For a few seconds she soared. Next she was churned around as if in a washing machine. Greg scooped her up and dragged her out to try again and again.

'Enough. I've not got the energy for anymore. Plus I've sand where sand should definitely not be,' laughed Annette.

'Where on earth did you find him Annette? He's great,' whispered Katrina when the men were at the bar ordering drinks.

'At the bottom of the garden. As you do,' joked Annette.

'What, like a fairy?'. They both giggled. 'He's fantastic Annette. All the single ladies of a certain age round here are on the prowl for a man. Yet you, up one pops in your garden in the back of beyond. You've landed jam side up there girl.'

'Oh no! Don't get the wrong idea. There's nothing going on. I mean, it's too soon after Alec. People would think me a shameless hussy.'

'Don't be daft. Anyone who cares for you would be pleased if you found someone. Anyway, in this day and age things are different. Why I'd swear that the women around here go in for rugby lessons. Any new man in town and wham! There's a race to tackle him to the ground. Poor beggars don't know what's hit 'em.'

Greg took Annette's bags in one hand and slipped the other round her waist as they slowly ambled back up the track.

'I always stop here on top of the rise just to look around. Isn't it fabulous? The landscape looks different at night. Look at how the shadowy clouds dance across the countryside when lit up by the moon.'

Greg dropped the bags and turned Annette toward him. They kissed long and hard.

Once in the house Annette kicked off her shoes and led Greg to the bedroom.

'I feel a little tipsy and very, very happy,' she murmured. 'I never thought I would feel happy again.'

Annette was aware of the morning sun glinting around the room. The shutters rattled. A wind was getting up. Slowly she opened her eyes and noticed a pair of men's shoes by the bedroom chair. Half propping herself up on her elbows she surveyed the scene. Clothes strewn everywhere. Guilt over-

*An Estate of the Heart*

whelmed her. She wanted to cry. Just then Greg walked into the room, a couple of glasses of orange juice in his hands.

'Morning. I had such a wonderful evening. Loved meeting your friends. What say we go into the village and I treat you to . . . ?'

'Get out!' Annette felt the anger welling within her. He was wearing Alec's towelling robe. How dare he? He'd showered. He must have used all of Alec's things and now he stood there in front of her in Alec's robe!

'What! Annette what's wrong? What have I done? I thought we'd had a good time yesterday.'

'You're wearing his robe! You are wearing my husband's robe! How dare you!'

'I'm sorry,' said Greg slipping the robe off and placing it on the back of a chair. 'I'm sorry. I really didn't mean to upset you.'

'Just go! I want to be alone!' Annette drew the sheet around her and refused to even look at Greg who dressed as quickly as he could.

'Right, I'm going Annette – but we really need to talk about this when you calm down.'

As soon as Annette heard the front door shut she threw herself onto the pillow and wept.

Unable to face Greg she feigned a headache and stayed in the house all day. That evening there was a tap at the door.

'Annette. We need to talk. Can I come in please?'

Opening the door, Annette led Greg to the kitchen in silence.

'I'm sorry Annette. I didn't mean to upset you or disrespect Alec.'

'It's not you. I shouldn't have snapped at you like that but …'

'But what?'

'I'm not ready to move on from Alec. It's all too soon. I think I was just lonely, you know. It's my fault. I probably misled you. It's all just too soon.'

'Just what is too soon? I've been alone for years and it's no fun I can tell you. From the minute we met there was a connection. You felt it too, I know you did.'

'Yes. There was, there is, a connection, but I cannot do it. I feel incredibly guilty.'

'Annette, I know you are still grieving for Alec, but what we have here is special. I'm certain of that. Some people never feel this way in an entire lifetime. We are so lucky. This is a good thing.'

They stood in silence for what seemed an eternity.

'Would it help if I went? I could continue my journey traipsing around the world, if that's what you want?'

'It is really. I do need to be alone to think things out. I've so many problems to sort out. What with planning permission or whether to sell off the land. I've been putting my head in the sand but I can't ignore things any longer. I can't deal with all this emotional stuff on top of it all. Do you understand?'

'Yes, I do. But Annette, when it comes to the emotional stuff, you just can't put a time on these things. You need to grab happiness when it comes, especially at our time of life. It doesn't mean you are discarding Alec to the scrap heap. He will always be in your thoughts and from what I have heard about him he'd certainly not want you to be alone. He'd want you to move on and enjoy your life.'

*An Estate of the Heart*

Annette shrugged.

'Would you like me to go? Today?'

'Yes, I think it would be best.'

'Shall I keep in touch?'

Annette shrugged again.


Over the next week Rico avoided Annette. He was angry with her for pushing Greg away. Annette began to drown her sorrows in the time honoured way. She was slopping about the house in an old kaftan, hair uncombed and drink in hand when there was a series of sharp raps at the door.

'What now!' Annette flung the door open and her jaw dropped. It looked like a lynch mob. Grandma Garcia backed by three men. Annette recognised them but only knew the name of one – Señor Lopez, a local councillor.

Grandma Garcia barged in. Making her way to the kitchen she sat heavily on a chair. Annette suppressed laughter at the old lady in black. Her bandy Nora Batty legs apart, rasping for breath as she tried to compose herself after the long walk up the hill. The men stood around shouting and arguing in Spanish.

Finally grandma banged her stick on the floor shouting, 'Cállate la suerte de ustedes. Vamos a seguir con esta.'

The men duly quietened and Señor Lopez took out a pile of official looking papers from a battered briefcase that looked, if Annette was not mistaken in her drunken stupor, as if it had a bullet hole through it.

'Señora Philippi. Señora Garcia has business with you. She has good idea.'

'What business? What idea?' Annette slumped into a chair opposite grandma.

'Manos a la obra,' shouted grandma getting impatient.

'Bien. Bien. Mantener a sus caballos,' retorted Señor Lopez equally sharply.

Annette raised her eyebrows questioningly.

'Señora, it about planning permission. You never get. It will be no good.'

'I know. I was thinking about selling the land in the valley.'

'¿Qué dijo?' asked grandma.

Señor Lopez translated. Grandma threw her hands in the air with expletives Annette needed no translation for.

'Señora Philippi, what if a business partnership between you and Rico? Rico get permission. Rico run business. You just take money.'

Annette looked at grandma who was nodding in agreement. At once Annette understood. Grandma did not want Rico leaving the village. Annette did not want him to leave either. He was like a son to her. She would miss him terribly. Annette nodded, she wanted to hear more.

Señor Lopez brought out a map. He pointed to a boundary marked in green felt tip.

'Esta área es para usted y la asociación de Rico,' said grandma as she jabbed her finger on the area.

'This area for you and Rico partnership,' translated Señor Lopez.

'Y esta área es para la casa y los jardines que quedan solamente para usted,' continued grandma pointing to another area marked in red.

*An Estate of the Heart*

'And this area is for house and gardens that remain just yours,' said Señor Lopez.

Annette sat back and smiled. She said nothing for a few minutes as they all looked on, in silence for once.

'Okay. Okay. I will talk to my solicitor. I like the idea.'

Señor Lopez started translating, but grandma had got the gist of it and was already on her feet cupping Annette's face with her hands and planting a great big kiss on her forehead.

Over the next few weeks a contract was drawn up between her and Rico making them business partners. Rico worried his grandmother was taking advantage but Annette finally got through to him that he would be doing her a favour. What could she do with the land down there?

One afternoon she heard a lot of angry shouting in the valley. She hurried down to see what all the commotion was about.

'Rico! Rico! Are you all right?' Annette was more than a little frightened at the sight of all these rough looking men surrounding Rico.

'Yes Mrs P. I all right. We discuss farming co-operative and how we make things work. Is okay. No worries mate.'

'I thought they were going to kill you. They look an angry lot.'

Rico translated and the men all burst into laughter.

'They say if they going to kill me you hear gun by now.'

Annette made her way back to the house. The bit of Australian lingo Rico had thrown in made her think of Greg. Where was he? What was he doing? She missed him more than she'd have thought possible. The months felt like years. She tried to take her mind off him by changing the house. What was it Greg had said? Take ownership, make it yours. Out went the heavy, dark, wooden furniture Alec had chosen and in came a lighter, more modern look. It did help. The house now felt hers.

Annette placed a vase of flowers in the guest room. Pete and Katrina were coming to stay for the weekend. The village was having a joint celebration for Rico's birthday and the business partnership.

'I can see why you don't want to move from here.' Pete sat dangling his feet in the pool. 'It really is a dream place. Bloomin' good idea too, this partnership thing. Let Rico do all the work and you sit back and rake it in.'

'Don't think there will be much raking in. Not till things get off the ground. It'll be more paying out for a bit I think. Still, I'm actually not bothered. I'm more pleased to be able to give Rico a start and it has definitely thawed things with old grandma. She smiles at me now,' Annette pushed her sunglasses back and looked at Pete. 'Another thing, I will enjoy having so many people about. It is great having such activity going on, I don't feel so alone anymore.'

'Well you wouldn't be alone at all if you hadn't given Greg the heave ho,' chimed in Katrina. 'You must miss him Annette. You seemed so alive when he was around. You had a spark about you.'

'Yes I do. I think about him all the time if I'm honest. In fact I was wondering about getting back in touch. What do you think? Do you know, Rico and he exchange emails and ring each other? I had no idea till the other day. He showed me some photos of Greg back home with his daughters and new grandson. Apparently he broke off his trip to go back for the christening. Expect he'll be settled back there now.'

*An Estate of the Heart*

Annette sighed. 'Well, guess we'd better start showering and getting ready for the night's festivities. They party long and hard this lot.'

'What on earth should I wear?' asked Katrina.

'Something not too tight and certainly comfortable shoes. Once the local farmers start flinging you around the dance floor you'll need all the stability you can get,' warned Annette.

'Is this the infamous grandmother bearing down on us then?' asked Pete as a crowd rushed forward to greet them.

'The one and only,' replied Annette.

Grandma Garcia rushed forward and planted kisses on Annette and shook hands vigorously with Pete and Katrina.

With slow deliberation grandma said, 'I, Perla Esmeralda Rosario Garcia. You Annut Pilipis. 'Ello.'

'Goodness. Your grandmother will soon be speaking English better than I speak Spanish,' said Annette to Rico.

Rico translated. The grandmother flung her arms in the air and shouted, 'Hablo Inglés mucho mejor de lo que usted habla español,' to the amused gathering.

'What did she say Rico?'

'My grandmother, she say she already speak the English much better than you speak the Spanish.'

That broke the ice and everyone was laughing.

Annette felt a slight tap on her shoulder. She turned. Greg. She felt as if she was falling into an abyss. Greg caught her.

She could not speak, just clung to him sobbing until he slowly led her outside where they could have some privacy.

'I thought I'd never see you again. I've been such a fool to send you away. Greg I'm so . . . '

'Hush,' Greg put his finger to her lips and then kissed her.

'How did you get here?'

'By plane of course.'

'No, you know what I mean.'

'I had an invite from Rico. I've been staying with Pete and Katrina. They picked me up from the airport last Wednesday.'

'What! You've all been plotting behind my back,' Annette gave him a playful punch.

'Yes. That and my daughters. They said they were sick of me mooching around the place. That if I loved the English lady so much I had better stop being an old wuss and get myself back there. So here I am. Are you pleased to see me?'

'More than you'll ever know. I just can't believe you're here.' Annette stroked his face and ran her fingers through his hair to check he was real. 'Please never leave me again.'

'Never.'

Greg cocooned her in his strong arms, the only sound they heard was the beating of their hearts.

'Well, I could happily spend all night just holding you like this but I think we had better get back and join the party. Think it's time we wished Rico, un feliz cumpleanos. See, I've been brushing up on my Spanish since I've been away.'

As they sauntered back inside to join their friends, Perla Esmeralda Rosario Garcia advanced on them.

*An Estate of the Heart*

'Regalo, for you, Annut y Greg.' Grandma thrust a gift towards Annette.

'Goodness! What can it be? I feel awful, Rico, I've not bought your grandmother anything.'

'Is okay Mrs P. My grandmother just happy I stay in village. You done much for her already.'

Annette carefully took off the blue wrapping paper and laughed. She held the present aloft for all to see.

'Look. Scrabble in Spanish. I think Perla Esmeralda Rosario Garcia has thrown down the gauntlet. We are now officially in competition.'

'Sí, una competencia entre yo Annut y Greg. Salud.' Senora Garcia raised her glass.

'Salud.'

# Collectability

Denis Marsden

He was sat on his mam's commode with a vague look on his face. He wasn't doing anything. He was just thinking. At sixty-five he was running the gauntlet of old age illnesses. Sandra could be his last chance. Catching sight of himself in the wardrobe mirror he straightened up, took a long look at himself. Well, he thought, new glasses, a haircut and shave would help. It was then he realised he did want to do something. Sitting on the commode must have set him off.

Later in his chair in the back room he sat with his feet up looking through the window. He notices his pale yellow toe nails have razored through his tartan slippers again. At last Monday's U3A meeting Sandra had made it clear. She said, Mr Mugglestone. He said, me name's Roy, call me Roy. She looked at him for some time, sniffed, then repeated. Mr Mugglestone there isn't an easy way to say this, I really don't like you and don't want any thing to do with you.

He looked at his reflection in the window. He smiled. He broke wind. He did another smile at his reflection. He thought, what's not to like about me.

His partner Rita had left him last year. He still saw her when he put a bet on – she works in Ladbrokes. He was doing her ironing and all he said was, There's some yardage in this nightie in spite of you spending all your time at weight watchers. And that was it, no more Rita.

Taking his mam's old teapot into U3A's collectability could sway Sandra he thought. I mean you never know. It's worth a try. He wondered about dyeing his hair, growing a moustache. Yes, yes he thought, it's far too early to give up on Sandra.

# Predictive Text

### Heather Shaw

'I know exactly what it'll be like,' Rosalind said. 'I should never have agreed to go.'

Celia looked up from the blouse she was ironing. 'Typical you,' she said through a hiss of steam, 'getting there before you've arrived.'

'Well, there's some chance of a handle on the future,' Rosalind said. She steepled her fingers. 'The past plays tricks. *What's past help should be past grief.*'

'Shakespeare.' Celia's tone was dismissive. 'Isn't it time you stood up to him? Anyway, what did he know about reunions?'

'I'll never get the clothes right,' Rosalind said. 'What do escapees from the third-age ghetto wear in public?' She shuddered. 'It'll be like hunting in packs, with opinions more instant than coffee.'

'You're not above an instant opinion yourself,' Celia said. She stared over the ironing board at her sister. 'Try not to let that shell get too thick.'

'I don't know you mean.'

'Oh I think you do, love.' Celia poured water into the iron.' You've been curled up in there for two years now, Rossie – since Hugh . . . That shell of bereavement smothers the real you. Come back to us soon.'

It wasn't the mention of her husband but the childhood nickname that had Rosalind forcing back the tears.

'Go to your reunion,' Celia said. 'Please.'

'It's not exactly a reunion. Just a get-together with the other students on the online course, a meeting.'

'Good idea.' Celia grinned. 'Travels end in lovers meeting.'

'Journeys,' Rosalind said, 'It's journeys. *Journeys end in lovers meeting.*'

'There you are then.'

Their laughter was the shorthand of siblings, a shared memory with no need of words. Both of them, Rosalind knew, would have a similar image in their minds.

They're on the back seat of the car, their white ankle socks gleaming above sensible sandals. The car's a buckingham-green Austin Thirty with semaphore trafficators that click out right or left like stiff yellow flags. In the front seats Mum and Dad are playing The Shakespeare Game.

'Dancing,' Mum says.

Dad whistles through his teeth and drums his fingers on the steering wheel. The traffic lights are red.

'He won't get that one, Mummy,' Celia says.

Mum looks at her watch. 'Ten seconds to go,' she says. 'Give up?'

Rosalind holds her breath. But Dad, and Shakespeare, never let her down.

The traffic lights turn green.

'Romeo and Juliet,' Dad announces triumphantly. *'You and I are past our dancing days.'*

Through the gap between the front seats, Rosalind sees Mum's hand cover Dad's on the gear lever. 'But we're not, my love,' she says to him. 'Are we?'

'You might enjoy yourself, ' Celia was folding up the ironing board. 'At the meeting thingie.'

'Once I get there, you mean?' Rosalind smiled.

'Where did you say it was?'

'London. The National Gallery. Shall I make us a cuppa?'

'That'd be great. You know where everything is. I'll just put this lot away.' Shirts and blouses swung on their hangers as Celia gathered them up.

This is a proper kitchen Rosalind reminded herself while the kettle hummed. Worktops hectic with jars and bottles, a pot of tawny chrysanthemums, recipes cut from magazines, a sponge cake cooling on its rack. And on the walls, a pin board ablaze with grandchildren's drawings, a calendar crammed with colour-coded arrangements – green for Celia, black for Gerry, their days a series of parcels waiting to be unwrapped.

Her own kitchen hardly earned the name. Slotted into a one-person apartment, with space for little more than a microwave oven and a slimline dishwasher, its tolerance of food was minimal.

*Predictive Text*

'Funny, the things that pop into your mind,' Rosalind said when Celia came back. 'D'you remember smocking?'

Celia was carrying a newspaper folded open at the crossword. 'I'm stuck on two down,' she said, sitting at the table. 'Seven letters.'

'Any particular seven?' Rosalind said, 'Or can I take my pick?'

'Very funny.' Celia chewed the end of the pen. '*Some would claim lessons are without a target,*' she read.

Rosalind poured tea into two Harry Potter mugs. 'Well, do you?'

'Do I what?'

'Remember smocking – on our dresses? It was the smell of ironing that brought it back. Mum had those iron-on transfers, rows of spots to guide the gathers on the dress yoke.'

'Smocking? I thought we were talking about you going to this re-union thingie.'

'You can't have forgotten those smocked dresses Mum made us wear. '

'I've not thought about them for years,' Celia said. 'The embroidery was pretty, but I was just about ready for a bra before she let me off the smocking hook.' She sipped her tea.

Rosalind said, 'Buds of breasts poking through the ruching.'

Celia spluttered. 'A charming thought to wash down the tea.'

'That's what comes of raking up the past.'

'You're the one who brought up smocking.'

Rosalind looked into her mug and said, 'Sorry, I should know better. All our yesterdays and that.'

'Off we go again,' Celia said. 'You can follow the way to dusty death if you like. I'm due at the bridge club.'

Rosalind grabbed her coat from the back of the chair. 'Aimless,' she said as she shoved her arms into the sleeves.

'Sorry?'

'Two down. Seven letters. It's inside the clue – aimless.'


The online course was Jane's fault, Rosalind thought on the drive home.

'I've found just the thing for you, Mum, based in the UK.' Her voice on the phone had been tantalisingly close, as if she were calling from the next room, never mind New York City. 'It'll keep you from getting into mischief.'

Rosalind damped down her delight at hearing her daughter's voice. No sense in sounding needy. 'You'll be coming out with the Dad-wouldn't-have-wanted stuff next,' she'd said. 'Do you know what time it is over here?'

So art history it was. Eight weeks of it. A tutored romp through the Renaissance – weekly assignments, websites of paintings to investigate. She hadn't expected to enjoy it so much. Words on the screen were all she had to do with her fellow learners. Good thing too, the world confined to a screen. But that was just her. Pound to the proverbial, none of the other students had their knickers in a twist about meeting up in the flesh.

Especially Roz.

Right from the start of the course Roz's opinions were very definite. Her assignments had bristled with them: of course

*Predictive Text*

Van Eyck's Arnofini painting wasn't a marriage portrait – any bride as demure as that in Protestant Bruges would hardly have advertised a well-developed pregnancy. If 'The Entombment' was an example of Michelangelo's painting skills, just as well he'd had a way with sculpture.

Roz wouldn't be sweating about mixing with complete strangers, agonising about what to wear, psyching herself up to venture into the maze of traintickets.com.

As she opened her front door, Rosalind decided that the woman probably looked like a cross between Margaret Thatcher and Delia Smith, well-coiffed and effortlessly efficient; make-up discreet but enhancing, clothes chosen with advice from a personal shopper, voice silky.

Roz had not only suggested meeting up but had access to a private room in the National Gallery. Mid-tour they could relax in comfort and experience a slice of café culture delivered to their persons from the modern European menu.

*Frailty thy name is woman* but not a woman called Roz.

Rosalind slapped her car keys onto the empty kitchen worktop. She wouldn't go. Why should she? Celia had talked about her being in a shell.

She was used to the cocoon she'd erected. No way did she need to get like that old fool King Lear – *a shelled peascod.*

There were two emails waiting; a call-you-later from Jane and something from a Peter Brandon. She was about to delete it, unread, when the subject line caught her eye: National Gallery trip.

*Do hope you don't mind my contacting you like this but I was interested in your comments about Hans Holbein. I'm planning to get to the Gallery half an hour before we all meet up, so that I can have a close look at his 'Ambassadors'. Kind regards, Peter.*

The moment Peter clicked on 'Send' he regretted the message. What did he think he was doing? Okay, he'd phrased and re-phrased the wording to remove any hint of, well what? The implication was there; he was inviting the woman to meet him, wasn't he?

He was wondering why he'd done something so out of char-acter, when the ringing landline phone provided the answer. If nothing else, being away in London for a couple of days would give him a respite from Sam, particularly if he 'forgot' to take his mobile. Before picking up the phone he armed himself with a chocolate digestive biscuit.

'Is that you, Dad?'

'This is where I live, Sam.' He held the biscuit under his nose, relishing the smell of chocolate. 'How are things now?'

Silly question, he knew only too well how things were with Sam. And if he forgot for one moment, this third phone-call today was about to remind him.

'It's just this offer for the business, Dad. I don't know what to do for the best.'

Peter ran his tongue over the knobbly surface of the biscuit. How could you love a person more than life, he asked himself, yet dread the sound of his voice? Swallowing his annoyance, along with a nibble of biscuit, he said, 'You must do whatever you think best, son. You're running the show now.'

'That doesn't mean . . .'

'It means, Sam that you don't want an old fogey like me hanging around.'

But that was exactly what Sam did want, someone to tell him what to do, make his decisions. Taking over a tailoring busi-ness wasn't easy for the lad, not with the market dwindling in the face of competition from China but the dress-hire side

*Predictive Text*

of things was on the up and the chain of fancy-dress shops was doing well. If the books weren't so healthy, the takeover offer wouldn't be as substantial.

Putting the phone down on the lad wouldn't do a lot for Sam's confidence so while his son re-invented the takeover wheel, Peter nibbled more of the biscuit, held the phone at arm's length and let his mind wander.

It wandered to art, the world of painting he'd recently discovered. What had happened to him over the past eight weeks was impossible to describe in words, especially these days when words hovered around the doorway of his thoughts like mercenaries waiting to see which side was likely to win the war. But fine art existed in a world beyond words, a world conveyed only by paint on canvas.

He'd had to come up with written answers to the assignments, of course, but the internet helped with that. Some of the other students were very inventive, unawed by the Old Masters. Take Roz. Never lost for words that one. The possibility she may be spouting absolute nonsense never seemed to occur to her. Said what she thought. Refreshing that was. Hence the email.

Sam's voice bleated from the phone. 'There are sixteen bales of the dark blue herringbone in the Maidstone stockroom, Dad and I'm not sure . . .'

Those artists knew about fabric, how it wrapped itself around the body underneath, fell in folds, caught the light.

Getting to the National Gallery had been no problem. Two weeks into the course, Peter had taken the train to Charing Cross then walked to Trafalgar Square. The course tutor had suggested that concentrating on a theme might help a rookie art viewer, so he'd started with paintings of the Madonna and Child.

There were lots of them, each with a totally different portrayal of how the poor lass was feeling. In one she looked worried at what she'd taken on, a girl who hadn't read the small print; in another she was embarrassed, as if the child on her knee had produced an unwelcome smell; in a third she was clinging to the baby as if someone was about to snatch him away. The variety was amazing.

By now the biscuit had all but disappeared.

'Are you still there, Dad?' Sam was fretting about a woman who couldn't decide what theme to choose for her fancy dress party.

Women were wonderfully unpredictable, weren't they? Sadly, for him, he'd only started to realise that on September 4th twenty-five years ago.

'I'm sorry, Peter.' His wife had been standing in the hall when he got home from work. By the living room door, a bulging suitcase, on the stairs their daughter Sarah thumb in mouth, pink teddy clamped under her arm, and ten-year-old Sam, clutching the banisters.

Life had white-knuckled poor Sam ever since. 'What d'you reckon Dad?' he was saying.

Peter licked his fingers. 'I reckon,' he said through the crumbs, 'at this time of day you should be with that family of yours, not slaving at your desk.'

'Lynn won't be in for be in for hours yet. Her job . . . well you know. And the kids are off somewhere or other.'

'Then why not get yourself home and have a nice meal ready on the table for when Lynn does get back? See you soon, son.' Peter put down the phone and watched the flex tie itself into knots on the hall table.

*Predictive Text*

Hark at him handing out marital advice, a quarter of a century too late for his own marriage. He'd lost his wife to a solicitor who got home before News at Ten. The pair of them were holidaying in Australia just now. Bondi beach, apparently. For some reason, his image of her was 1978 vintage, a little round face surrounded by bubbles of blonde curls, and a green and white spotted sundress in some horrible synthetic fabric.

Plenty of water under the bridge since then, too much of it solo sailing.

Roz wouldn't have a round face. He imagined her long in the jaw, a bit horsey even, like a lot of those intellectual women. But he wouldn't mind that, would he? It was personality that mattered, not appearance. He may already have seen her on his trips to the National Gallery, of course, but he wouldn't have known who she was.


Next morning Rosalind booted up the computer and found the file with the short personal profiles students had sent in at the start of the course. The suggestion of adding photos hadn't been taken up, thank goodness.

Peter Brandon – Divorced. Recently retired from running his own business he said. Looking for a new interest. Hence the course.

Interest? Here came the bard again, King Lear – *We will divest us both of rule, interest of territory*. Celia had told her to stand up to Shakespeare but why challenge the best wisdom on offer? Why risk *a sea of troubles* when you could come safe home?

What had she put in her assignment about Holbein that made Peter B want to meet her? His sideways invitation to look at The Ambassadors with him suggested diffidence, a man unsure of his territory but you never knew. He could be one of those blokes who pretended shyness to prise out women's mother instinct, wore crumpled rugby shirts that begged for someone else to iron them. On the other hand he could be a military type, blazered and tied in regimental colours. His assignment answers did have that stiff, rehearsed tone as if he felt more secure offering someone else's opinions than exposing his own.

There she went again, making assumptions. What had Celia called it? Getting there before she arrived. Look where that had got her.

She's lying in a Cornish hotel bed pretending to read Macbeth; the Scottish thane is not the only one to murder sleep. Beside her, Hugh, eight hours into the role of husband, lies with his back to her, snoring gently.

 Her flatmates at university were amazed when she told them. 'Engaged to Hugh Fennerton? Who's the cat that's got the cream then?'

Sour cream as it turns out. Her kind, affectionate fiancé – let's wait till the wedding night, darling, much more romantic – has little inclination for what he's just called 'Duty done then.'

Henry V – *Our expectation hath this day an end.* How naïve can you be?

Little did her sister know, Rosalind thought, how long she'd been inside this shell of hers. Why didn't she divorce him? Jane, the honeymoon baby that's why, arriving with a bundle of compensations, and before the second wave of Feminism gave women options.

Now and again duty was done, hurried and disappointing, but there was always his kindness, not to be sneezed at. Kill me not with kindness – who said that? Not Shakespeare so it didn't count.

Did some woman divorce Peter Brandon, she wondered, find him unsatisfactory and have the courage of her convictions? Poor chap.

On the morning the group were due to meet, Peter peered at the board in a coffee shop round the corner from the National Gallery. So many fantastic choices. Whoever hankered for the good old days had surely never spent their teenage years making one cup of weak, frothy coffee last all evening? Mind you, a dollop of All Shook Up on a juke box wouldn't come amiss. Why the heck hadn't he stayed at home?

He chose his coffee, added a cinnamon croissant to his order and waited for the machine to whisper and slurp its way to a cappuchino. He took a seat by the window. The woman at the next table was filling in the last answer of a crossword –*The Independent*, same paper as his own. He studied her reflection in a handy mirror. Slim build, short grey hair in one of those fashionable styles that look natural but probably took ages to achieve. Her straight, dark skirt looked smart. Nice bit of cloth that, good tweed never let you down; the cream jacket was a brave choice for the grimy city but the casually knotted silk scarf spoke of someone who knew how to create the effect she was after. Very nice it looked too. Was she watching him? Reflections worked both ways. Peter opened his paper and hunted for the crossword.

One across – *To achieve the goal,* he read, *sounds like pussy is happy to take up a position.* What the dickens was that all about? Sounded mucky. He felt in his inside jacket pocket for a pen.

'Quite a challenge today – the crossword.' There was no-one else in the place so the woman must be speaking to him.

He cleared his throat and pointed to her finished grid. 'It doesn't seem to have given you any trouble.'

'It's taken me longer than usual,' she said.

'I'm new to this milarky,' Peter heard himself say. What was he up to? He'd never done a cryptic crossword in his life.

The woman smiled at him, a bright smile, the sort he could do with on a day like this. 'Do you want a start?' she said as she got up to go.

'Wouldn't say no,' he told her.

'One across,' she said, 'it's purpose.'


Rosalind, sitting round the corner from The Ambassadors, kept the painting in view. She wasn't entirely sure why she was here but her plan to take a look at Peter, before she committed herself to meeting him, gave her an escape route should she need one.

She looked at the painting on the nearest wall – The Tailor by Giovanni Battista Moroni. She hadn't heard of him before but she liked this work, the idea that an ordinary chap could catch an artist's interest. In the picture the tailor looked up, scissors in hand, and considered her as she was considering him. Above a doublet of fine cream wool, his attractive, bearded face was serious. What would his sixteenth century mind make of her, waiting alone here for a man she'd never laid eyes on? Respectable women of his world didn't do things like that. Was he a forward thinker who'd understand how she felt? Not that you could take much seriously from a chap wearing such voluminous trunk hose, like a pair of enormous, red Chinese lanterns round his bum.

*Predictive Text*

A man was standing to one side of The Ambassadors, glancing at his watch. No sign of rugby shirt nor regimental tie. Above well-cut jeans, his dark sweater strained a little over his tummy. His jacket was tweed, his trainers new, and expensive. It was the man from the coffee shop.

He turned to look at her as she walked towards him, 'It's you,' he said, smiling. His words tumbled out, 'I didn't know it was you – in the coffee shop I mean. I didn't know if you'd come, if you'd think I had a cheek, asking.'

Rosalind smiled at him. 'We crossworders need to stick together.'

He seemed about to say something but changed his mind. Awkwardness hovered.

'I liked . . .', he said.

'What was it . . . ?' she began.

They laughed.

'This is a wonderful painting,' Rosalind said, pointing to The Ambassadors. 'Much bigger than I'd realised. Splendid, aren't they? *Courtiers of beauteous freedom* you could say.'

'Come again?'

'Sorry, bad habit.' Rosalind stepped closer to the picture. 'I really can't work out this skull thing though.'

Peter frowned. 'You've changed your mind then?'

'How d'you mean?'

'Well . . .' Peter hesitated. 'What you said in the assignment . . . it suggested quite the opposite.'

'Remind me, would you?' Rosalind said.

'You said the skull was obviously a mistake on Holbein's part. A moment of madness you called it.'

A finger of doubt pointed its way into Rosalind's mind. 'I don't recall saying anything of the sort,' she said. 'It certainly doesn't sound like me.'

Peter's face was turning redder than the Moroni tailor's trunk hose. 'Oh my god,' he said. 'You're not . . .'

Rosalind felt herself stiffen. 'Whom did you think I was?'

'You're not Roz, are you?'

'No,' Rosalind declared. 'I most certainly am not.'


Peter watched her stomp off. This is what it felt like then to  prick your own balloon, dig a hole and drop yourself in it. Now what? His instinct was to run, disappear back into his life leaving not a trace. Trouble was, the only way out he knew of was through the entrance hall, the very place where the group would be gathering in . . . he glanced at his watch . . . five minutes. Perhaps he could creep past them? Wait till they'd started their tour of the gallery then leg it?

But why should he? A guided tour, lunch in a private room and a lecture from one of the curators was what he'd paid for and that's what he would have. Damn the woman. Whatever her problem, it wasn't his fault. How she'd managed to steal his email he didn't know but anything was possible. Shame though – she was a looker.


Rosalind muttered her way towards the entrance hall. How dare he? How could he think . . . ? The stupid idiot.

There was she, flattered by his interest, leaving her cosy nook and dragging herself to London. Tricked, that's what she'd been, tricked into thinking he was really nice, when all the time . . . *In forgery of shapes and tricks*. How could she have been so trusting? And he'd not filled in a single answer in the crossword.

She stopped for a moment to look at Titian's The Death of Acteon – turned into a stag by Diana the huntress and devoured by his own hounds. Serve him right.

The voice bouncing round the entrance hall was jolly. 'My group to the left here, please. Hurry up guys and dolls,' demanded a woman with a pudding-basin, ginger hair-do. 'Don't be shy now.'

Shyness had surely never troubled the speaker, Rosalind thought. No-one who left the house looking like an explosion in a jumble sale could ever have encountered the monster of self-doubt. The woman wore a tartan kilt, under which dripped layers of elderly lace, topped by a gold satin blouse with sparkly bow. Over this, a black, thigh-length coat was crawling with embroidered dragons and the furry creature draped around her neck had surely breathed its last in some ancient, murky forest. Her legs were clad in vivid blue leggings, her feet in what could only be called plimsolls.

From the depths of a frayed carpet bag she pulled out name-tags.

'Rosalind Fennerton?' she yelled. 'Peter Brandon?'

Rosalind gawped. This, was Roz?


Peter took his name-tag and hung it round his neck. 'Roz, is it?' he said . . . Not so much horsey as jolly, he thought, and a free spirit when it came to clothes. This was a woman who might well have decided views on Holbein but the idea of discussing them with her was not appealing. Floor you with her carpet bag soon as look at you, probably.

The woman beamed at him. 'That's me. Rosamund by birth, Roz by nature.'

A pinprick of light hovered in Peter's mind, an idea of what might have happened to his email. Keeping as much distance as possible between him and the looker on her high horse, he scrabbled in the folder he'd brought with him. Somewhere in here was a list of the student email addresses.

Under the spell of the beauty hanging on the walls —Massacio's Virgin and Child, Botticelli's wonderful colours and the sinuous angel Verrocchio had created to accompany Tobias — Rosalind's fury began to dissipate. Roz proved a capable leader, knowledgeable without being pretentious, and her job in the gallery's conservation studio meant she could share the sort of snippets not found in gallery guidebooks. Rosalind wondered if her wacky comments on the course had been by way of playing devil's advocate. Even her gratingly cheerful voice and odd appearance hardly seemed an issue in the face of her enthusiasm.

By lunchtime Rosalind had begun to think she'd been unfair to Peter Brandon. He'd kept well away from her all morning so when coffee was served after a delicious lunch, she was surprised to find him at her elbow.

'Have you got a minute?' he said.

His look was wary, a man returning to a firework that had gone off once and may not yet be benign. She arranged her face into an encouraging expression.

'Only I think I may have worked out what happened,' he said, 'with the email.'

'The one you meant to go to Roz?'

*Predictive Text*

He glanced at her name-tag. 'You're Rosalind, right?'

She nodded.

'Look,' he glanced at the other students, 'how d'you feel about having a walk? The lecture doesn't start for a while.'

'You'd risk being alone with me?' Rosalind said.

'I'm game if you are.'

They left the Gallery, walked under Admiralty Arch and into St. James' Park. Side by side, they stood on the bridge over the lake, both of them clutching the railings. Rosalind looked down at the two pairs of hands, between them a length of flaking grey paint.

'I can explain,' Peter began.

'I'm sorry I was so offhand,' she said.

Without looking at her he said, 'Ladies first.'

Rosalind sighed. 'It was being mistaken for Roz,' she said. 'It sounds stupid. I know, but . . .'

In the middle of the lake a quacking squabble broke out on Duck Island, a mother duck protecting her young. Covered by the rumpus, Rosalind made her confession. 'I'd decided she was everything I wasn't.'

She sensed Peter turn his head. She knew he'd heard her. She rushed on. 'I'd pictured her, you see. I always do this, imagine how things will be.'

'Me too,' he said. 'What did you think she'd be like?'

'Oh you know, sophisticated, at ease with life, expensively turned-out,' she said, '*So perfect and so peerless.*'

'Another quotation? Like the one about The Ambassadors?'

'Shakespeare I'm afraid. I do that too.' She turned to him. 'What did you think she'd be like?'

'Horsey.'

Rosalind's giggle joined Peter's guffaw and their laughter rang out over the lake. Peter reached into his pocket and pulled out a bag of sweets. 'Sherbert lemon?' he said. When they'd both embarked on the journey to the fizz, he went on, 'Not much good at this prediction milarky, are we?'

'I can usually rely on Shakespeare though,' Rosalind said.

'*Perfect and peerless* you mean?'

'Ferdinand says it to Miranda, in The Tempest.'

'What sort of chap is this Ferdinand? Reliable?'

'He's the love interest,' Rosalind said.

'There you are then. A man with a mission you might say. Anyway Shakespeare could make him say anything, couldn't he? It's the made-up characters talking, isn't it, not the big man himself?'

What now? Rosalind thought. This could well be a pivotal moment, a moment when I might collapse in a heap at the thought of a lifetime spent worshipping at the wrong shrine. Below her the water sparkled; beside her was the nicest man she'd met in ages. What she said next was more than important . . .

She laughed. 'Do you know,' she said, 'In all these years I've never looked at it like that before.'

'First time for everything,' Peter said. 'But look, I wanted to explain – about the email?'

'I'm listening.'

*Predictive Text*

'It's the computer. Once you start to type in the email address you want, it finishes it off. It's called Predictive Text.'

'And?'

'And your email address comes before Roz's, alphabetically on my list. You're RosalindFennerton@ . . . and she's RosamundCarpenter@ . . . I didn't check properly.'

'You mean,' Rosalind said, 'the computer knew better than you did where you wanted the message to go?'

Peter was looking straight ahead. 'I rather think it did,' he said.

Rosalind felt the warmth of his hand beside hers on the railings and when she looked, there was no flaky paint between them at all.

# The Secret Life of Madeline Greatorex

### Patricia Stoner

Her hair was ash blonde, gleaming in a fashionable pageboy cap. Her hands were smooth, the nails unpolished, short and square-cut but immaculately manicured. Her skin was unlined, her eyes grey-green and she was sixty four years old.

God, how she hated it. Not the being old – that in itself was, on reflection, quite pleasant. She knew she was more poised, more confident and happier in herself than she had ever been. She knew, too, that she looked a lot younger than her age. What was it they said: 'Sixty is the new fifty.' No, she had no problems with being 64.

What she resented was the perception. The way anyone over the age of 35 was written off, became invisible.

'What the kids of today don't realise,' she was fond of saying to her closest friends, among whom she allowed her language to slip, 'is that we old fogeys in our sixties are children *of* the sixties. We've been there, seen it, done it and *taken off* the T-shirt – and long before they were even thought of.'

Her closest friends concurred. They had been there, seen it, done it and taken off the T-shirt with her. They still called her Loony. It was a logical, though hardly original, extension of her name. Madeline, Madds, Mad . . . Loony.

No-one in her professional life called her Loony. She was Miss Greatorex to most, Madeline to a chosen few. Her boss alone called her Maddy. She called him Mr Cecil. Everyone in the company, from the lowest post room junior to the managing director himself, called him Mr Cecil. He had been Mr Cecil since time immemorial, even though he was now Lord Goldstein.

The young man in the outer office coughed gently. He was clutching a bound script, and she could see that his palms had left damp patches on the cardboard cover. It wasn't surprising that he was nervous. A personal interview with the chairman of the most prestigious independent television production company in the country was enough to make anyone nervous.

'Mr Cecil will see you shortly,' she told him kindly.

She glanced out of her window. From her 11th floor office she had a panoramic view of the Thames. The river flowed sleepily at low tide and the London Eye shone in the late-afternoon sun. Expertly she assessed the sky. The weather forecast for the weekend had been mixed. After an exceptionally hot and dry June, July was starting out cooler, with cloud and occasional showers most days.

Nothing wrong with a few showers, she thought; less dust and more mud. She grinned to herself. What would her colleagues make of the cool, polished Miss Greatorex gloating over the possibility of mud?

The door opened and Edward Savile walked in without knocking. It was not a privilege she would have accorded

160    *It's Never Too Late to Fall in Love*

anyone else, but he was the managing director. And he was Edward. In spite of her very best intentions, her heart gave a little flip.

She had been in love with him since she was 22, a shy ex-grammar school girl fresh out of secretarial college. Even then Edward had been tipped for the top. The news documentary strand he produced for the ITV Network was controversial and challenging, not afraid of tackling the sensitive issues of the day.

Of course, he hadn't noticed her then. And, as they made their separate ways up the corporate ladder over the next 40 years, their relationship had developed into one of detached mutual respect.

Now he glanced over at the young man in the outer office, and nodded approvingly. 'So Mr Cecil agreed to see our young Shakespeare, then? I'm glad. He's got a really good script there – it'll knock their socks off at the Network. Let's hope they have the b . . . , er, guts to commission it.'

The light on Madeline's console blipped discreetly and she signalled to the young man to go into the Inner Sanctum. 'Good luck,' she whispered as he walked past her desk, and gave him an encouraging wink. He looked faintly startled. She occasionally forgot she was supposed to be a dragon.

'So, have you any plans for the weekend, Miss Greatorex?' Edward said, settling himself in the chair the young man had vacated.

'Yes, as it happens. I am meeting a few friends in Wiltshire.' As if on a wide-screen television she saw the images that crossed his mind; lunch at a boutique gastro-pub followed by a vigorous walk with the dogs? Or perhaps a country-house weekend on someone's estate? She smiled and said nothing.

*The Secret Life of Madeline Greatorex*

'Oddly enough, I plan to be in Wiltshire myself this weekend,' Edward said. 'Perhaps we'll run into each other.'

I sincerely hope not, she thought but didn't say. The idea of meeting Edward in those circumstances filled her both with horror and an overwhelming urge to laugh like a, well, like a Loony.

'Perhaps we will,' she said.

As she left the building that night she saw Edward again, getting into his late-model Range Rover Vogue. She approved his choice but, as she climbed into her silver Audi R8, she wondered not for the first time if he even knew what that small second gear lever was for.

Saturday dawned cloudy and cold, and it was not long after dawn that a transformed Madeline emerged from her Putney house. Gone were the designer suit, the sheer nylons, the trademark Jimmy Choos. Gone was Miss Greatorex: she was all Loony now. Her faded jeans were cut for comfort, not style. Her padded blouson sported a Land Rover green oval and the same logo adorned her battered baseball cap.

She checked her watch. She was meeting the gang at 9:30 in the car park by Stonehenge, then they would drive in convoy to the Plain. Better allow a couple of hours for the drive to be on the safe side. If she left now, she would have time for a bacon sandwich at the truck stop on the A303.

She opened the doors of the double garage that flanked the house. Her Audi gleamed quietly in the half-dark and, sitting next to it, was the love of her life.

The Series 2 Land Rover had seen better days. The front wing was dented and there was a chip in one half of the split windscreen that would turn into a crack if she didn't do something about it soon. The dark green paintwork was clean – she had taken her Karcher to the mud after their last outing – but dull and scratched.

She noticed that the rear number plate – MAD 1 – was slightly bent. She had grounded badly coming down the Steps – a steep, rocky path in the Devil's Punchbowl. It must have happened then.

She slid into the driver's seat, cursing as usual as the cracked vinyl snagged on her jeans. The key turned smoothly, the engine coughed into life. As she pulled away a gleam of sunshine broke through black clouds, giving the sky the hectic brightness that threatened a storm.

By the time she was nearing Stonehenge the rain was coming down in torrents. The windscreen wipers on the ancient Land Rover did their best, but she could hardly see the road ahead.

As she turned left into the Stonehenge car park she could see her friends, hunched gloomily in Kagools and Barbours, huddled round flasks of coffee. 'Nice day for green-laning,' she called cheerfully as she drew up.

And then, suddenly, it was. The rain stopped. The sky still loured but a feeble ray poked its way tentatively between clouds. Loony's weather, they called it. Somehow, she had the magic touch. No matter how foul the weather, whenever Madeline turned up it got better.

She was the last to arrive, so within a few minutes they had all climbed into their vehicles – in some cases wiping puddles off the seats as canvas roofs proved as reliable as ever against the rain. They set off across the road and onto Salisbury Plain.

If anyone asked Madeline to describe what it was like, green-laning on Salisbury Plain, she'd say, 'It's a minefield.' Which was, literally, true. The land belonged to the MOD and vast

*The Secret Life of Madeline Greatorex*

swathes of it were out of bounds to civilian traffic. You needed an experienced leader to get you through safely.

On the other hand, it was for the most part extremely boring. Flat open countryside didn't offer many challenges to seasoned off-roaders. But it was convenient for everybody, and the occasional mud puddle or rocky slide kept things from being too tedious.

After about half an hour the lead car veered off to the right, and Madeline realised with a lift of her spirits that they were headed for Dawn's Ditch. It was the steepest bit of terrain on the Plain and, after a heavy rain fall, the ground had the consistency of a quagmire. On one famous occasion last October, her friend Dawn's Discovery 1 had become so deeply embedded that in the end they had had to call on a passing DAF army truck to give her a tow out. Since that day, the spot had been known as Dawn's Ditch – and Madeline had carried a heavy-duty tow rope on her front bumper.

The convoy halted abruptly on the edge of the wooded area leading down to the Ditch. This in itself wasn't unusual: probably someone had broken down. Peering ahead, Madeline expected to see the inevitable raised bonnet and the inevitable jeans-clad bottoms sticking up as their owners disappeared head-first into the intricacies of the engine.

Instead, there seemed to be an unusual amount of kerfuffle and arm-waving going on, and several people she didn't recognise. Dave galloped back down the line towards her. 'Loony! You're needed!' he yelled, waving her forward. 'Some eejit in a poncy motor 's gone and got himself stuck in the Ditch. We'll need your tow rope to get him out.'

She edged the Series cautiously round the stationary vehicles and drove down towards the Ditch. Sure enough, a mud-spattered Range Rover had got itself firmly stuck in the mud

164        *It's Never Too Late to Fall in Love*

at the bottom. A mud spattered Range Rover which, curiously, she seemed to recognise.

'It's OK, Ted, the cavalry's arrived,' someone said. 'Be thankful that it's a Land Rover and not a blessed Toyota, like last time.' Madeline shuddered – oh, the shame of being towed out by a Toyota. Carefully she positioned her car in front of the stranded Range Rover and the driver got out to attach the tow cable.

He was the last person she expected to see on Salisbury Plain, but even in the khaki combats and the heavy military-style green sweater she recognised him at once. This, she thought, was going to be interesting.

Dave was obviously the self appointed master of ceremonies. 'Easy, now Loony. Easy does it. Slowly back . . .' he shouted at full volume, as if she didn't know perfectly well how to tow a car out of a ditch. Engaging four wheel drive and low box she eased backwards, the cable taking up the slack until she felt the pull of the heavier vehicle against her own.

Slowly the Range Rover came free. She continued reversing until she was sure both cars were on firm ground, and stopped. The driver got out and detached the cable, then came round to her window to thank her. His double-take was delicious.

'Ted?' she said, her voice breaking on laughter.

'*Loony?*' his expression matched hers.

Later they sat in the pub garden with their respective groups. The buzz of Land Rover chatter was all around them, but they had other things to discuss. 'Have you any plans for next weekend, Miss Greatorex?' he asked. 'Do you know, Mr Savile, I rather think I have,' she said.

# How Little Time

### Cedric Parcell

The pilot of the Wellington bomber had a premonition from the moment they took off that things were not going to go well. Their target was a factory outside Milan and they were carrying a lot of extra fuel – the old Wimpey was not really designed for such long range flights. She was sluggish with all the extra load and they didn't arrive over the target until the main force had left. They could see that the previous aircraft had done their job and they lost no time in dropping their bombs into the circle of fire beneath them and turned to head for home. But the fighters were waiting for them and they were set on by a couple of Focke Wulfs. A shell from one of them hit amidships and put the hydraulics out of action and after that the pilot had very little control over the plane: he knew there was no question of getting them back home.

They were flying in bright moonlight over mountains and there was nowhere flat enough to ditch. But he thought he saw a patch of cultivated land ahead. It was too late to bale out so he told the crew to hang on tight and he would try and put her down, but he soon realised it was impossible... they crashed on a hillside and from that moment everything went black. He remembered nothing more about it for a very long time.

Apparently they had come down in an area where the Partisans, guerrillas fighting against the Germans, were in control and they were quickly on the scene. They told him later he was the only survivor – all the rest of the crew were killed. How he had survived was something of a miracle. He must have been the luckiest man in the world not to have died with the rest of them. But he was very badly injured. The Partisans took him to a farm house outside the village of Montepalagio and found a local doctor to have a look at him – he didn't give him much hope. He had a badly shattered leg which he eventually had to have amputated, severe injuries to his head and a lot of internal injuries. Nobody expected him to survive, but somehow he held on.

By this time the Germans were looking for him. They had found the wreckage and taken away the bodies but they knew the pilot was unaccounted for and they were searching the villages for him. He had to be hidden and for days he lay under a pile of straw in the loft of an old farm building while the Germans poked around.

Eventually he was strong enough to be moved and they smuggled him into a safe house in one of the villages where he was looked after by an Italian peasant and his wife. They were the kindest and most gentle folks he had ever known; they looked after him as though he was their own son and if it hadn't been for Guiseppe and Maria he would never have survived.

He stayed with them for the rest of the war. He was in such a weak state that it was months before he had the strength to hobble about on a pair of crutches which Guiseppe made and they did everything for him, fed him, tended his wounds, washed and cared for him, all for not the smallest reward.

They were a wonderful couple and he owed his life to them. If the Germans had found him they would have shot the Italian couple, and he would surely have died in a prison camp.'

Stuart Castleton disliked the charity shops which had sprung up along the High Street. Fifty years ago, when he had first come to live in Listfield, these premises had been occupied by newsagents and tobacconists, fishmongers and men's outfitters, small shops that gave a useful service until they were pushed to the wall by the multiples and the supermarkets. He had once or twice ventured through the door of the local Oxfam but he remembered it in its former existence as Fred Smith's Manshop where he had bought his shirts and underwear. Fred had been an ex-R.A.F man like himself and Stuart had been very sorry when he went out of business, like a lot more had. They had been replaced by charity shops, which no doubt did a very good job, but Stuart had reached an age when he preferred things as he had always remembered them.

One day however, he dropped and broke an ornamental salt cellar, part of a cruet set that his late wife had been very fond of. It had been given to them as a wedding gift in 1949 and by now the firm who made them had long gone out of business, so there was little hope of finding an exact replacement. Somebody suggested to him that he might be lucky and pick up a second-hand one at Oxfam or the Hospice Shop. He tried them both along with several others, poking around among the miscellany of ornamental vases, fruit dishes, old vinegar bottles and Woolworth's glassware but without any success.

He was feeling tired and frustrated and all the walking he had done that morning had made the stump of his leg play up. He was on the point of abandoning his search when he

*It's Never Too Late to Fall in Love*

noticed a box of framed pictures which had once hung on the walls of somebody's drawing room. He had done a bit of painting in his youth and pictures interested him. Riffling casually through the contents when one of the paintings made him look twice. He picked it up and held it to the light, examining it almost in disbelief; it depicted the village green at Daneswycke, a small village on the Yorkshire Wolds, with the church on the hill and the George and Dragon pub which sold Tadcaster Ales back in the 1940s. He was amazed to recognise the painting as his own work, one which he had done during the war when he was stationed with the R.A.F. near Driffield and he had given it to a friend as a memento.

It was marked modestly at £2 which he handed over to the lady in the twin-set and pearls who insisted on wrapping it in bubble paper before putting it into a plastic bag bearing the logo of the charity. 'Hardly a masterpiece', he murmured apologetically, but he little knew then the significance which that small purchase was to have. On the bus home he took it out and had a good look at it. Yes, it was his painting alright, and he scratched away a bit of the grime in the bottom corner to reveal his initials S.C. and the date 1943. Where could it possibly have been for the past fifty-five years, he asked himself?

When he got back to his bungalow he made himself a cup of tea and sat for some time gazing intently at his picture. Of course, he remembered perfectly well to whom he had given it. Margaret Yates was the kind of girl it would be hard to forget. Despite the passage of more than half a century, and even after a long and happy marriage, he still thought of her from time to time. In 1943 she was a lovely twenty-year old WAAF with a complexion so perfect that she reminded him of the girl in a Vermeer portrait. Her parents had a small farm close to the airfield and he remembered the day she took him home and introduced him to them, good honest yeomen farmers, the 'salt of the earth'. Stuart who was himself brought up in a farming community felt immediately at home with them.

His squadron had been sent up to Daneswycke-on-the-Wolds, a wartime airfield a mile outside the town in the Spring of 1943. It was at the local pub, the George and Dragon, where the aircrews gathered when off duty, that he had met Margaret one evening. He had been immediately attracted by this lively girl with the plain Yorkshire accent who was so full of life and fun. They had sat and talked all evening and got on so well with each other that he had asked her if he could take her out for dinner at the Bell in Driffield. She had hesitated.

'The Bell is very posh and expensive', she said. 'It's alright for officers like yourself, but I'm not sure if they would like it for you to take in a mere WAAF.'

'Nonsense!' he had replied. 'We don't go for all this class stuff where I come from. On the sheep farms of New Zealand one man's as good as another and if he can afford to take his young lady to the best places that's OK by everybody else'

Over dinner he had told her something about himself. He had been born on his father's sheep farm in Otago on the South Island of New Zealand and at the outbreak of war in 1939 he had decided to come to England and join up, as his father had done in the First War. But instead of choosing the New Zealand Rifles he opted for the R.A.F. After training to fly heavy bombers he had been posted as a sergeant pilot to 158 Squadron stationed in the North of England. He had carried out a number of bombing raids against targets in the industrial Ruhr of Germany and had been fortunate on a couple of occasions to manage to limp back with a badly damaged aircraft. The squadron had suffered heavy losses during the winter and was short of officers, so Stuart, somewhat to his

170     *It's Never Too Late to Fall in Love*

surprise, had been put up for a commission. He was now flying as a Pilot Officer but rank made not a jot of difference to him – he was one of a six man crew and they worked together as a team – he just happened to now have a single ring on his sleeve instead of three stripes on his arm.

Memories of the war came flooding back as he looked at the old painting and prompted him to do something he had not done for many a long day. From a battered old suitcase in his wardrobe he took out the souvenirs of his days of active service and sat for some time mulling reminiscently over them. There was his R.A.F. log book which recorded every one of the forty five operations he had carried out, from late 1940 until the night in 1944 when they suddenly ended. He picked up his 'wings' which he had unstitched from his uniform and kept safely in the back of his log book, and he opened the small box which contained his most prized possession, the D.F.C. medal which he had received belatedly, long after the events of the night of the 7th of March in 1944. Among the papers was an envelope with a few fading photographs and there she was! A smiling, happy girl with her arm linked through his on the farm at Daneswycke on one of the weekends when she had taken him home. He was in his uniform but she had changed into civvies, a slim-fitting summer dress that showed off her figure better than any uniform ever could. How lovely she had looked on that May morning so long ago.

All that summer they had been inseparable. He had bought a small open-topped Morris 8 sports car from a fellow officer and he had taken Margaret all over the place. Together they had rambled along the winding coastal paths at Bempton where huge colonies of seabirds nested on the high cliffs, wheeling and screeching in the wind, they had explored together the antiquities of medieval Beverley, and the

*How Little Time*　　　　　　171

conservative charms of Filey, and they had danced late into the night at the Spa Royal Hall in Bridlington.

Sometimes they had taken a picnic into the country and she had watched him as he painted – he was, he claimed, little more than a 'dauber' but she thought he was pretty good. In between he had flown with his squadron, always returning safely with the dawn. He disdained to carry a rabbit's foot or other superstitious charms in his pocket as many aircrew did, insisting that Margaret was his charm and protector, and that as long as he had her love he would be safe. And he had been until that fateful March night.

Stuart lay awake for a long time wondering how his painting of Daneswycke-on-the-Wolds had found its way to a charity shop in Listfield. He didn't sleep very well these days – his prosthetic leg was giving him trouble again but it was the mystery of the painting that kept him awake that night. He wondered if the lady in the shop might be able to remember who had brought it in.

He went back the next day taking the painting with him. It was a different assistant on duty that morning and she seemed rather less snooty than the one who had sold him the painting. He introduced himself and asked her if she had any idea who might have brought it in.

She looked hard at the painting and said she couldn't recollect who the donor might have been. 'These old pictures don't sell very well and we might have had it in stock for quite some time,' she said, 'but I'll have a word with the manageress when she comes back from the bank and see if she can throw any light on it'.

Stuart kicked his heels for a while until the other lady returned and she too had a good hard look at the painting. No spark of recollection dawned but just as Stuart was about to give it up as a bad job, she suddenly remembered a man about a month ago bringing in a whole load of stuff that an elderly lady wanted rid of and she was pretty sure the painting had been among the items. But that was as much as she could tell him: people seldom gave their names and addresses when they donated their cast-offs and bric-a-brac.

But she offered Stuart a practical suggestion. 'I have a friend who works on the Listfield Chronicle and she may be able to help. The papers are always on the lookout for an interesting story and if you tell her your tale she might agree to write a bit in the paper and the person whose painting it was may come forward'. The idea paid dividends. The following week a man telephoned Stuart with the information he wanted.

'That painting belonged to my mother who is now in her seventies,' he told him. 'She has had to move into a retirement home recently and I helped her to clear her house.'

Stuart held his breath and asked the caller, 'Does your mother's name happen to be Margaret?'

'Yes, it does'.

'And did she originally come from a village in East Yorkshire?' he asked.

'Exactly right. Daneswycke-on-the-Wolds, which is the village on the painting'.

The man gave Stuart the name of the retirement home to which his mother had gone, but warned him that she was not in good health and it would be advisable to phone the home before attempting to get in touch with her. Stuart promised he would do so.

The Green Gables Retirement Home was a large Victorian house built around the end of the 19th century and had formerly been the home of a local industrialist who had

*How Little Time*

made his money out of brass ornaments. It had undergone a great deal of alteration since those days, and after being used as a private school, and later standing empty for many years, it had been bought by a developer in the 1970's and converted into its present use as the final staging post in life for a number of elderly residents.

Margaret Grantham arrived there on a chilly November morning in 1997 and the sight of the gloomy mansion depressed her enormously. She had never expected to be ending her days in such a place. When her husband Matthew had died suddenly in his early sixties she had moved down to the Midlands to be near her only son. She sold their house in Wakefield and bought a bungalow on the outskirts of Listfield, only five minutes away from Christopher and his family. He had done his very best to look after his mother but as her health and mobility deteriorated she became increasingly in need of help and it had become too much for him and his wife, both of whom had full-time jobs.

Margaret was not short of money for her father had left her a substantial sum and she had the pension from the bank where Matthew had been a branch manager. She could well afford to pay for residential care, but it was the thought of being confined with strangers, and dependent on paid assistants to help her through her everyday living which upset her. She had not realised that the love and support of the family, on which the aged parents of earlier generations had been able to depend, was no longer an option. She had struggled on her own for as long as she could but when she fell and broke her hip it had been decided that she needed professional care.

It was not that Christopher and his wife Frances were uncaring but they had the responsibility of three growing children who made big demands, both physically and financially on their parents. Margaret offered no reproaches and did her best to accept her lot and settle down in Green Gables, but at heart she was a sad woman. In fact she had been that way for quite a long time.

Her married life had not been entirely happy. At twenty she had lost the man with whom she had hoped to spend the rest of her life; her brave lover who had disappeared on a night raid over Northern Italy and nothing had ever been heard of him. On that night in March 1944 her life too had almost ended. Night after night she had cried herself to sleep. As soon as her pregnancy became apparent she had had to tell the WAAF officer and had been discharged from the R.A.F. She had lost the man she loved and at the same time she lost the friendly companionship of service life. She returned to her parents' farm in Daneswycke and moped in despair.

It was an unexpected gesture on the part of Matthew Grantham which changed things. He was a boy from the village with whom she had grown up and they attended the same grammar school in Bridlington. She had always liked him as a gentle and kind friend but they had very little else in common. Where she had been an outgoing and fun-loving girl, Matthew had been a quiet and bookish lad with few friends, but he had for many years harboured a love for her which he had never dared declare. Now, with the birth of her child only a few weeks away, Matthew had offered to marry her and bring up the child as his own.

She had asked herself many times over the years whether she had done the right thing in accepting his proposal but they lived in an age and a society which still looked askance at unmarried mothers and for the sake of her parents' respectability she had agreed to marry the young bank clerk. They were wed at Daneswycke parish church in October 1944 and Christopher was born on Christmas Eve. He was the only child she was to have.

*How Little Time*

Over the years Matthew made his way up the ladder at the bank and she had accompanied him on a number of moves to different branches in the North of England. She was a conscientious wife, doing her best to further her husband's banking career and trying to share his interests but somehow their marriage seemed to lack that spark of vitality that she so longed for. At times she dreamed about what life might have been as the wife of a New Zealand sheep farmer and her heart still ached for the young man who had flown out of her life without even a chance to say goodbye. The painting he had given her, and which had hung in her bedroom for years, was the only reminder she had of him.

When Mrs. Goodrich, the lady in charge of the home came and sat beside her in the residents' lounge, Margaret Grantham was about to receive the biggest shock of her life.

'I've just had a telephone call dear, from a man who says he knew you during the war.'

Margaret sat up straight in the chair. 'Really? What was his name?'

When the matron told her she nearly fell off the chair.

'But that's impossible!' she gasped, 'Stuart Castleton died in 1944. Somebody's having us on.'

'I don't think so, dear. Did he give you a painting of the village where you used to live when you were a girl?'

'Yes, he certainly did. It hung on my bedroom wall for years.'

'Well, it seems he's got it now – says he found it in a charity shop right here in Listfield'.

The matron's words left Margaret's head in such a spin that she thought she was going to faint and Mrs Goodrich called one of the girls to bring her a glass of water. As her mind cleared Margaret began to digest the message which had dropped on her like a bombshell.

'But how did it all come about? Stuart was posted missing, presumed dead, after a bombing raid in 1944 and nobody ever had a word from him. We eventually had to accept that he had been killed and his body never found. How could he possibly turn up now after all these years?'

Mrs. Goodrich was caring but firm. 'Look dear, this has obviously come as a great shock for you. Mr. Castleton naturally wants to see you again, but he promised your son that he would telephone first to find out if you wanted to see him. Why don't you sleep on it and tell me in the morning if you want to see him. If you do, I have his telephone number.'

It was the following afternoon that they met. Mrs Goodrich considerately vacated her small office and sat Margaret in her chair before she brought Stuart to her. It was for both of them a more emotive experience than they had ever known in their lives. Words completely failed them as they stood facing each other with the tears streaming down their cheeks. He took her sobbing in his arms and held her until all emotion was spent and they could talk coherently.

Now for the first time she heard what had happened on that night almost sixty years ago, the night Stuart and his crew did not get back to Daneswycke. That, above all else, was what she had waited all these years to know.

He held her hand tight and began in that soft New Zealand accent she remembered so well, to try and recall all that had happened.

Margaret was reduced to tears by the description of his suffering. The effort of recalling the events of those terrible months quite exhausted Stuart. Mrs Goodrich had brought

*How Little Time*

them both a cup of tea and they sat in silence for some time before Margaret spoke.

'And was there no way that word of what had happened to you could have been got back to England?', she asked.

'None at all', Stuart replied. 'We were in such a remote part of Italy, high up in the mountains, and I was in too weak a state to think about anything but surviving. We had no idea what was going on in the outside world until one day a Jeep with American soldiers drove into the village and they told us that the war was over. They arranged for an ambulance to pick me up and I was flown to a military hospital in Frankfurt where they had to amputate my leg and fit me with an artificial one. From there they flew me home to New Zealand.'

'Oh, my God. What you must have gone through', she said. Her voice softened and she quietly asked the question that she had to know the answer to. 'Did you think of me in all that time you were in Italy?'

'Think of you? There was never a day, Margaret, when you were out of my thoughts. It was the hope of seeing you again that kept me going through it all'.

She turned her head away, as if afraid to ask to ask, 'How did you learn that I had married somebody else? It must have come as a shock'.

'It really did. As soon as I could get to a telephone in Frankfurt I phoned the farm and your father told me you had married a young man from the village – I couldn't believe it at first.'

'I had no idea you had phoned' said Margaret.

'I asked your father to say nothing. There didn't seem any point in stirring up old memories. I realised that you must have thought me dead and married this chap on the rebound'.

'No Stuart, I assure you that wasn't the way it was at all. Of course I thought you were dead, as everybody else did, but I didn't marry Matthew for that reason'.

There was a long silence between them until she continued.

'When you spoke to that man on the phone yesterday, who did you think he was?'

'He told me he was your son,' he replied.

'He IS my son . . . and yours too!'

Stuart sat for a moment in stunned silence. As the impact of what she had just told him sunk in it was almost too much for the old man to bear. The blood drained from his cheeks and his chest tightened – she was afraid he was about to have a heart attack. She put her arms around him and comforted him. 'Can you ever forgive me Stuart for not believing you were still alive?' she pleaded.

'Forgive you my darling? What is there to forgive? I am the one who needs forgiveness for making you pregnant and ruining your life.'

'No, no, you didn't ruin my life,' she cried through her tears. 'In all the years as he was growing up I looked at Christopher and saw you. The child was my salvation'.

There was much more to be said but the emotions of the day had been as much as either of them could take. He promised to come again the next day and they would tell each other the story of the years in between.

Over the next few days the missing pieces in the jig-saw were fitted together. He told her how he had returned to his

*How Little Time*

father's sheep farm in Otago, broken in health and spirit by the war. He knew he would never again be able to follow an active life and resume his work on the farm and he made up his mind that he would return to England and try and find work that he could cope with.

The British government had introduced a number of schemes to assist returning servicemen to settle into a career and teaching was one of them. He had not been to university, as had few of the men of his generation, but a twelve month emergency teacher training course was on offer for those with a secondary education. He had been sent for a year to a Teachers' Training College and later took his place at a school in Listfield to teach English and geography. It was there that he met and married Molly, a nurse who had taken good care of him over the years. To their deep regret, they had never had children for his wartime injuries had made this impossible. But they had enjoyed fifty years of companionable marriage without any regrets.

Margaret in turn told him of her married life with Matthew Grantham, omitting to dwell on her disappointments and the lack of fulfilment in their marriage, but she had accepted Matthew's self denial in marrying a girl who he knew did not love him and bringing up her child. She bore Matthew no grudge for the empty and unfulfilled years she had endured.

When he died Margaret was still comparatively young. At sixty-five and living in the new age of equal opportunities, she was able to find many practical ways to enjoy life to the full. She had joined a number of organisations offering opportunities for friendship, and perhaps a little more. She had met other men but most of them had disappointed her. After years of subordinating her dreams and ambitions to playing the role of a bank manager's wife, she valued her new-found independence and living alone held no terrors until, unexpectedly, arthritis had struck her down. She knew there was no cure for this degenerative illness but she had enjoyed long periods of remission and the newest drugs minimised the effects. It was the fall while out shopping that had been the final set-back – a broken hip meant she could no longer look after herself and made the sunset home inevitable.

Stuart could see that life in the sombre confines of Green Gables Retirement Home was depressing her and it seemed unlikely that she would ever settle. He took her out for lunch two or three times a week or to a matinee at the theatre but his lack of mobility restricted him.

'If it wasn't for this bloody tin leg of mine we could go out more often, walking and joining coach trips, visiting National Trust houses and things like that!'

'Well', she reminded him, 'Douglas Bader had two tin legs and it didn't stop him from flying in the Battle of Britain.'

'You're right', he said, 'We shouldn't let our handicaps stop us from enjoying what little of life we have left'.

It was this conversation that prompted him to put to her the proposal he had been thinking about for some time.

'I don't see why you shouldn't get out of this place and come and live with me. We could look after each other and I'm sure we could get more out of life if we were together'.

She took no persuading at all and moved in with him the following week.

And now life took on a real meaning for both of them. With Stuart at her side Margaret was soon a different woman. She forgot about all her aches and pains and her energy and enthusiasm returned; she worked with him to turn his disorganised bungalow into a happy home for two; they bought a small car which she was able to drive; they planned outings

*How Little Time*

and short holidays and best of all, the nights were no longer lonely for either of them as they snuggled down in the king-size bed which they had chosen together.

The happiest outcome for both of them was to become part of a united family. Christopher and the children readily accepted that the new man in their lives was the father and grandfather of whose existence they had never dreamed. When they heard the full story of his life and his heroism in the war they were immensely proud to be his descendants.

And finally, Stuart and Margaret took the big step they had waited for sixty years to make. They married at the village church in Daneswycke where they had spent so many happy hours in their young days. They honeymooned on the Italian lakes and Stuart even arranged for them to be driven up to the hill village of Montepalagio to meet the children and grandchildren of Guiseppe and Maria who had saved his life in the dark days of 1944.

Stuart and Margaret both lived into their nineties – so little time together, but golden years at the end of their story.

# A Good Sense of Humour

## Margaret Kitchen

Sitting in her favourite lunchtime café, sipping her second skinny latte, Glenys was trying to work out whether she had a good sense of humour. She was reading the relationship advertisements in a magazine, which implied this was an essential quality for a good relationship.

She was, however, uncertain how a sense of humour could be properly measured. If there were a Richter scale for humour (similar to earthquake measurements) she wondered how often she would make a 6.8. Or would she more routinely produce a 3.9?

Glenys had never kept a record of what she found funny but she was conscious that she sometimes laughed at jokes that were barely amusing. She did not like to offend people who thought they were hilarious.

She tried to remember how often she had really laughed in the previous week. Office life was passing through yet another crisis of change, so there was not much humour during the working day. Her friend Christine had sent a postcard from Mexico saying she was running away with the local Latin lover, but that had produced more of a grimace than a smile, because Christine had done something similar almost forty years previously and it had not turned out to be a great success.

She could recall nothing on the radio or television that had caused much of a giggle, but maybe her memory is not what it was. (Or maybe television is not what it was.) She had, however, managed a slight titter when the attractive, young, male manager of the café had commented on the beautiful day outside. In fact it was raining stair rods and the manager, who came from Poland, was learning how to joke about the British weather.

All in all, Glenys felt it was not easy to tell whether she had a GSOH – a good sense of humour – which might lead to a happy liaison. When she was in her twenties and in no need of a magazine to find a date, these were called lonely hearts or matchmaking services. Glenys was not sure whether she wanted to make a long term, committed match. However, a few weeks away from retirement, with an empty nest at home, she felt she would soon be in need of some companionship. She felt willing to give an encounter with a man another whirl, before settling for a life of new activities, primarily with her women friends.

Her divorce was so ancient, she could scarcely remember to whom she had been married and encounters with men in recent years had not been durable. Work and colleagues had long provided company and stimulation, so she had not needed to worry about being solitary. Loneliness was, however, looming ominously and she knew she had to make an effort to avoid it.

After some months of trawling the internet and studying magazine and newspaper advertisements, she had become fluent in the language and acronyms of the relationship services. She WLTM (would like to meet) someone with a GSOH as a priority but so far she had lacked the courage to respond to any man in want of a 'companion for fun and friendship and perhaps more'.

Nor had she marketed herself yet, although she had made several stabs at trying to describe herself. She was poignantly aware that her appearance, rather than her impressive CV, was the most critical factor. Being black, rather short and definitely what the ads described as 'cuddly', she was uncertain how marketable she was in the predominantly white media she was researching. Adding that to her approaching age of 62 and more than a few grey hairs (which she stubbornly refused to dye), she was beginning to feel rather ridiculous about the idea of using dating services to find a companion.

Her women friends divided into two camps about her idea of using the relationship ads. Some urged caution and wanted her to find friends through mutual interests. However, as reading and gardening were her main interests and not sociable occupations, this would mean taking up new hobbies.

Other friends thought she should try the dating services and not worry about her age because, they said, there were plenty of men of a similar age who had lonely hearts. They begged her though, to make sure they knew where she was going if she went out on a date.

A first date was not going to come about, however, until she grasped the nettle and wrote a reply to one or more of the advertisements. She was uncharacteristically procrastinating because she was concerned that an attachment might be more trouble than it was worth. It would be very pleasant to have a male friend in her life, but a greater attachment might mean she would have to sacrifice her hard earned independence while she was still healthy enough for adventures.

*A Good Sense of Humour*

'What you do?' her thoughts were interrupted by the good-looking Polish café manager who was peering at her magazine as he removed her cup from the table.

'Just Reading a magazine,' she replied laconically, turning the page so he could not see the list of hopefuls in search of romance. 'And I'll have another one of those please,' she indicated the latte. She felt no compulsion to rush back to her disgruntled office. She doubted she would be sacked for being late just four weeks from retirement.

The young man walked back to the counter to fetch her drink and she watched his slim hips swirl as he progressed. She would not, she felt, have a clue what to do with a gym-honed body like that, but he would look very good on her mantelpiece.

When he returned he pulled out a chair and sat down at the table. There were only two other customers remaining after the lunchtime rush, so he was able to make the most of a slack period.

'I am Peter, I see you reading every day. I know what you read,' he reached over and flicked the page of the magazine back to the dating ads before Glenys could prevent him.

'No need to feel shame,' he said. 'Everybody needs somebody.'

Just before her eyes welled up with tears, Glenys wondered if he was going to offer himself as a date.

'I know somebody you would like.'

'You do?' she replied with astonishment, scrabbling for a tissue.

'Yes, I watch you and I think this good lady would be nice for my father.'

186          *It's Never Too Late to Fall in Love*

'Your father?'

'Yes'. He did not enlarge on his response.

'Does your father live in this country?'

'Now yes, soon who knows?' The broad shoulders shrugged. 'He make much money here. This is his café, he has other business so I come to manage this. I am learning English at a school also.'

Glenys had been aware that the café had recently changed hands but she did not think it was a gold mine. Perhaps the other business made more money.

'You like meet him?' Peter inquired.

Glenys looked down at the dating ads. 'Does he have a good sense of humour?'

The young brow furrowed as Peter translated the question and thought about it.

'Yes!' he declared triumphantly. 'A Polish sense of humour.'

Glenys knew nothing about Polish humour. She knew very little about Poland at all.

'Is he divorced?'

'No, my mother died,' Peter replied in a matter of fact manner.

'I'm so sorry.'

'It was long time ago, she was very ill.'

'And your father never married again?'

'No, he was too busy making money for me and my two sisters. We are all here in UK now and we have jobs, so he can relax. He need a nice lady like you.'

*A Good Sense of Humour*

Glenys was flattered that somebody so young thought she was nice but she felt his father might prefer something beyond niceness.

'What does he look like?' she asked, watching Peter carefully as he groped for a description in English.

'He is maybe a bit tall, blond once but now grey, handsome I think.'

Glenys gained the impression that Peter had described his father that way before and decided he must regularly tout for girlfriends for him. She finished her drink and gathered up her magazine.

'Well perhaps I'll see him around,' she said sternly, handing him the money for her food and drinks.

'I can arrange meeting,' Peter said, looking anxious as he went for her change.

'I bet you can,' her face was stony now.

Peter turned and saw her face. He realised she was cross. 'I am serious. I think you think I do this before. I don't.'

'But you're very good at it.'

Peter looked perplexed. 'Look, write here something about you. Like the advertisements. I give it to my father, he can reply.' He held out his notepad and pen.

Glenys felt she would never get out of the café and back to work if she didn't satisfy his request. She seized the pad and wrote:

Tall, friendly, slim, F, GSOH, WLTM man who likes a wild time.

'Tell him to leave his reply here,' she said airily, handing back the notebook and leaving.

188　　*It's Never Too Late to Fall in Love*

As she walked back to her office, she felt sad that she would be unable to return to the café that had given her sustenance in her final working years. It had been a comfortable bolt-hole in the middle of the working day, energising her for the afternoons ahead. She also regretted putting in the bit about a wild time and hoped this man would not try to track her down. She really only wanted a pleasant time.

Back at her desk, bolstered by her bizarre encounter, Glenys dashed off a letter to a box number she had circled while she had been eating her lunch. The ad had read:

*Easy going M. 53, not bad looking, seeks F, age not an issue, for relaxing times.*

He sounded like Glenys's sort of man.

Three days later, walking to work past the café, she was accosted by a reproachful looking Peter, who had apparently been looking out for her.

'You did not come back for your reply.'

'Er no, I've been busy. I'm retiring soon. I have to finish a lot of work first.' She did not know why she felt she had to offer an explanation.

'I have it here. My father will be in the café for lunch, same time as you.'

Peter handed her the piece of paper and strode off, trying to muster his dignity as he went. Would the father look like the handsome son? Glenys's curiosity was mounting.

She read the note: *Tall Polish man, own business, 46, WLTM nice woman with GSOH who likes food.'*

She imagined the Polish father and son grappling with the language and acronyms of the dating ads. Perhaps Peter had a British girlfriend who had helped them. Some trouble had

*A Good Sense of Humour*

obviously been taken with the reply. Glenys recognised the humour in the composition. Peter's father was highly unlikely to be 46. She thought he would be about her own age.

As she walked on, she reflected that very soon she would no longer need a café. She would be making her own light lunches and eating them alone, at home. So, ignoring caution, she decided she would go back to Peter's father's café at lunchtime.

'He's not arrived yet,' Peter explained, as he indicated a free table by the window. He had an English grammar book tucked into his apron, perhaps he had a test later. She ordered a salad and a latte and pointedly settled down to read the news section of her newspaper.

'He's still not here and not phone too, I'm sorry,' Peter said later as he cleared her plate away looking very ashamed and waving away the payment for her meal. She stood up feeling only a little let down. At least her would-be suitor had not run away at the sight of her, unless he had peeked through the window.

'I think maybe very busy,' Peter muttered, his English deteriorating with embarrassment as he trawled through his text messages one more time.

'No problem,' Glenys shrugged.

'Where you work?' Peter asked with a note of desperation in his voice.

So close to retirement now, it hardly mattered whether she divulged her business address. She could always call Security if the missing father harassed her.

'Over there,' she pointed to an office building across the road. 'But tell him not to worry, I'm not offended. I'm busy too, I must go.'

*It's Never Too Late to Fall in Love*

'Your name?' Peter called after her.

Still feeling reckless, she told him.

Just after four o'clock, as she was contemplating a walk to the sweet machine to satisfy her afternoon sugar craving, reception called up to say a man had arrived, asking to speak to her. She replied that she would come downstairs. She did so via the sweet machine, pressing the wrong button so it dispensed a larger bar of chocolate than she would usually buy.

She walked into the lobby and was directed by the receptionist toward a short man, about her own height and age, with a grizzled appearance and friendly, smiling face. A few blond strands were still visible among the mainly grey head of hair.

As she approached him, he held out a single pink rose. 'I am Palach. I am very sorry I missed you at the café. I had a problem and I had forgotten to bring my mobile phone from home this morning. I also apologise for my pushy son. He worries about me. He has done so since his mother died.'

Glenys could not help but smile at him in return, he seemed to be entirely sincere. 'I recognised you from your description,' she joked, noting his good English as she accepted his rose.

Palach laughed. 'I see you have a good sense of humour. I recognise you too from your description but I have to tell you that I think I am too old for wild times.'

Glenys giggled ruefully. 'Me too really. I do like food though.' They both looked at her large chocolate bar. 'But I've never eaten Polish food.'

'Do you like Indian food?'

'Very much.'

*A Good Sense of Humour*

'Good. So would you like to go and have an Indian meal when you have finished work and we can see whether we want to be friends?'

'Why not? Yes I would like to,' she grinned at him.

Walking back to her office, relishing the prospect of a date with this apparently kindly man, she reflected that he certainly had a good sense of humour, which she now realised was an essential asset in the dating game. She had no idea what would come of this initial encounter but she rather suspected it would be more interesting to her than taking up golf.

# Stranger Love

### Carol Homer

Nancy sank onto the wrought-iron seat with a sigh. It was such a relief to be out of there. It had all become too much – the crush of people, the laughter, the back-slapping, the raising of glasses. It had just made her feel even more miserable; she didn't belong here. She wasn't ready for all this.

It was too soon, that was the trouble. It had only been eighteen months after all. Eighteen months of tears, grief, anger and depression and she had hardly been out at all in that time. She had become unused to being amongst people, even the supermarket was an ordeal. Everywhere she went she felt people's eyes upon her. She just wanted to hide herself away.

This wedding had been far too much to ask of her – there must have been a hundred people in that room, hardly the 'intimate affair' Myra had promised her. 'You've got to get out there again,' Myra had said. 'This wedding is just the thing – nobody will be interested in you, Darling, They'll all be looking at me.' Nancy smiled at the recollection – typical Myra. And of course she had been right. All eyes had been on Myra, who looked fantastic, nowhere near her sixty-four years and of course all these theatrical types were completely self-obsessed. However, that didn't stop Nancy being as paranoid as ever. Once or twice she thought she had caught someone looking at her for just that little bit too long and felt sure she saw recognition, even pity in their eyes.

In her eagerness to fade into the background, Nancy had chosen a three year old dress of such 'good taste' that it made her look dowdy. She hadn't even bothered to have her hair done, so she, in contrast to Myra, looked every one of her sixty-three years. Amongst all these soignée women in their latest designer outfits she felt herself standing out as the poor relation she had become. Nobody knows and nobody cares who I am, she thought; nobody has ever cared who I am, I was only ever HIS appendage – someone useful in the background. But now she was out in the open, exposed and vulnerable and she didn't like it. She should not have let this happen.

In the end she could stand it no longer and had fled, slipping in and out of the throng like a shadow – to the cool of the terrace, to an isolated bench with a wonderful view of the ornamental lake. At last, solitude and the cool air of the late afternoon came to her aid and she began to feel calmer. Almost without realising she was doing it she slipped her elegant, strappy sandals off and rubbed her swollen feet. She hadn't worn anything that wasn't flat and sensible for so long that fashionable shoes were agony. Oh the relief – never again would she sacrifice comfort for style. Why should she care what her feet looked like – nobody else did.

It's so beautiful here, thought Nancy, wiggling her toes to bring the feeling back. Trust Myra to get married in one of the loveliest stately homes in England – only the best was good enough for her. Rumour had it that Charlie had tried to buy this house for her, but even the great Charlie Goodman couldn't persuade the earl to sell, even though he had been reduced to hiring it out to the plebs (only rich plebs need apply) for weddings. To find husband number four at sixty plus wasn't at all bad, but to snare a millionaire – well that was Myra for you – she always managed to fall on her feet. I hope, thought Nancy, that she doesn't mess this one up by – well, being Myra. Perhaps the thought of all that financial security will keep her on the straight and narrow this time. Myra was her oldest friend, complete opposites though they were, but Nancy had no illusions about her. Still, Nancy was very fond of Myra, they had been like sisters. Myra always used to say they complemented one another – 'I'm fire – all passion and heat – and you, Darling, you're water – calm on the surface with hidden depths.'

Nancy had never envied Myra her glamorous lifestyle – some would have said that Nancy's life had been nearly as glamorous in its own way, although so much of had been nothing but tedium and playing second fiddle to HIM . At least Myra had played second fiddle to no man. She had always been the star of the show, on and off the stage, but Myra's life had always seemed so exhausting to Nancy – all that intrigue, all those lovers, always in the spotlight. No, it wasn't envy that she felt, but it did seem so unfair that Myra, despite her dubious history had snagged yet another husband, and a millionaire to boot, when faithful old Nancy, who had done everything that was asked of her without ever making a fuss or causing the slightest upset . . .

Tears sprang into her eyes and she brushed them away angrily. She must not go over all that again. She wondered if there would ever come a day when it ceased to hurt. When, she thought, will I get my life back? But what life? She could hardly remember a time when she had been herself and not just HIS wife.

*Stranger Love*

Nancy swallowed hard and stared at the view, making a conscious effort to pull herself together. She would have to go back to the reception; she didn't want to upset Myra on her wedding day. She would sit here in the cool breeze for a while, take some calming yoga breaths and then she would go back, play the part of a happy guest and best friend. She would give an Oscar winning performance in there. She just needed to centre herself. She closed her eyes and breathed in.

An ugly hacking cough broke the silence. Nancy opened her eyes and saw, with a feeling of dread, a man walking towards her along the terrace. Not him again! He was tall, well over six feet, not thin, but rangy and loose-limbed. He looked about seventy, Nancy thought, although it was hard to tell. He had a thick head of white hair, combed back from his forehead, which gave him a slightly theatrical air. She had seen this man at the reception, had noticed him at first because he had arrived very late and was so inappropriately dressed. He was wearing an old green tweed jacket, with leather patches on the elbows and sagging pockets and brown cord trousers, faded at the knees. She had thought at first that he had wandered into the reception by mistake, but he had been warmly greeted by Charlie, the bridegroom, (although not by Myra, Nancy had noted) and had proceeded to make himself at home, talking unselfconsciously to the guests and grabbing a glass of champagne every time a waiter passed anywhere near him. The shocked or amused looks he received from the other guests hadn't seemed to faze him at all. He had been completely at ease and Nancy had accorded him a grudging respect for that. There was something about him that seemed familiar to Nancy, but it seemed unlikely they had met before. Surely she would have remembered.

At first, Nancy had thought it was her imagination. But there was no mistaking the glances he kept throwing in her direction, deliberately seeking her out with his eyes; several times he had seemed to be making his way towards her through the crush. She had managed to avoid him. With growing apprehension she surmised that he must have recognised her, (surely neither Charlie or Myra would have given the game away. They had been so protective of her). No. He was one of those dreadful people who thought they had a right to rake through the muck heap of her recent past, just because her photograph had been in the papers. He was too old to be a journalist, surely, just a prurient old man, who'd dine out on her for weeks, have a good laugh with his friends at her expense. Well, it wasn't going to happen – good God, was she allowed no privacy? Not even at her best friend's wedding? He had been the catalyst, precipitating her panic-stricken escape to the terrace, still clutching her empty champagne glass.

And now he had pursued her out here. Or was this just another attack of paranoia on her part?

As the man approached, Nancy noticed he had an unlit cigarette between his lips and was patting the pockets of his jacket. 'Bugger,' he said as he stopped by her seat.

Nancy opened her eyes wide in surprise. She hadn't been expecting that. It was, if nothing else, a novel approach.

'Damn and buggery,' he said, then, as if noticing her for he first time, he said, ' Haven't got a light have you?'

Nancy bridled, she didn't like bad language. It was one of her 'things'. She stared up at the tall figure, shading her eyes against the sun. 'Are you following me?' she asked, surprising herself by her boldness.

'Of course not.' He frowned and took the cigarette from his mouth. 'I just need a smoke after all that hoo-ha in there, but I seem to have forgotten my matches. So – have you got a light?'

*Stranger Love*

It just so happened that she had bought a disposable lighter and a packet of Marlboro Light that morning. She hadn't smoked since university, but she had bought the cigarettes in the desperate hope they might help to calm her and least give her something to do with her hands, forgetting that there was practically nowhere you could smoke nowadays. All she had to do was tell him she didn't have a light and he would go away. Simple. But her mind was distracted, trying to place him. Where did she know him from? His whole bearing was confident, slightly theatrical. Well, they were all theatricals here. Chances were that he had been on television – she didn't often go to the theatre these days. Yes, thought Nancy, she must have seen him on television. His shoes, she noted, although well-worn, were hand-made and highly polished. Her mother had always maintained that you could judge a man by his shoes.

The man was staring at her intently and tapping his foot. 'Well, have you got a light or not?' Although curt, his voice was mellow and cultured. Without realising what she was doing, Nancy reached for her bag. She held out the lighter and the man snatched it impatiently from her. She was struck, firstly by the rudeness of his gesture and then by his hands – although his fingers were heavily stained with nicotine, he had beautiful hands - wrinkled and spotted with age, but still beautiful. How strange to notice the hands of a complete stranger, when, for the last eighteen months, she had hardly noticed whether it was day or night. Again she struggled to place him. Where had she seen him before? Something nagged at the back of her mind – perhaps not an actor, maybe an eccentric academic –the kind that appeared on arty documentaries on the BBC.

With a grunt of satisfaction the man lit his cigarette, sucked in a lungful of smoke and exhaled it through his nose, his eyes closed in pure bliss. He pocketed the lighter and then, to Nancy's horror, came and sat beside her. She moved away slightly, his jacket reeked of cigarette smoke. He offered her the packet, 'Smoke?'

Nancy shook her head. 'I don't,' she said. She felt the beginning of a headache and the now-familiar panic when faced with a social situation. He, on the other hand, seemed completely at his ease, staring at the view and smoking peacefully. Who was he and what did he want?

She was weary and her brain was working in slow motion. Was she being paranoid or had this man followed her out here? The sensible thing to do, of course, was to simply stand up and say, 'I think I should be getting back to the reception now.' He wouldn't follow her, bother her in front of all those people. But if he did? She would have to make a fuss – draw attention to herself. Just go, she told herself. Just get up and go. The trouble was that her feet seemed to have grown a size larger and it would be a struggle to fit her shoes back on. Besides, she had somehow managed to kick them under the seat, which would mean some unseemly scrabbling about, possibly on all fours. She still had some pride left. She could not leave without making a fool of herself: nor could she stay here, barefoot and tongue-tied without making a fool of herself.

The man took a last drag and threw the cigarette end down on the ground. Nancy stared at it in disbelief. How could he be so loutish as to sully this beautiful place? She felt it almost as a personal insult. She stared at the cigarette end, lying smouldering on the marble slab, as though it were a symbol of all that was wrong with her life.

He was coughing now, a disgusting kind of cough. A stomach-churning smoker's cough. Oh don't let him spit, thought Nancy – please don't let him spit. The thought of it made her want to retch. She would have to move away from him,

*Stranger Love*

right now, even if she lost every shred of dignity – what there was of it.

He was lighting another cigarette, with her lighter, she thought irrelevantly, which he pocketed again. He held the cigarette packet out to her again and she shook her head. 'I don't smoke.' He blew a stream of smoke with obvious enjoyment. Stretching out his long legs and leaning back with his arms on the back of the seat, he said suddenly, 'So, what do you think about this wedding. Bloody farce, eh?'

'What on earth do you mean?' Nancy looked up, startled. She had been engaged in probing around under the seat with her feet, trying to locate her shoes.

'I give it a year, tops.'

'What on earth do you mean?' she turned to stare at him, her eyes wide with indignation.

'Well, for a start there's Myra,' said the man, turning and looking at her properly for the first time.' He stuck out his hand, 'I'm Clive, by the way.'

Reluctantly Nancy shook his hand. 'I'm . . .' she hesitated for a split second, wondering whether to give him a false name, 'I'm Nancy.' It wasn't worth lying, she decided, lies always came back to bite you on the bum, as HE used to say. 'What do you mean about Myra?'

'Well, you know our Myra. She hasn't got the best track record has she?' He leered at Nancy and gave an exaggerated wink.

'She's not had the best of luck I will admit,' said Nancy on the defensive. 'She's made a few unwise choices.'

'Fourth time lucky – and how! I just hope she doesn't mess him about, like she did the others. We go back a long way Charlie and me, he's been a good friend and I wouldn't want

200  *It's Never Too Late to Fall in Love*

to see him get taken for a ride,' just for a moment there was a note of genuine concern in his voice.

'And Myra is a good friend of mine. I happen to know that she absolutely adores Charlie.' Nancy crossed her fingers behind her back.

'Hmm. Hard not to,' said Clive lazily. 'Charlie is absolutely adorable. Funny thing that – millionaires often are.'

Nancy felt her face flush with indignation. 'What gives you the right to judge Myra's motives? You don't know the first thing about her.'

'That's where you're wrong,' he waved a beautifully manicured finger at her. 'I've known Myra for a very long time. We were good friends once. Very good friends indeed, if you know what I mean,' and he gave her another wink.

'It hardly matters, does it, if it was all in the past?' she said, and added waspishly, 'I told she'd made some bad choices.'

Clive clapped his hands over his heart, 'Touché,' he said and grinned. 'It's not that I've got anything against old Myra as such. We had a lot of fun together. It's just that it's hard to believe she's fallen for a bald, overweight seventy-six year old who's three inches shorter than her, hates going to parties and whose main interests are orchids and cats.' He coughed and threw the second cigarette end down to join the first.

' You make him sound irresistible.'

Clive was silent for a moment as he looked for his cigarettes. He took one and offered the packet to Nancy. This was beginning to irritate her more than his chain smoking. 'I don't smoke,' she enunciated slowly, as though to a deaf person. He gave her a puzzled look, shrugged and shook another cigarette from the packet. 'Charlie has been like a brother to me,' he said seriously as he patted his pocket, looking for

*Stranger Love*

the lighter. 'We've always looked out for each other. I just think he could have done better for himself. Why go for an old broad like Myra – she's sixty if she's a day and let's face it . . . er . . . Nancy, she's not exactly a luscious peach anymore – more of a dried-up old prune, filled out with a lot of silicone and Botox. If he was going to marry a gold-digger there's any number of cute dolly birds out there who'd be more than up for it.'

Nancy felt something strange beginning to happen to her. She was tingling all over, from the soles of her feet to the top of her head. She could feel the hackles rising on the back of her neck and hear the blood singing in her ears. It was so long since she had experienced anything but flat, grey depression that she did not at first recognise the feeling. It was anger. No, more than that, it was rage. Red rage. How dare he? How dare he disparage her dearest friend? How dare he drop litter and smoke and cough and be generally so vile? How dare he have such beautiful hands and such a lovely voice. How dare he? She stood up abruptly and glared at him with such ferocity that he should by rights have gone up in smoke. 'Dolly birds?' she spat. 'Who talks about dolly birds nowadays? There haven't been dolly birds since the sixties. You old fool.'

'Okay, whatever. You know what I mean.'

'I do indeed,' she said through gritted teeth as she gathered up her bag. 'Give me my lighter.'

He looked at her, bemused, 'Sorry?'

'My lighter,' she barked, 'It's in your pocket. Give me my lighter.'

He shrugged and handed the lighter over, 'I thought you didn't smoke.'

'I don't,' she said. 'But I might want to start.' She bent to retrieve her shoes, which she managed fairly gracefully, no hope of getting them back on however, so she carried them in one hand, grabbed her bag and began to walk away, barefoot, with as much dignity as she could command. 'And another thing,' she stopped and turned back to Clive, who was sitting with an unlit cigarette in his mouth. 'My friend is not a dold gidder.'

She turned and continued her progress.

'Nancy,' called Clive.

She turned round, 'What?' He was holding out her champagne glass, 'I think you might need this.'

She glared furiously, ' You are a . . . a . . . cad!' His deep, mellow laughter followed as she walked away. She couldn't stop herself from thinking what an attractive sound it was, which made her so angry she could practically feel steam coming out her ears.

Nancy's anger carried her through the rest of the evening. It helped her bear the pain of cramming her feet back into the elegant sandals. It gave her the courage, when they sat down to the formal meal, to engage in conversation with the other guests on her table and to find them charming and not at all threatening. It helped her to sit taller, look people in the eye and almost enjoy herself.

She tried not to look in Clive's direction, but occasionally, despite herself, she stole a glance at him. He had been placed on a table at the other side of the room, with a bevy of beautiful young women and seemed to be enjoying himself she noticed. Every time she looked he seemed to sense it and would look up to meet her eyes – every time he caught her looking, he would raise his glass to her and give her one of those lewd winks, rekindling her anger. He looks like he's

*Stranger Love*

getting sozzled, she thought – a boozer as well as a smoker. Disgusting.

The evening ended respectably at midnight and Myra came to say goodbye to Nancy, 'At last, you've got some colour in your cheeks and some sparkle in your eyes.' She gave Nancy an affectionate hug. 'You look really pretty. I told you this evening would do you good.'

Nancy said nothing. She was reluctant to admit it, but she did feel better. Perhaps she had turned a corner.

' About Clive . . .' Nancy began, it was still bothering her, that feeling of recognition.

Myra made a face 'Oh I hope he hasn't been annoying you. Don't take any notice of him, Darling. He's a hopeless case.' She shrugged and sighed, 'Charlie's very fond of him. Apparently they were at school together. So what can you do?'

'But you and Clive . . . ?'

Myra blushed furiously and avoided Nancy's eyes. 'I admit we had a fling, but that was centuries ago.' She looked up boldly and her eyes glittered, 'Who wouldn't ? He was gorgeous. Hard to imagine now.' She stared into the distance, suddenly lost in thought.

Nancy felt something stir, something akin to jealousy.

There was a flurry of goodbyes and air kissing as the newly-weds left in their limousine and Nancy, standing alone amongst all these couples felt the familiar lump at the back of her throat. The mood that had sustained her all through the evening had evaporated. She felt herself deflating like a balloon – her feet hurt, her head ached and she just wanted to go home. Couple after couple had passed her, calling out their goodbyes and she was now the only person left. The car that Charlie had promised to send for her had not arrived.

204 *It's Never Too Late to Fall in Love*

Unable to bear the solicitous hovering of the earl's butler, Nancy went outside to wait. There was a car parked outside, a guest's car, not the limousine she had been promised. Nancy had no interest in cars but she recognised this as a vintage Jaguar like the one Morse drove in the television series. It was too dark to see properly, but Nancy thought she could make out a figure in the driving seat. Then she heard the familiar cough and saw the flare of a match. The old fool! What does he think he's doing. He's had far too much to drink to be driving.

Rage took hold of her again. She marched across the gravel, ignoring the pain in her feet and yanked open the door of the car. 'Get out!' she commanded.

Clive squinted at her and then he smiled, the lopsided smile of a drunk. 'Nancy! My love, get in. Have a ciggy.' He held out the packet.

'I don't smoke,' she said automatically. 'Clive, you can't drive. You're completely sozzled.'

'Pissed as a judge,' Clive agreed.

Nancy winced at the language and began tugging at his sleeve, 'Get out. You're not driving anywhere in this state. We'll get you a taxi.'

Clive shook his head, 'Can't afford a taxi.'

Nancy sighed, 'I'll lend you the money.'

Clive shook his head, 'No need. Got nowhere to go. Going to sleep in the car tonight.'

'What do you mean you've got nowhere to go?'

'Homeless.' Clive said lugubriously. 'Without a home. Roofless . Houseless. Indigent. In short – up shit creek without a paddle. Was going to touch old Charlie for the price of a hotel, but didn't get round to it.'

*Stranger Love*

Nancy tutted, 'Don't be silly Clive. There must be somewhere you can go. You cannot sleep in the car.'

Clive yawned, 'Don't worry. Done it before – I'll just hunker down in the back. Real leather seats. Quite comfortable really.'

Nancy didn't know what to do. Her instinct was to leave Clive to sleep it off in the car. He wasn't her problem. Walk away, Nancy, she told herself, he's nothing but trouble. There was something, however, that kept her from doing that. She didn't know why, but, even though she had known him for only a matter of hours, had hardly even spoken to him, she felt a connection – as though she had known him for years. Nancy was still standing there, debating what to do, when the long, dark shape of a limousine swept up to the entrance of the house.

A liveried driver got out and was about to climb the steps when Nancy made up her mind. 'Hey you,' she called, 'Over here, quickly.'

The driver approached. 'Mrs Nancy Heatherington?' he enquired.

'You took your time,' said Nancy impatiently, reflecting that if he had arrived half an hour ago she wouldn't be in this position now.

'I apologise Madam. There was an incident on the motorway.'

'Yes, yes,' said Nancy. ' Look, there's been a change of plan. This gentleman will be accompanying me. Give me a hand to get him in the car.'

'Whassgoinon?' Clive seemed to become more inebriated by the minute.

'You're coming home with me for tonight,' said Nancy.

Clive gave her one of his lewd winks.

'For crying out loud, pack it in,' said Nancy, 'I've had enough for one night.'

Clive put on a mock serious face and allowed himself to be manhandled out of the car.

The driver's face remained impassive as he helped Clive into the limousine. His whole bearing conveyed that it was none of his business if Nancy wanted to take a drunk home with her. His job was to drive her – to hell and back if that was what she required.

In the limousine Clive fell asleep immediately, his head on Nancy's shoulder. She prayed he wouldn't be sick. The reek of cigarette smoke was making her feel queasy herself so that the thirty minute journey seemed interminable. At last they were there and she and the driver managed to extricate Clive, who was now singing 'I'm getting married in the morning,' from the car. He stood swaying and looking up at the Georgian façade of the house while Nancy found her key. He gave a low whistle, 'Nice pile,' he said. It was when the driver had left and they were inside the house that Clive suddenly seemed to sober up quite considerably.

'Going away?' said Clive, looking at the boxes piled high in the wide hallway.

'Selling up,' said Nancy abruptly. 'Moving out next week.'

Clive said nothing as he followed her into the kitchen.

'Coffee and lots of it,' said Nancy. She busied herself, filling the kettle, turning away from him to hide her face. The realisation of what she had done was beginning to dawn on her. She was appalled at herself – bringing a complete stranger home to spend the night. She was alone in the depths of the country, miles from her nearest neighbour. In darkest Hampshire nobody can hear you scream, she thought.

*Stranger Love*

Strangely, though, she was less worried about being raped and murdered than about the etiquette of the situation. What would they talk about at breakfast?

Clive had seated himself at the kitchen table. 'Forget coffee,' he said, 'I need something stronger.' His voice was no longer slurred and he looked alert, hardly drunk at all.

'I think you've had enough,' said Nancy, getting the coffee cups out of the cupboard. 'It's coffee or nothing.'

Clive shrugged. Reaching inside his jacket, he pulled out a silver hip flask and unscrewed it. 'Want a swig?' he proffered Nancy the flask. Tight-lipped, Nancy shook her head and spooned instant coffee into her cup. She really didn't want coffee either. Her head ached. She wanted to go to bed, but didn't know how to broach the subject without eliciting a lewd response from Clive. She couldn't cope with that at the moment.

Clive smacked his lips and wiped his mouth with the back of his hand; he held the flask upside down to show it was empty and sighed.

'I'll go and make up a bed for you,' said Nancy.

'No hurry,' said Clive, stretching expansively. 'Why don't we sit here and get to know one another over a nightcap. You must have something around the house. You're not teetotal are you?'

'Fine,' said Nancy and put down her coffee cup. If she gave him enough alcohol he'd pass out. She stomped out of the kitchen and returned immediately with a bottle of whisky. 'There,' she said, banging it down on the table, 'Drink yourself to death for all I care.'

Clive gave a low whistle of approval, 'Laphroaig. Haven't been able to afford this in a long while.'

'Be my guest,' said Nancy. 'I'm going to make up the sofa for you.' She turned to leave the kitchen, but Clive grabbed her hand. 'Nancy. Nancy Heatherington. Please stay and have a drink with me. I need company tonight.' He began to open the bottle.

Nancy froze and turned to face Clive, her face dark. Here came the anger again – it was the only emotion she seemed to be able to feel in his company. 'You know who I am. You've known all along. You've been following me all evening and now you've wormed your way into my house.' She came and stood over him, 'Well, you can just get out right now,' she spat. 'You can get out and sleep under a hedge for all I care. I don't know what your game is, but you'll get nothing from me. Tell that to your friends on *The News of The World* or whatever rag you're spying for. Get out right now or I'm calling the police.' She was quivering with anger and noticed, with surprise, that she was actually shaking her fist at him. Did people really do that?

Clive put up his arm to shield his face. 'Hold on there Nancy,' he said, 'I don't know what you're talking about. I had no idea who you were until that driver called you Mrs Heatherington. Am I supposed to know the name? Sorry, but I've never heard of you.' Clive's expression was one of bewilderment.

'Yeah right,' said Nancy hesitantly. He did look innocent, sitting there, comfortably ensconced at her kitchen table. She didn't know what to think anymore. Suddenly her anger subsided and she realised how foolish she sounded. This was Charlie's friend, and however annoying and ill-mannered, she had to take a chance on him. She collapsed into a chair slumped over the table, all the fight gone out of her. She was so tired.

'Okay,' said Clive, reaching for a couple of glasses from the worktop. 'Tell me why I should have heard of you Nancy Heatherington. What have you done?'

Nancy raised her head and sighed, 'I suppose you've never heard of James Heatherington, ex Minister Without Portfolio, who was on trial for fiddling his expenses and spending it on setting up his lover, male lover that is, in a love nest in Chelsea. That James Heatherington.' She stared at him defiantly. 'Tell me you've never heard of him.'

Nancy waited as Clive poured two whiskies and pushed one towards her. 'Sorry, Old Love,' he said, sipping appreciatively. 'Can't say I have.'

Nancy looked at him in astonishment, 'Where have you been? On the moon? It was in all the papers for weeks. The press have been practically camped out here. I've been followed, door-stepped and photographed, all because of that . . . that . . .' 'Cad?' offered Clive with a grin, then seeing that his humour wasn't appreciated he went on, 'I've been holed up in the South of France. My ex wife has a villa down there she lets me use when she's not in residence. 'Fraid your fame didn't extend that far. I don't get the English papers.'

Nancy stared at him. She was inclined to believe him. 'So why have you been stalking me?'

Clive looked hurt. 'I haven't been stalking you. I just liked the look of you. At the wedding – you looked nice, you were on your own, I thought it would be nice to talk to you.'

Nancy shook her head. No there had to be more to it than that.

'Look,' said Clive. 'I'd had a hell of a day. I'd been to an . . . interview . . . about a job, which I don't think I got, by the way. I was feeling low and pretty lonely and there you were.

You stood out from the crowd and I just wanted to get to know you.'

'Oh yes,' said Nancy sarcastically, 'I stood out all right.'

Clive sighed, 'Yes you did. In a good way. You weren't one of those stick insects in designer dresses – with their faces so full of silicone and Botox that they dare not sneeze. You looked like a real woman. A woman not afraid to act her age. I just liked the look of you. I thought you'd be nice to talk to. Now have a sip of your husband's excellent whisky. Where is he by the way?'

'Ex husband and he's in prison.'

'Here's to him,' said Clive, raising his glass.

Suddenly Nancy felt herself relaxing. She had absolutely no reason to feel safe with this man, but she did. She experienced that feeling of connection again. She took a cautious sip of the whisky. 'Okay, so tell me about you, Clive, I don't even know your surname.'

'Clive Roberts,' he said.

'And what do you do. Aren't you a bit old to be going for interviews? If you don't mind me saying so.'

Clive sighed, 'It was an audition actually. I'm an actor. They wanted someone to play a retired professor – hence the getup,' he gestured to his clothes. 'I didn't have time to change. I drove up from France yesterday and spent the last of my funds on a B&B last night.'

An actor! She knew it! 'Have I seen you on television?' she asked, 'I thought you looked familiar.' Was that all it was then – she felt connected because she'd seen him on television.

Clive shifted uncomfortably, 'I haven't done much lately. Been living abroad, as I said.'

*Stranger Love*

'You do look familiar though,' said Nancy.

Clive cleared his throat, 'You might possibly have seen me in films. I had a couple of successes in the sixties. I was Ralph Donne then.' He looked away, embarrassed.

Nancy stared in disbelief. 'You're Ralph Donne?' Clive nodded and turned to meet her gaze. Of course. It was all there. Why hadn't she seen it before – the high brow, the straight nose, the chiselled chin and those brilliant, blue eyes, faded now, but still beautiful. She had sat for hours as a teenager, staring at his poster on her bedroom wall. She had dreamed about him at night and fantasised about him during the day. She had no idea what had happened to him after that. There had been no more films with him in the starring role. He had dropped off Nancy's radar and she had missed him, but then James came along. As Clive reached out to pick up his glass, she had to stop herself from stroking his beautiful hand. Ralph Donne – in her kitchen! She felt like a teenager again. She almost asked him for an autograph.

'I didn't know you'd had an affair with Myra,' she said. Suddenly she couldn't bear the thought of it.

'It was just a fling,' said Clive. He sounded tired. 'It meant nothing.'

'So,' said Nancy, trying to recover her equilibrium. 'Why did you give up acting? What happened?'

Clive shrugged. 'Life happened. Women and whisky happened. The film industry is very fickle. I got by on walk-ons and voice-overs. Let's not go there eh?' He stared up at the ceiling.

Nancy didn't pursue the topic, it didn't really matter. He was Ralph Donne. 'So what's this part you're up for then. Is it a film?'

*It's Never Too Late to Fall in Love*

He shook his head, 'A bit part in a daytime soap.' He shrugged, 'It's rubbish and the pay is peanuts, but I need the money – simple as that.' They sat for a moment in an uncomfortable silence, then Clive seized the whisky bottle and filled their glasses. 'Come on. Let's finish the Cad's whisky. It's the least we can do.'

They sat all night in the kitchen, drinking and talking. Clive was, of course, a magnificent raconteur. By morning Nancy's eyes were red and her head ached, whether from the whisky or the laughter, she was not certain. She had not laughed like that, she realised, with James. She had never felt so at home with a man. As the sky lightened, Clive stretched and yawned, then he took Nancy's hand and looked into her eyes, 'This isn't the first time I've watched the dawn come up with a woman,' he said softly, 'But it's the first time with a woman as beautiful as you.'

'That's a line from *'Stranger Love*,' Nancy said, smiling. 'What a cheat you are.'

'Guilty as charged,' said Clive, 'but why waste a good line – especially if it fits the bill.'

Nancy held her breath, not wanting to break the spell. She was here, in her own kitchen, with Clive Roberts, but in her mind she was on a tropical beach with Ralph Donne.

Gently Clive touched her face, brushing his fingertips across her lips, 'You have a beautiful mouth, Nancy Heatherington,' he said softly.

She had fantasised about this so often as a teenager. Now she was with her teenage fantasy and very soon Ralph was going to try to kiss her. Well, she thought, it wasn't going to happen tonight – not even the romance of kissing Ralph Donne could compete with the reek of cigarettes and whisky on his breath. But soon, when she'd found him a toothbrush

*Stranger Love*

and a razor, well, then she'd see. The girl she had been had looked forward to a life full of romance and laughter – the woman she had become had been pretty short on both. It wasn't all her husband's fault, after all she had allowed it to happen. She had married under false pretences, that was the truth of it. She had been dazzled by James; she had convinced herself he had something of Ralph Donne about him. She didn't know what would happen in the future and she wasn't going to let her herself be taken in again. She wasn't a teenager now and she knew Ralph was really Clive with all his annoying habits, but she liked Clive. She didn't think she had ever actually liked James. He had never been able to make her laugh like Clive had. And then there was the gay thing – that had put a strain on their marriage although she hadn't realised it. Poor James, he must have been very unhappy. Well, she thought, as she looked fondly at Clive, nodding over his empty whisky glass and looking every one of his seventy-odd years. He's no teenage fantasy now, but it doesn't matter. He's better than a fantasy. He's real and I really like him – warts and all. I'm not too old to take a chance. There was just one thing she needed to know. She touched him lightly on the hand and he started awake, 'Clive,' she said, 'You're not gay are you?'

*It's Never Too Late to Fall in Love*

# *Rendezvous*

## Malcolm Peake

The time was fast approaching four o'clock. The day, the one on which we met, by chance, forty two years ago. And the weather not dissimilar to how it was then. What was left of the daylight was fading to a dull grey colour, the sky overcast and the surrounding air miserably cold; a bone chilling breeze drifting in off the Irish Sea. The sun was sinking low on the horizon, its final rays casting a silver luminance over the water, the waves half heartedly lapping against the sea wall.

I stood waiting on the second tier of the promenade. The North Pier wrapped in the reflecting brightness of light bouncing off the surface of the shimmering sea. With my leather gloved hands I gripped the collar of my overcoat and tugged it up as far as it would go; preventing the ice cold air creeping down into its warm inner recesses. As I did so I reflected on the clothes we had been wearing when we first met. Me, I was wearing my wrinkled double breasted de-mob suit – she, a camel haired coat that enveloped her entire body and was so long it all but dragged on the ground as she walked.

On the promenade below me a few people were silhouetted in the last of the cold November light. An older couple, he in his anorak she in a thick winter coat. They were slowly ambling along, no other purpose in mind it seemed to me, than to eke out the last few strands of daylight before finally retreating indoors. As I waited I wondered if earlier they had sat on a bench looking out to sea, content in their own company, musing over the past and chewing over what remained of their future. I could see them, in my mind's eye, sitting there, eating sandwiches that had been wrapped in tin foil with a thermos full of hot tea; maybe a triangle of moist fruit cake to pull apart and share. Lucky devils!

Directly in front of them and walking in the same direction a couple of blokes on their own, wives perhaps left behind knitting in a warm B&B. Not young from the look of their stature, their gait the tell-tale sign of age. Both wore woollen hats pulled down low to protect the tips of their ears from the bitter, biting cold. Coming towards me a dog pulling at its leash grasped tight by a young boy accompanied by his dad; no doubt heading home to mum. But these unknown people the only ones, as yet, walking in my direction.

A man on his own with his back hunched up, his head bent forward, his face turned out of the icy westerly breeze, was walking away from me towards the pier, hands safely tucked away deep in his duffle coat pockets. In the far distance, just rounding a left-hand bend, where a gentle slope began to take you back to town, a couple walked south. Heads erect, arms swinging in perfect unison as though marching to the sound of a military band. It was from around this bend that she would come. As yet I couldn't see her.

The first time I'd seen her I had been standing where I was now. On the exact same spot, as she came in my direction. From time to time she'd stop, look about, as if not altogether sure of where she was. I remember seeing her withdraw a handkerchief from her coat pocket; tears suddenly cascading down her face. I could see her now as she turned towards the sea and appeared to stagger. She threw out both arms to clutch the rail that separated the dark, deep, murky looking water from the safety of the promenade. Without thinking I hurried down the steps to help her. In my haste, half way down, I missed my footing; I slipped and fell arse over tit the rest of the way. When I came to she was kneeling over me, concern etched deep on her face, wiping away the blood that trickled down my face.

That was how we met.

As today only a few other people were out and about. I recall I tried to smile and say thank you. She always disagreed with this recollection saying that I grunted and winced. After a while I gathered myself together and she helped me to my feet. At first, as I tried to stand, I felt light headed. However, even as the fuzziness retreated and my mind refocused I said nothing as with one arm around my waist she helped me to a wooden bench. I can't ever remember telling her that, from the very beginning I'd been reluctant, even then, for us to be apart.

Feeling altogether less wobbly I thanked her for her assistance and asked why she had been in such distress, near on falling over the seashore railings. The latter she said, with a faint smile, was because as she turned to go back the way she'd come she had twisted and broken the heel of her shoe; the culprit a crack in the promenade paving. The turning and the simultaneous breaking of her shoe had thrown her off balance, she told me, and she'd reached out in need of some immediate support; hence the grabbing of the metal rail. During this explanation she withdrew from her coat pocket the broken item which she must have been retrieving during

*Rendezvous*

my headlong descent down the steps to the esplanade. But that didn't explain I said in a quiet undertone, the copious tears she was shedding prior to the mishap with the heel of her left shoe.

At this she looked away seaward and her face took on a remote expression. To change the subject and to relieve her anguish I suggested that a cup of tea might help us both. At first she was reluctant to concede but with a little nudging she agreed. As we attempted the short walk to the café, me still a little dazed – her walking lopsidedly on her broken shoe – both of us clinging on to each other for mutual support, she ask if I was local. I told her no. I explained that of late I had been a member of His Majesty's Armed Forces, recently returned from Germany; that I originated from Stoke on Trent, to where I planned to return tomorrow. It turned out that her family originally came from Congleton, not that far away, just down the road. They had moved to Blackpool just prior to the start of the war in 1938 because of her mother's continual ill health.

I ordered our tea at the shop counter as she found us a table by the window. Once we were both sitting down an awkward silence prevailed which was only broken when tea was served. She took sugar and milk while I drank mine as it was poured, having got used to it that way, I explained, while serving the King abroad. With the ice once more broken she asked why I had been standing on the top promenade and I felt compelled to tell her the sad tale of my visit to Blackpool.

My mate Arnold, with whom I had survived most of the war, had been brought up in an orphanage just up the coast. He was a great bloke but bored the whole platoon silly with never-ending stories of his childhood spent mostly playing on the sands hereabout. He bought his packet just as we were making our last advance on Berlin. I didn't tell her that

*It's Never Too Late to Fall in Love*

I'd just ducked down when the sniper's bullet tore a bloody, great big hole in his chest. Just before he slipped away, I said, as I once more saw Arnold lying dying in the blood stained mud, he handed me a metal cigarette tin. Inside were a few sea shells wrapped carefully in cotton wool. His last wish was that I return the shells to the beach from where he had collected them before being, as he always said 'asked to help out in getting rid of Herr blinking Hitler and his mob'. So here I was, I said, and later when the tide once more receded, I would go down onto the sands and carry out Arnolds dying wish.

By the time I came to the end of my story tears had once more formed in the corner of her eyes and I felt responsible for having caused her further distress. She dabbed the tear drops away using a white silk hanky on which pinkish blotches, hints of blood from dabbing my scratches, were visible. Gathering in her emotions, a small, restrained, self-conscious smile appeared on her face. When sure of having her feelings in check, she murmured, 'Isn't that strange', and began to tell me why, she too, had come down to the seafront that afternoon.

Last year, on this very day, her mother, who was at this time in a wheelchair, had asked her to wheel her down to see the sea once more. At first she had been reluctant, because, like today, the weather was inclement she said. But her mother had insisted, and so she had finally agreed.

During their journey she frequently stopped to tuck in the blanket around her mother's legs and feet lest they got too cold. On the last occasion, just where she had broken her heel, she stooped down to adjust the blanket again and to ask her mother if she was warm enough. Having tidied the blanket she looked up into her mother's face, only to see that life to which she had been clinging these last few years, was gone.

*Rendezvous*

I distinctly remember, even after the passing of forty-two years that we sat for a few moments, each wrapped in our own thoughts, invoked by personal memories, before quite out of the blue I surprised myself and asked her to join me for dinner. And you may think us daft, a little loony perhaps but every seven years since then, on the dot, we've played out the charade of our first meeting in celebration.

As these memoirs seeped into my mind a tram car came rolling past, the clatter from which brought me back to reality. I looked at my watch it was now nearly ten past four. She had never been late before.

But this year I knew she wouldn't be coming.

So for the very last time I descended the steps to the seashore, taking great care not to fall, to the place where she had had her stumbled. I stood by the rusty, paint flaked rail playing out in my mind our happy life together; the grey murky sea ebbing and flowing below. From my pocket I withdrew the heel of her broken left shoe and, with tears in my eyes, I hurled it as far out to sea as I could.

# In Sickness and In Health

Gwen Anderson

I'm still in and out of my peaceful place – it's where I prefer to be – I'm comfortable there. Then I slide out into a thick fog. I open my eyes and people I don't know talk to me. Some bend over and kiss me and squeeze my hand. I wish they wouldn't. I wish they would go away. The woman cries – makes my cheeks wet when she kisses me. I can't wipe it away, but I can feel it. They go away then – except my guardian angel – he stays – my quiet man – with his crossword or his book. He's always there – I don't know who he is – although he looks familiar. When the mist comes down – I open my eyes and he smiles at me – a lovely crinkly smile. I try to smile back. But before I can achieve it – I'm back in my solitude. Once, when I opened my eyes, he wasn't there, just strangers – talking to me. I was devastated and immediately slipped back into my comfort zone. When I opened my eyes again – there he was his grey head bent over his book. He looked up and caught my eye. 'Hello sweetheart' he whispered, smiling. I tried so hard to smile – but nothing came. I wanted to move my hand – I so wanted to reach out towards my guardian angel. I was so upset and slid away into my peaceful place where I could cry and no-one would know. Once when I opened my eyes there were two children there, standing by the bed with a very tall man. They looked familiar – but I couldn't place them. They all kissed me on the forehead and went away. My quiet man was still there – his presence seemed to wrap me in a blanket of tranquillity.

Sometimes a nurse swishes the curtains round my bed, gives me a wash all over and changes my nightie. That leaves me feeling lovely and fresh. That's when the quiet man brushes my hair. I try so hard to keep my eyes open to look at him but I can't summon the will to keep myself from drifting away.

Strange people play music and hold up photographs for me to see through the fog. That annoys me and I just want them to go and leave me with my quiet man. He never annoys me – he just sits there reading – watching over me – as I slip in and out the awful fog. But knowing he's there somehow calms me. I just wish I knew who he was and why he sits by my bed everyday. I'm getting used to his features – his grey hair and his glasses, his kind eyes and gentle hands.

Today the nurses made me sit up with extra pillows behind my head. It felt strange. I've been lying flat for so long. I find I'm spending more time in the fog and I'd rather go back to my safe place but I can't find the way. It's very disconcerting – I hate the fog. The nurses are talking to me as if I am an idiot – enunciating every word as if I were four years old.

'Your daughter is here', they say. 'Isn't that nice?'

Daughter? I didn't know I had a daughter. It's the tearful one.

'Hello Mum – you're looking much better', and she kisses me. I recognise her perfume. I've smelt it before – but where – and when? I suddenly have a glimpse of a laughing child. Is this her?

*It's Never Too Late to Fall in Love*

After she's gone my quiet man stands beside me.

'I think you're feeling a little better today – eh?', he says – so wanting it to be true.

I try to nod and am amazed when my head actually moves – and then an absolute miracle happens – the awful fog that has enveloped me for so long – slowly melts away – and I know who I am – and also who my quiet man is.

I turn my head towards the man I have loved for 52 years – who has been sitting beside me all these weeks – my guardian angel.

'Hello darling', I say – and stretch out my hand.

# Second Time Around

### Gillian Lazar

She'd been in the middle of a dream about Nick; years ago in their youth. They'd left their folded clothes by the sand dunes and like children, raced each other down the beach. Just before they reached the first cream-topped waves washing the sand, he turned back and took her hand. They trod water until, where the beach shelved, they'd plunged waist deep into the cobalt sea. She gasped with the sting and pain of the cold.

Something woke her. Luxuriating in the unexpected warmth of the bed, she stretched out her hand for him. Her hand explored the sheets and finding only emptiness, memory flooded back. The years had gone dipping over the horizon and, more recently, Nick had gone too. She'd tried to help him fight the illness but he'd lost, they'd lost and she'd been left alone with decisions to make and time on her hands.

At first she thought she'd have to join the little band of widows, sharing suppers, shopping, theatre outings, complaining on the Autumn Sunday when the clocks went back, at the unfairness of that extra hour in a day already too long. If only Nick and she had had a child. Other widows had Sunday lunch with their children and baby-sat for the grandchildren.

It was on a chilly March Sunday, when she took a walk up the lane, unsure where she was going. At the end, past the cars lined up on the demolition site and the scrubby trees that shielded a cricket field, she reached a wrought iron gate. Beyond was the deep roofed tithe barn that held the local Museum, a reminder of a rural past. A notice announced *'Jazz on Sundays – 12.30 – 2.00'* and from the barn there was the sound of clarinets and the insistent beat of a drum.

She was drawn in, stepping through the huge barn doors to an enveloping warmth and resounding rhythm. About 50 people sat in rows or at tables, drinking coffee whilst they listened to the three-piece band on a small stage at the end of the timbered building. She settled herself for the rest of the performance and at 2.10 when the band finished and people began to disperse, she went to the counter to get herself a coffee.

That was how it began. Leaning on the counter she talked to the woman in the kitchen behind. She was small and quick, moving like a bird, in little swoops over her territory. She told Jessica about the activities carried out: exhibitions, talks, tours of the old Manor House and school visits.

'We're always short of volunteers,' she said. 'There's a waiting list for helpers to set up exhibitions. They've got enough gardeners, but we always need more helpers for refreshments.' Jessica took the form home, filled it in and in due course had her interview with the Museum Manager.

She chose to work on Sundays, two or three afternoons a month. The Manager was delighted and she had a trial run with a veteran volunteer. She mastered the coffee machine with its litany of options, 'latte, cappuccino, mochaccino'

*Second Time Around*

etc, slow in its response and spluttering in execution. Most prices on the new electronic till were quickly covered by scanning the bar code, although occasionally the red flashing 'eye' remained obstinately closed. She was always busy during the jazz sessions and the Assistant Manager helped by clearing the tables.

During the afternoon, there was a regular trickle of families who came in from the park to buy ice cream and visitors to the exhibitions. There were regulars too, a disabled man who rode a tricycle; a woman who left directly the jazz was finished; Mike, a cheerful character with an encyclopaedic knowledge of planes and steam trains. Shortly, before three o'clock one of the two guides, would arrive to take a tour of the Manor House whose ghost stories were particularly popular.

After the departure of the jazz fans, there was time to chat to the visitors when they stood at the counter making their selection of drinks and snacks. On hotter days, when the doors of the chilled cabinets were kept busy, she'd get requests for something stronger.

One summer afternoon, a good-looking man, possibly in his early sixties like herself, said, 'I suppose there's no chance you've got a Liquor Licence yet?'

'I'm afraid not,' she laughed, and he assumed a mock tragic expression.

'What no reward for a tough afternoon's cricket,' he indicated the boy rummaging in the ice cream cabinet. 'He's worn me out. It was only the thought of a cool lager that kept me going!'

She smiled back at him, recognising a latent energy in the man who looked far from exhausted. Involuntarily, she noted the grey hair, eyes green against the suntan. He had the erect posture of a younger man, perhaps the natural outcome of a lifetime of sport and fitness. There were downward lines from nose towards chin, a slight thinning of the mouth which might indicate ageing rather than a tendency to meanness.

She felt the blood rising in her cheeks and was quick to turn away to get his order for a chilled coca cola. With her back turned to him she bent to take the ice-cold can from the cabinet and standing up, caught sight of her own face in the mirror above. One or two blonde-tinted strands of hair had escaped the ribbon tie behind her head and curled around her face; the flush of the skin was soft and becoming.

He turned to the boy, still going through the Magnums and Cornettos. 'Come on, Ben, you're keeping the lady waiting.' She fancied an edge in his voice but didn't quite understand. Ben seemed to gauge the time he took, hesitating a few seconds more but not enough to irritate the man who must, she guessed, be his Grandfather.

Ben laid the Magnum bar on the counter and looked up at her; wide blue eyes, sensitive mouth, dark hair flopping untidily over his forehead, dark eyebrows like his Grandfather's.

'Hallo,' she estimated he must be about ten. She accepted the £5 note the man offered and gave him the change.

'This is Ben, my Grandson. I'm Andy.' He held out his hand. 'You're new here, aren't you?' Ben turned away to look at the toys and puzzles for sale on the shelves.

She shook his hand. 'Yes, I've been coming for about two months.

'Good of you to give up your time,' he looked at her speculatively.

'Nothing good about it, I like coming,'

*Second Time Around*

'Time can hang heavy on a long Sunday, I know' he said. She looked at him irritated; whatever his circumstances, at least he had a Grandson.

'Oh but I'm on my own, really on my own,' she said with finality.

'No family?' his voice was gentle.

'My husband died two years ago. We both regretted we had no children.'

'Children can bring their own problems.' He looked down at the counter and she wondered whether he was offering consolation or merely a statement from his own experience.

'Ben looks a very nice boy,' she said. 'Yes, he is.' He began to talk about the exhibitions. The one he'd enjoyed most was on the history of astronomy with a final section on space travel. It was appropriate, she reflected, that his own eyes seemed to look beyond his subject, as if scanning distant space. 'I've thought of volunteering to help set up exhibitions,' he said. 'But there are other things that crop up . . .' He didn't elaborate further.

Soon a group of children came in, jostling around the ice cream cabinet. 'Hi, Ben,' they acknowledged him briefly and she saw his eyes followed them wistfully. Immediately, she became busy with serving them and a queue formed behind. Andy raised his hand in farewell and smiled as he gathered Ben and moved away. 'See you,' he mouthed.

At home, she was irritated that her mind kept slipping back to this casual encounter with a stranger. A woman past sixty who'd been married to the love of her life. A man in his seventh decade and a grandfather, too. It was ridiculous. 'See you,' just a phrase. She remembered when a couple of decades ago people had started saying, 'See you later'. But it seemed, 'later' no longer meant later that day. Three or four

*It's Never Too Late to Fall in Love*

weeks might elapse before meeting again. 'See you,' unqualified by time, could mean a matter of years, if ever! There was something restless about him too. He'd been chatting to her when he suddenly called Ben from the ice cabinet as if anxious to get away.

The following Sunday she dressed casually but carefully. The week had passed with chores, supper with Sandra and shopping and lunch with Jane. Over chicken and piri piri salad, Jane regarded her curiously, her head on one side, 'Has anything happened?' she asked. 'There's a gleam in your eye.'

'No, same old life,' said Jessica with apparent conviction.

On Sunday, neither Andy nor Ben appeared. The afternoon was uneventful; the jazz average; the tricycle man had his usual latte and Mike expounded to her on the Fighter Aircraft of WWII. The following Sunday she didn't go to the Museum as she had accepted an invitation to lunch with an old school friend and her husband.

Three weeks after her meeting with Andy, she was on duty again. This time she didn't tempt fate by taking special care over dressing; but nevertheless, she chose a tee shirt in cerulean blue which seemed to restore her eyes to the deep blue of her youth.

It was nearly 4.30 before he arrived, on his own, with no sign of Ben. He looked worried as he stood at the counter to order a cappuccino. 'No Ben today?' she enquired. 'My daughter's taken him out,' he said. The decision did not seem to please him and she refrained from asking more.

He seemed abstracted and the mood of their first meeting was missing. There were several interruptions and even using the skills of the practiced listener to draw him out, she was getting nowhere. Then, as he noticed out of his corner of his

*Second Time Around*

eye, a couple of visitors come in through the door, he said, 'Look Jessica, it's impossible to talk here, would you feel like having coffee with me sometime. Or what about lunch? You're retired – well officially,' he looked round the kitchen. 'I am too, apart from some freelance work. I've nothing on now,' he added quickly. 'Well, how about lunch?'

'Lunch would be lovely, Andy,' she answered lightly, not wanting to betray a naïve enthusiasm. Since Nick had died there had been other offers but either she had not been tempted to accept or had gone and spent the time wishing she was with Nick.

'Let's try that new French place in the High Street,' he suggested and they settled on Wednesday at 12.30.

Wednesday was sunny and warm and when she arrived he was sitting at a table by the windows that opened on the old street. He stood up for her with the old world courtesy so often scorned by the young men of today. Or, she sometimes wondered, were they just confused by the new Feminist women who have rejected gallantry and courtesy in favour of an uncomfortable sort of equality.

'It's good to see you relaxing instead of slaving over a hot kitchen counter.' She read the admiration in his eyes as he looked at her. He made a practised selection from the wine list, they ordered their food, shellfish for him, steak, rare, and salad for her.

'Tell me about yourself, ' he said without preamble. 'Later,' she parried, smiling, 'You go first.'

'There's not a lot to tell.' As he settled in his chair, his face became serious. 'My wife died a few years ago. I have a daughter, who's divorced and, as you know, a ten year-old grandson, Ben. I spend a lot of time with them. I'm retired but sometimes I go away to do research.'

'Research? That sounds intriguing.'

'For the books,' he said. 'Didn't I tell you I'm a writer?'

'You know, you didn't tell me.' She looked at him in mock reproof.

'Well I guess I've learned to keep it quiet. It raises such expectations. I'll never win the Booker or the Costa. After all, I'd take a bet you've never heard of me. Andrew Daley?' He handed her his card.

'Well no,' she admitted. She was beginning to apologise for her ignorance but she saw that he was laughing at her embarrassment.

'Well, that proves my point.'

He began to talk about his life and it had been an interesting one. He'd worked on oil-rigs in his youth, travelled the world, and been a news correspondent for a while.

Whilst they waited for the sweet course, he leaned forward, taking her left hand and as his fingers brushed her wedding ring, he said, 'No more prevaricating, tell me about you.'

So she told him about Nick; the time they'd lived in Mexico; their holidays; walking, climbing; she noted his approval of their active life. The time they found the Iguazu Waterfalls in Brazil, 'the best in the world,' she insisted. 'Well I always thought Niagara is overrated,' he said. They both laughed.

'We had it all,' she said . . . 'except a child that is.'

'After such a perfect life, wouldn't a child be a bit superfluous?'

'Oh, but a child would be a visual reminder of him.'

'But what if the visual reminder turned out to be of someone from your mitochondrial DNA thousands of years ago?' he

*Second Time Around*

asked. Genes study was another of his interests and he had a way of looking at her long-held beliefs more pragmatically.

They sat on over coffee. They found they liked the same music; Van Morrison, Simon & Garfunkel, Celine Dion, opera that stopped short of Wagner. She was surprised how much he made her laugh, how conversation flowed.

After the lunch he drove her back home, accepted a cup of coffee and as he got up to leave, he kissed her on the cheek and then again, gently brushing the skin of her upper lip. She was stirred, as she knew he was, but neither would trespass further on this first, delicate moment.

'See you,' he said with that crooked smile of his and was gone.

Next Sunday at the Museum, she was unusually busy. A group of boys came in, noisily shoving each other and shouting. Suddenly on the fringe of the group, she recognised Ben. They circled the counter and cabinet, holding up items and demanding, 'How much? As they grabbed the sweets, and waved them around, she became confused and angry. 'Put those down,' she shouted. 'One at a time.' A boy started juggling the KitKat bars whilst another mimicked her, 'Put those down.'

There was a lot of arguing and jostling; someone swore. Panicing, she was struggling with the till scanner which wouldn't respond, when she heard a scuffle. 'Good on yer,' the biggest boy shouted. Suddenly Kate, the Assistant Manager, materialising as if from nowhere, cried out, 'Stop that, you thieving little so and so!' She scooted across the room and dragged the boy back, kicking and swearing.

She emptied packs of sweets from his hands and pockets and pulled his head up. 'Ben!' Jessica was horrified. 'Get out the lot of you,' said Kate and, trading insults, they slowly retreated. 'As for you,' she still had hold of Ben, 'You're banned for good and I'm seeing your Mother about this.'

After the boy had gone, she begged Kate to let her speak to his Mother. 'I know the family a bit, please let me deal with it.'

'OK, but you'd better get this sorted. We've had too much trouble from those kids. They're making us look like idiots, an easy touch for shoplifters.'

After the Museum closed she took out Andy's card and went round to the address – a neat Close of suburban semis. There was no reply when she knocked on the front door but she could hear sounds of a television through the window, so she waited. At the third ring, the door opened slowly and Ben peered round, reluctantly. 'Mum doesn't want to see you,' he said. From the sitting room, a voice called out, 'I'm ill, send them away.' He motioned to close the door but Jessica was insistent. 'I need to speak to your Mother, NOW!'

He led her into the sitting room where his Mother lay on the sofa. Her face was pasty-pale; her dark hair scraped untidily on top of her head. The room was littered with empty cans, cups and magazines. From the sofa, she looked up at Jessica, resentfully. 'Who are you? How dare you barge your way in here?'

'I came about Ben, Mrs Daley. I'm afraid he's been caught stealing sweets from the Museum and we had to ban him.'

She lounged back against the sofa. Well, you've got the name wrong for a start. Daley's my father's name. My name's Ryan. Mrs Lucy Ryan.

'Sorry, Mrs Ryan, I'm Jessica Long from the Museum. But the fact remains, your son's been caught shoplifting.'

Lucy raised herself on the cushions. 'You can't run that bloody place and because a few sweets are missing, you come

*Second Time Around*                                                233

here blaming my son. You've got a nerve! Ben never has sweets, his father was diabetic and we don't want him to go the same way.'

'But he eats ice cream, I've seen him.'

'You come round here, telling me about my son. Get out.'

'Please Mrs Ryan, I 'm not trying to interfere but I don't think you understand the seriousness of the situation. This time the Museum Manager caught him and asked me to come to talk to you. But next time it might be a Store Detective and trouble with the Police. Besides,' she added, 'when he was caught he swore like a teenage yob.'

Lucy stood up, shouting, 'You bloody old cow, effing busy-body,' leaving no doubt where Ben had picked up his bad language. As the decibels rose and Lucy swayed, her hands, shaking with rage, the door was suddenly flung open.

Seeing Andy standing there, Jessica sank into the armchair with relief.

He stood surveying the scene for a moment. Ben took a step back but he never took his eyes off his Grandfather. Lucy collapsed onto the sofa, pointing at Jessica. 'She's here accusing Ben of stealing and threatening us with the Police!

'But that's not what . . .' Jessica started to say. Andy cut her off as he loomed tall above her. 'I don't remember inviting you to come here, questioning my family,' he said. If you have a problem with Ben, you should have come to me about it. This isn't your business, this is my family and whatever needs sorting out – I'll do it.'

He opened the door for her and stood waiting. As she passed him, she saw the lines of anger on his face and the lips thinned to a mere line. The door closed behind her as she heard the finality of his words. 'Goodbye Mrs Long.'

*It's Never Too Late to Fall in Love*

Back at home, she regretted mishandling the whole incident. She'd seen with her own eyes his troubled daughter which explained Ben's unhappiness and his clumsy attempts to join a gang. It also went some way to explain his Grandfather's moodiness. But she was still hurt and angry.

She met Jane for lunch and after her gentle probing admitted, 'Yes, I did meet someone, but it didn't work out.' She put her fingers against Jane's lips, to stop further questions. 'Not now, some day, maybe.'

Sunday afternoons at the Museum resumed. She hinted to Kate that she was thinking of resigning but Kate was horrified. 'You've been great, honestly I don't think we can manage without you.

As she came out of the gates one Sunday evening, there was a figure waiting for her and startled, she recognised Ben.

'I know I'm not allowed in, Miss. But I wanted to say I'm sorry for taking that stuff. I mean, really sorry.' He gulped and she saw his genuine shame.

'Thank you, Ben, I appreciate that.' She bent down so their faces were level. 'I didn't want to load all the blame on you. I know it was the other kids egging you on. I was just afraid one day you could end up in worse trouble, with the Police.' He nodded and sniffed, drawing his hand across his nose. She searched for a tissue and then spontaneously put her arms round him and hugged his thin body to her. Without actually responding, he submitted to this treatment and agreed to go home with her to see her husband's model race cars.

Together they explored the cars. Then he told her he wanted to be a historian, that's if he wasn't an archaeologist or an explorer. 'I'm going to travel like Grandad,' he assured her. She told him that they could fix it so he was allowed back into the Museum.

*Second Time Around*

Then, after a while, he stood up and said that he'd better be going. At the door, he turned, 'Grandad's sorry too.'

'What's that, Ben?' She was startled.

'I know Grandad's sorry for the way he told you off. I got it even worse when you'd gone.'

'He didn't just tell me off, he kicked me out.'

'It's not easy for him. Mum's been ill since Dad left. Instead of going travelling, he has to spend a lot of time looking after us.'

'I appreciate you telling me this, but I've no reason to think he regrets anything he said.'

The following evening the phone rang. 'It's Andy here.' He sounded hesitant. 'I wondered if you were all right?'

'I'm fine, thank you,' she answered crisply. There was a long pause which she had no intention of filling.

'Look,' she heard him swallow, 'I've made a real mess of things. I didn't mean to insult you. I completely over-reacted.'

'Well thank you for the apology. So long as you know that I had only the best of intentions. But I'm a bit busy now, so you'll have to excuse me.'

'Jessica, please. Just let me explain'

'I understand that your daughter is unwell and you have problems. There was no need to send your Grandson along to soften me up. Now I really must . . .'

'For God sake, Jessica. Please give me another chance – meet me just once and then if you still feel the same, I promise I'll never bother you again.'

They arranged to meet the following evening at a Pub overlooking the lake two miles away. It was a real summer's evening. Geese returning home to roost, formed an inverted V formation against the deepening blue of the sky; the water of the lake was calm and dark.

She had planned to be tough and uncompromising. 'There's no need to explain anything. I understand that your life is complicated with things of which I have little or no experience. I think we should go our own ways.' She had expected protests and pleading but the honesty of his answer took her unawares.

'You're right of course. And that's what I thought when I saw you in the house with my difficult daughter and my lonely grandson. I vowed it was only fair to send you back to the shrine of your memories.'

'What do you mean "shrine of memories"?' She was stung by his words.

'You're not living life, Jessica. You're trapped in the dream of your past love. What can I offer you in my messy life to compare with the idyllic life you shared with Nick! If you had a live boyfriend it would be so easy; I could fight him for your favours, 21st Century style – Sudoku, Thai boxing, golf. Let the best man win! But how can I compete with a dead hero?'

'This is the moment for you to get up and go,' he suggested. But she sat on with him in the fading light. He told her how his son-in-law had run off when Ben was six years old. Lucy couldn't and seemingly, wouldn't, get over it. She'd lost several jobs, because of her habit of mixing anti-depressants with drink. Jessica saw his life shaped by the neediness of his descendants and sympathised.

They finished their drinks and went for a short walk along the shoreline. As her foot hit a stone at the edge of the beach she stumbled and cried out. He put out his hand to steady her

*Second Time Around*

and then he took her in his arms and began to kiss her. He did it expertly as if he'd kept in practice and she was glad of it. They kissed again, then gently, he released her. 'I know you're not ready for another relationship but I'll wait,' he said. 'We can take time to get to know each other – take things as slowly as you want.' She was aroused but at the same time she felt wholly safe, held close against his chest.

He'd come so lately into her life but Jessica knew she was beginning to care for this man. Nick was part of her youth when love was idealised and free. This second love which had come so unexpectedly in their Third Age was different; it was a love that comes encumbered by the baggage of pre-made relationships. Yet, they would try to find a way to make it work.

'You'll say it's much too soon to know, but I love you,' Andy whispered. As if he had read her mind, he hugged her and vowed, 'somehow, against all the odds, I believe we can work it out'.

'Yes, I know we can,' she answered with conviction. Then, with a flash of his own wry humour, 'even if it's a bit of a roller coaster on the way.' She smiled and reached up to meet his lips.

## *Stardust*

Jean Dorricott

The notice over the inboard crematorium read:

*A Clean Departure*

*No Body Litter Permitted in Space.*

*Press X to Sanitize Corpse*

*On Completion Red Light Flashes*

*To Eject Dust, Pull Lever*

*Religious Departure – See Online Manual*

Daudi dragged Basila's emaciated body into the pod. His wrinkled face expressed no emotion as he waited for the red light to flash. A momentary hesitation, then he ejected his wife's dust.

They used to joke about clean departures. An uneasy joke, for the two of them were running their ore transport business alone now, without the support of grandson Joe.

As Daudi returned to the control console his anger at Joe's desertion returned. Why wasn't he there to help load his grandmother's body and share Daudi's grief?

He stared at the space-monitoring screen, but Basila's final atoms were too minute to register.

'Stardust returned into stardust,' she'd mumbled, her face and body contorting with pain. 'A clean . . .'. She didn't have strength to complete the phrase but she tried to smile, and the memory broke his heart.

She would never return. No planet, no solar system, no galaxy held any memory of her. He gripped the console with gnarled fingers. He groaned, beat his fists wildly against Manual Control. The space truck lurched and tossed submissively, but he didn't care because nowhere in all Galaxy would he hold her close again.

'Forget me,' she'd said.

Forget? Draw down the shutters on over three-quarters of a century?

How beautiful she'd been when they first met in Nairobi, their birthplace. Her black skin glowed with vigour, her hair was darker than the storm clouds across the African plains and the smile on her face as welcoming as the rainbow after the deluge. They'd had their ups and downs, of course. Even occasional permanent partings, followed by rapturous reunions. He struggled to fill his mind with memories of her laughter, but the last pictures of her twisted face and racked body were imprinted too strongly to be erased. Cholera 126, a bacterial disease contracted while loading up titanium on their last planet. Stomach cramps, fever and wasting diarrhea, but the inevitable dehydration easily treatable with salt and sugar dissolved in distilled water. Combined, essentially, with an antibiotic, since 126 is one of the real nasties plaguing interplanetary travellers.

But – no antibiotics on board.

Yes, Basila had intended to replace the kit. Three years ago their daughter Rhiad had used the last dose when she emigrated to settle with her son Joe, his wife and their adult children on an earth-greened planet circling Proxima Centauri. At the time it had seemed such a happy trip. Joking and laughing – no realisation there was already a rift between them.

Basila had said sadly as she lay sick, 'I did know things weren't right. I hid it from myself.'

'If only. . .'

Tears had fallen weakly from her eyes. 'If only. . .'

And if only they'd replaced the antibiotic. If only the painkillers hadn't run out she wouldn't have gone through . . . oh heaven! He'd go mad if he thought of those last days when all the spacelink medic's advice had failed, and he could only provide the water treatment and soothe her headache with his rough workaday hand and wait the inevitable. And she hadn't been that old. A hundred is getting on a bit for an interplanetary trucker maybe, but until the family breakup grandson Joe, being merely fifty-one, had done the heavy work. And the old ship was cheap to run. Daudi stared round at the comfortable chipped and cracked fittings in dirty blue and cream. Homely, used. Not your new fangled factory spaceship, immense and safety compliant.

Why hadn't the family space trucking enterprise been enough for their grandson?

Joe chose the worst of times to tell his grandparents. Out on a small nondescript planet only important for its rare

*Stardust*

ores. Loading monazite sand rich in holmium, a hazardous element likely to cause explosions and fire. Not the best moment to say, 'I've been accepted as pilot for Interplanetary Truckers Inc.'

Basila, always excitable, exclaimed, 'You can't desert us!'

'Better pay, Gran.' Joe sounded nervous? Angry?

'We'll meet that,' Daudi said, though of course they couldn't. Not even if he and Basila took deep cuts.

'Far superior accommodation.'

Basila was shaking now, tears in her dark eyes. 'We've always been comfortable, haven't we?'

'Just look at the mucky old ship. Unsafe. Unhygienic.'

His grandparents stared around them. They had to admit she'd seen better days.

'Modern equipment,' Joe added remorselessly. 'Not forever breaking down. How many days do we waste repairing a rig that should've been ditched years back?'

'Told you we should modernise,' Basila shouted at Daudi. 'Told you, time and again.'

'We can't afford it, you know that. Don't you think I'd give anything to renovate her?'

'That's about it,' Joe expostulated. 'You take on low paid jobs that no one else in all Galaxy would be fool enough to touch. High risk jobs, at that. How many times have we skimmed major disasters in the past earth-year?'

'We've always come through,' Daudi said.

'You aren't listening to me, are you? You're a danger to yourselves and to me and I'm not standing for it any more.

I've helped you out. I've done my stint. It's time you both admitted you're too old to carry on with this job.'

The interminable process of breaking up their long partnership was hot-tempered and both Daudi and Joe swore and cursed each other. When it was complete Basila and Daudi's meagre pensions had disappeared into the greedy maw of the legal profession and the old space ship had become ever more unreliable and expensive to repair.

The rift spread to the rest of the family.

At last Basila cooled down enough to contact her daughter Rhiad through space-link, seeking reconciliation.

'There's nothing the matter,' Rhiad replied coldly. 'Really, Mum, you're just imagining things. Joe just wants his own life.' And finally, 'The problems are all in your mind. You sort them out.' Then silence. And nothing since from any of them.

All that was over for Basila now. Daudi felt momentary relief that she was at peace, followed by the harsh realisation he must carry on alone.

A red warning light flashed on the panel in front of him. Its insistence irritated him and he slammed his hand across it.

Why, oh why, did Basila have to leave him just now? Suddenly he was angry with her, then sick at the thought of informing Rhiad. Would she be indifferent? Cut him off without listening? He didn't understand his own daughter anymore.

He was too tired to think. Brain dead.

The space-truck shrieked its alarm siren and he turned down the intrusive volume.

*Stardust*

He contacted space-link. When the girl at central control replied he panicked and logged off again without asking for a connection to Rhiad.

The red light continued to flash and an image of the space ship's exterior flickered across the screen, warning of structural problems. The old bus's hull had recently been covered with smart paint, and now when it vibrated excessively the resin coating flexed, generating electricity in its piezoelectric ceramic particles. So the warning light often malfunctioned, and Basila had covered it with an old rag when she was at the control.

Daudi picked up the rag.

Basila was standing behind him. He spun round, then realised she was not, never could be there again. The tiny space ship was as empty of her as the black hole at the heart of the Galaxy.

He must, he must inform Rhiad. What could he say?

The ship jolted violently and started spinning slowly. Lights were flashing all round him. Just like fireworks at Thanksgiving, he thought irrelevantly. Casually he fumbled with emergency controls and reactivated spaceguides, distance and speed checks, and finally the external monitors. And that was when he realised part of the left hand stub wing had sheered off. As he zoomed onto the damage he saw the complete hull billowing like the sluggish waves made by hunting crocodiles in Kenyan lagoons. The whole damn ship was starting to disintegrate. Adrenaline surged through his body, waking him at last to his danger.

Where in the universe was he?

Near the totally forbidden area of Galaxy Central Zone. No, not just near the most dangerous part of the Galaxy, but within the actual boundary. At the edge of the black hole where its massive jaws sucked in any fool-hardy molecules in range. His space ship was beginning to spiral. Soon it would contract into itself, crushing him in its frenzied spinning.

He was violently sick. Even as he coughed on the sour taste he speculated frantically on fluid dynamics and the complexity of black holes, cursing himself for rejecting refresher courses on space travel emergencies.

Hammers rained down on his head, his brain shrinking under the increasing pressures. Eventually his skull would disintegrate and mangle what was left. A heavy chill engulfed his chest, cold as outer space where Basila's stardust danced.

What use was his existence? This was as good an end as any to grief. He relaxed and let go his hold on life.

As he stared into death's darkness he saw the void was not empty. Little specks glided past, like motes in the eye's vitreous humour which gyrate out of focus across closed eyelids. Dust of eternity, without form, jiggling with the Brownian chaos of bluegreen bacteria under a microscope. He peered more closely. There was, after all, some shape to the particles' motion. He thought of a flock of pink flamingoes rising from their soda lake or gazelles bouncing away from danger in a liquid harmony of movement.

Lightheartedly, the particles danced together into a golden column, compacting into a human form with an intimate presence he couldn't name. The face was brighter than the sun so he dared not look at it, but he heard her voice – whether in his ears or his heart he couldn't say. 'Go back,' she said, 'go back.' Surely he knew her, but she was different now. Force and power flooded from her, pushing him roughly so that he began to spin again, rewinding himself out of darkness and into a place of nondescript blue and cream

*Stardust*

shapes. On a black screen stars were still spiralling but ever more slowly.

He was sick again, a slimy green vomit from his empty stomach all over the cushions of the ship's rest area. When he became fully conscious he forced himself to stagger to the controls. Earth style gravity had been restored and the ship was on autocontrol. He checked the left stub wing and found that the smart repairer had done its job as well as could be expected, closing the torn membranes and extruding an inelegant replacement wing, sufficient for landing.

He looked round the old ship, seeing it with his grandson's eyes. Yes, it was time both he and it retired. Joe was right to leave them. Remembering their final argument he was ashamed. He'd begin by apologizing to Rhiad.

He sighed deeply as he checked his position relative to Aldebaran. Amazingly he was in the precise area where he'd deposited Basila's remains. For a moment his mind veered away from remembering his loss, like a man unable to touch the stump of an amputation for fear of appalling pain. Then he realised he felt only sadness. Great sadness, but no longer despair.

Central control was calling him urgently.

'And where have you been?' The girl's voice was shrill with unusual fright.

'I think I slipped into Galaxy Central.'

'You sure did. Real panic here, man. Lost contact completely. How's Basila?'

He told her.

'Oh god, I'm sorry, Daudi. But you've had an awesome escape.'

*It's Never Too Late to Fall in Love*

'I don't know how I got away.'

'Black holes don't devour everything. Some of the gas molecules that get sucked into Galaxy Central distort the surrounding magnetic field. That disturbance releases matter further out. I guess a shower of stardust fell into oblivion while you were on the very edge. Merely a few grams of dust can dislodge a small spaceship like your old bus, so you were pushed away into safety. It's the nearest to a miracle I've heard of.'

'Sure. A miracle,' Daudi said as nonchalantly as possible. 'Get me Rhiad, will you?'

# Ménage à Troisième Age

### Stephanie Richards

Hello my dear friend,

How are you both? How is your newly retired other half managing with all his free time? And more importantly, how are you managing a newly retired other half with a lot of free time?

You have asked me to tell you what both of you being at home at the same time is going to be like. Well, let me share with you a few scenes from our life in a 'ménage à troisième age' . . .

I have to start with the fact that we are still married and still speaking to each other. Or should that be repeating things to each other. One of the most common phrases in this house these days is 'Did we have this conversation?' After 35 years you do tend to develop a special language with each other, only now it's not so much breaking conversational boundaries, more like going over the same ground in a louder voice.

Both of us being at home after years of being out at work is turning out to be, how can I put this, well let's just say there's the usual balance of pros and cons that come with a whole new lifestyle.

We definitely enjoy not having to get in a car and drive to work every day. I will never miss searching for a parking space each morning. It already seems a strange idea that we would kiss goodbye on the drive each morning, get into our cars and bingo! that was it for 'Couple Time' until the evening.

Right up there in my top five not working list is being able to do different things in the day, rather than work all week and have some variety only at weekends and evenings.

I embrace the bliss of empty shops, and the quieter roads. The pleasure of going food shopping in the day, rather than after work, is huge, although obviously this is a pleasure I have all to myself, as shopping trips are all hypothetical to men. The Lord and Master (hereafter referred to as L&M) did try and completely flummox me the other day by paying me his complete attention when I was talking to him. Scary stuff and a brave try, but I was not fooled by his apparent interest and readiness to become involved with a trip to go food shopping. Buying the paper and six bottles of wine do not a weeks shopping make, but at least the concepts of shopping trolley and automated checkout have been introduced to him. I have found myself changing the way I shop as well. Not just a ready meal snatch and grab bulk trip, but using shops in the village and buying fresh ingredients. I'm working on not caring how long it takes or how heavy it all is to carry or how much it costs. Can you believe how long it takes to prepare fresh peas from pod to table? Not to mention estimating what quantity you need. Frozen peas are much easier to use! Change like this can come as a bit of a shock when you have spent years whizzing a trolley round a superstore and then paying by credit card. Handing over cash

*Ménage à Troisième Age*

makes you realise what you are spending. I dare say that the exercise and fresh air from walking up and down the High Street is good for me and it sure beats doing a big shop on a Friday night after work.

I'm delighted to say that the 10 minute speed library trip is but a distant memory. I seem to have retained the job of book selection and delivery as one of my solo tasks. Not a problem as I do enjoy taking my time choosing the chick lit that I read almost exclusively these days (enough serious stories in real life). I also choose the L&M's thrillers and sci-fi stories. There should be a joke in there somewhere about thrilling aliens, but not just now. However he does read the books himself, so its not just about me.

The L&M is doing some consulting work from home so he is still a bit of an inbetweeny in the retirement stakes. But I feel sure that his attitude and outlook is already perfectly poised to embrace the 100% free time regime that he fondly imagines is awaiting him. My subtle, well not very subtle actually, hints as to how a shared domestic job load is a happy job load have so far been met with incomprehension or his favoured response of selective deafness and the nod and smile approach.

Yes, I know that a lot of this sounds like my mother talking, but that is one of the most strange and wondrous parts of all these days. I am turning into my mother whether I want to or not. Don't be shocked . . . but I now talk to people in shops . . . I know, I know, all those years when I would go 'OMG ma, why do you have to talk to everyone'. Now I do it. As for my handbag collection, well suffice it to say it has met and exceeded hers by some distance. But I am not the only one who has embraced the timelessness of acting like our parents did. As a woman you surely know that men have the ability to be mildly bewildered about a lot of things. . .

*It's Never Too Late to Fall in Love*

about how one minute it's all about driving the fastest car or drinking the most pints and how now, the prospect of a sit down on the sofa after dinner with the paper no longer is the sort of thing his father did, but a damn good idea. Mind you, I don't expect his pa drank red wine while he read the paper, but the rest of the analogy holds good.

The L&M has rediscovered making things. Some of which are quite useful. His bits of wood collection, has, as he always said it would, come in handy. There is much repair work undertaken (some finished) and several innovations around the house that are both useful and completed (do notice my use of irony there). Much more time is now allocated to football on TV than before. Hard to believe that there was more time available, not to mention more football to choose from, but there you go.

We both, and this is one of the few areas to which this applies, work well in the garden together. Albeit in different parts of the garden. I am constantly surprised by just how different the male/female approach to a job, any job, is. No, I shall resist the temptation of elaborating on that. Or pronouncing on who has the better approach of the two. You need some surprises to look forward to.

But back to the garden. Blackcurrants and gooseberries that I used to leave for the birds I now pick and cook . . . and we eat them! I prune roses, whether they need it or not. I have planted bulbs. Who knew that I would ever have the time or more importantly, the inclination, to do these things.

L&M has begun to use his garden power tool collection rather than just rearrange it in the shed and has so far not cut through the hedge trimmer flex again. His scorched earth pruning policy still holds sway. Following the lone success of his cutting a rose to ribbons last year only for it to bloom magnificently this year, I have held my tongue on that one. I

*Ménage à Troisième Age*

expect the space where the mallow was will soon fill up. But the periods of time that the lawn mower is actually mowing are becoming longer and the enforced dismantling time (after stones run out in front of the blades) is becoming shorter.

Living with a man all day and all night isn't necessarily hell, but it can seem like it. Living with one who believes that the fairies perform chores like changing the toilet roll is definitely a circle of hell, if not the core.

I know it's hard to believe in a rational man, (just reread that and yes, it is hard to believe in a rational man but you know what I mean); but at least he is consistent. The fairy mindset continues with the self making bed, items putting themselves into and removing themselves from the dishwasher; 'you mean you have to put a tablet in there?'. The fairies also make food appear in the fridge, frequently being thoughtful enough to bring enough food so that some can go in the freezer; ' the thing with the ice lollies in?'.

How foolish of me to think that it was enough to simply put a load of washing on when the fairies had filled the washing basket to the brim. Especially as they have always taken care to include the garment debris from the surrounding carpet that hadn't actually made it into the bin. Of course I now know that instead I should  focus on quantity, not quality (or colourfastness) by ensuring that the machine is filled to within an inch of its capacity . . . or should that be a millimetre . . . must go metric one day.

I'm informed by L&M that a full machine will save electricity, money and the planet.  Luckily the washing machine fairies are well versed in the sequence of events required to make the change from in dirty to out clean and the third portion of this magic trio, the putting away. Their comments on the saving electricity/money/ planet question have not been recorded.

*It's Never Too Late to Fall in Love*

Appeals to refill the sweetener dispenser nearly produced an attack of the vapours . . . his not mine, I hasten to add. And I'm disappointed to have to tell you that my master class on putting the sweetener in at the same time as the tea bag as the best way to A, not forget to do it and B, this will help you not to put two in, did not produce the rapt attention and follow through that I was expecting. Don't get me started on his ability to leave only one, the last, tissue in the box, cheekily peeping out just over the top (the tissue, not the L&M).

Obviously there are high spots. The sheer pleasure of sitting down to eat lunch together in the middle of the week is hard to beat. Think of all those working years when lunch meant sitting in the car for half an hour and eating a shop bought sandwich. Now I can even have an ice lolly for lunch if I feel really daring. So much more nutritious than a sandwich! No? You surprise me!

To balance the relaxed ambience of lunch together, only consider the advantages of me having my own time and motion expert on call 24/7. I was quite happy making it up as I went along, as I have done all our married life. And all our unmarried life as well for that matter. That hippy time in the 1970's . . . how long ago that seems. The not being married time. . . I still find it hard to say 'living together' or 'living in sin' as it was known then. Neither of us wanted our parents finding out about our joint address. But I expect they guessed. Now I'm old enough to realise that they weren't stupid, but we no doubt were, thinking they were, if you know what I mean. How much easier it is to be a rebel these days. All you have to do is smoke a cigarette or eat a lot of burgers. Neither activity was considered daring or living on the edge in the 1970's. Anyway. This isn't going to turn into a comparison of life in the 1970's and life now. We both know which era was best.

*Ménage à Troisième Age*

Our new way of life at home together can get fraught and claustrophobic and tense, but I suppose the old way of life did too.

Suffice it to say I had to explain after one clipped conversation recently that the wringing motion of my hands was not in fact tension, but hand cream.

If I were honest, I know that adjusting to being in captivity at home will take him time, just as it is taking me time.

So what is the darker side to this bucolic idyll for two? You know how we have always lived well together? How we endured the work/life balance being seriously tilted in favour of work whilst we were actually working and now the hope is to tilt it in favour of house and consultancy work with small w and life with a capital L. Unfortunately there are things you never discover or don't notice about your darling husband until you are elbow to elbow in the house all the time; rather than your quality time consisting of a fond farewell in the morning and sitting down to a meal together in the evening.

Don't worry, no habits on either side (I hope) that we can't cope with, but dear me, the honeymoon is supposed to be the period of revelation, but it is small beer compared to being ... how can I put this, 2 x 3rd-agers x 1 house x 24/7/365.

Possibly, and I doubt this very much, there may be a few, small habits of mine that could be construed as annoying or impractical or inefficient, BUT when set against the man of the house, well I wonder how the romance has lasted this long.

That IS meant as a joke. True romance is still loving the man you married 35 years ago when you are both at home all day.

Never mind the seven ages of man. What about the three ages of love and romance? Falling in love and getting married when you are young is lovely and it certainly felt a natural progression to being together, even in the heady days of the 1970's when it was so uncool to wear a suit, never mind being wed in a church. Then you have the working years, when for so long you are stressed mortgage paying ships that pass in the night. And when money isn't a problem, time is. So finally you reach what is now called the 3rd age. And, if you have been careful and lucky with the years that have gone before, you can enjoy the not working, not paying a mortgage and the being together times.

My conclusions to all this?

Simple.

Enjoy it.

Enjoy it each and every day.

Enjoy the time together.

Enjoy, as much as possible, your different ways of doing things.

Enjoy knowing you are always right.

Enjoy smiling while he enjoys knowing that he is always right.


And enjoy the peace and warmth and joy that being older, together and in love brings.


Love from us both. xxx

*Ménage à Troisième Age*

# Acknowledgements

Primarily I have to thank the judges who each read through more than twenty stories and rated every one according to their not inconsiderable experience as writers and teachers. I am particularly grateful to Maggie Smith (National Adviser for Creative Writing for the University of the Third Age/U3A) for her advice in setting up the competition and for her help in spreading the word to potential entrants. Francis Beckett, Editor of *U3A News*, has also been very helpful in this respect, as has Laura Wilkinson of *hagsharlotsheroines.com* (women writers) network who also helped with finding judges. We are also grateful to *gransnet.com* (and, again, with the help of Maggie Smith) for introducing their readers to the book.

Thanks to Mig for her patience as she persevered to get just the right image for the cover and to my son, Adam Norton, for his stunning sunset photo.

Finally, thanks to all those friends who's brains I have picked as I contemplated Third Age Press's first step into fiction.

*Dianne Norton, Managing Editor, Third Age Press*

# The Judges

### Mary Essinger-Rogers

My first novel, *Wounded Bird of Paradise*, was published when I was 68; nice things DO happen to older people. Note the semi colon; I do not use it enough. *In My Fashion*, about starting work in a dress factory came next followed by *How to be a Merry Widow* (published by Third Age Press) but I had to use my maiden name for that, didn't want men queuing up at the door wanting to marry me. My latest book is *Mary Writes Comedy*. It has just occurred to me that I have not written any fiction since I became a widow. I wonder why?

## Amanda Sington-Williams

Amanda is the author of *The Eloquence of Desire* published in 2010 by Sparkling Books. She won an award from The Royal Literary Fund whilst writing this novel. Her short stories have been published by Ether Books, Sentinel Literary Quarterly, Writing Raw, Bridge House Publishing and selected for readings at several literary events. Her poetry has also been read on BBC radio. She has an MA in Creative Writing and Authorship and teaches novel writing in Brighton. More information about her can be seen on her website: www.amandasingtonwilliams.co.uk

## Maggie Smith

The author of three books on Mid-life Career Change, for the past ten years Maggie has been National Adviser for Creative Writing for the University of the Third Age. She tutors at Summer Schools and study days and has compiled a handbook for U3A Writers Groups. Maggie recently had a story in Story Slam at Queen Elizabeth Hall as part of the Festival of Britain 60th Anniversary. She is attempting to make time for her own writing and intends to complete her memoirs while there is still time.

## Alan Wallace

Alan Wallace has a varied background in theatre. Three years ago, he joined the U3A Forest Hill Writers' Group, which produced *Deadline Thursday*, a collection of stories and verse by its members. His account of a trip to China is shortly to appear in another U3A anthology, this one devoted to travel writing.

# The Authors on The Authors

**Gwen Anderson** (*In Sickness and in Health*) I've been writing all my life and have written dozens of short stories and poems – some of which have been published locally. I belong to a writers' group – I paint and play bridge. I'm 85 but certainly don't feel it! One of my poems has been read on the radio.

**Paul Chiswick** (*Lightning Never Strikes Twice*) was born in 1951. Following two successful careers in Civil Engineering and IT Sales, he is now semi-retired, filling most of his time by writing. He lives with his wife in a north Warwickshire village. You can read more about him and his writing by visiting his website www.paulchiswick.com

**Jean Dorricott** (*Stardust*) spent her early years on a farm in North Wales and studied agriculture. She worked on different farms, then taught immigrants in Birmingham where she met her husband. Three children, numerous foster children, teaching in special education followed, along with published short stories, a novel and a non-fiction book.

**Margaret Foggo** (*The Last Verse*) I am 85 years old and expect I am the oldest contributor to this anthology. I have been writing for about six or seven years with the very minimum of success but I enjoy it enormously together with reading, gardening and long lingering lunches with friends.

**Carol Homer** (*Stranger Love*) I have always been interested in the arts – writing, drawing, crafts. A voracious reader from infancy, I am not fussy abiout great literature. I'll read most things. Give me a good story and I'm happy. When I can't find something I want to read, I write it myself.

Born in Carlisle in 1949, **Brenda Jackson** (*An Estate of the Heart*) lived in Cyprus for much of her childhood. Working in Australia she spent time in the outback and on Lord Howe Island; feeling lucky to have experienced the Short/ Sunderland flying boats. After a year in USA she now resides in North Yorkshire.

After a dissolute twenties, octogenarian **Peter Johnson** (*Life Class*) entered London book publishing, his career for several years. On retirement, he ran an art gallery while painting and drawing himself. He published a novel, *Making Waves,* (Macmillan) and art books (Search Press) and articles in several magazines. He lives in Hadleigh, Suffolk.

**Margaret Kitchen** (*A Good Sense of Humour*) is a former journalist who likes writing and reading short stories. She is an active member of Aughton and Ormskirk U3A in Lancashire, enjoying learning, socialising and chairing the publicity committee. Now the baby boomers are retiring she hopes to see more 'Third Age' fiction being published.

**Ed Lane** (*Life Without Grace*) I've been a soldier, a graphic designer and now a writer. My first novel *A Circling of Vultures* is on Amazon with profits going to 'Help for Heroes'. The second *Terrible Beauty* will be out in October 2011.

I live in Lincolnshire with my wife, Barb, and Airedale Terrier, Cooper.

**Gill Lazar** (*Second Time Around*) Marrying a Freedom Fighter from the Hungarian Revolution seemed romantic, reckless Mother thought. Forty-odd years brought happiness, a beautiful family, an OU Degree – but unfulfilling work. After having articles published, in 2009, I joined a WEA Creative Writing course and U3A Groups. This is my first published short story.

**Denis Marsden** (*Collectability*) I am a 69 year old (could pass for 67) retired tea sales man. I enjoy writing with the Doncaster U3A writers group, it's great fun. My fear is this could make me famous, I could become big headed, young girls will flock to me, I might, you never know, run off with a pop star. My wife (Julia) after of 48 years married doesn't seem bothered by this possibility!

**Norma Murray** (*A Cat About the House*) An early career in teaching, and the demands of a busy family life, left Norma Murray little time to write creatively. Only a chance encounter with an online writing group and the enthusiastic reception her work received from other bloggers, led her back to her first love, writing stories.

**Cedric Parcell** (*How Little Time*) a Yorkshire man now living in Sutton Coldfield served throughout the war in the RAF, mostly in Egypt. As a civil servant after the war he worked for number of years with the Commonwealth Office in Kenya, Malawi and Bermuda. He joined the local U3A. in 2001 tutoring courses in family history and creative writing and editing the house magazine 'Sage'. He has written a number of books including two recent novels.

**Malcolm Peake** (*Rendezvous*) Since retiring I've spent a lot of time writing stories and taking photographs. In respect of the latter I've had a number of photographs published/exhibited. *Rendezvous* however, is the first short story to be published – others have made it to the 'short list' in competitions.

**Stephanie Richards** (*Ménage à Troisième Age*) I spent my working life surrounded by students, computers and concrete. Now I live with my husband in a country cottage in Sussex. At last I have the time to learn French grammar properly (thank you U3A) and to visit France as often as possible to practice my new skills.

**Heather Shaw** (*Predictive Text*) Reaching the Third Age gave me a wonderful chance to concentrate on what had been an occasional hobby – writing fiction; U3A offered the challenge, and support, of meeting other writers locally; the online Short Story Course, first as a student and then, for a time as a tutor, provided stimulation.

**Patricia Stoner** (*The Secret Life of Madeline Greatorex*) ives with her husband in West Sussex. They have a Brittany Spaniel called Purdey and a collection of Land Rovers, some of which work.

**Jane Walker** (*Spot On*) lives in Somerset and is a member of Street and Glastonbury U3A. After retiring from a career as a Maths Teacher, she joined a creative writing group and has enjoyed writing poems and short stories. Other interests include sun dials and campanology, so a story set in a church tower seemed a good idea.

**Denise West** (*Dancing Round the Med*) I have lived all of my life in Sheffield and would describe myself as a 'city girl'. Now in my third age with five grandchildren I still love rock and blues music, the theatre, cinema and art. As an avid reader I have always loved words but lately writing for my U3A group has opened up a new world to me. I find it liberating to shape other people's lives for a while.

**Sue Wilson** (*Copperplate*) joined Three Brethren U3A in Galashiels two years ago so that she could play in the handbell ringing group. Music and creative writing have always been important to her. She is a pianist and church organist who writes stories, poetry and songs just for her own entertainment.

# THIRD AGE PRESS

... an independent publishing company which recognizes that the period of life after full-time employment and family responsibility can be a time of fulfilment and continuing development ... a time of regeneration

**Third Age Press books are available by direct mail order from** Third Age Press, 6 Parkside Gardens  London SW19 5EY **or on order through book shops or from Amazon UK**
dnort@globalnet.co.uk     www.thirdagepress.co.uk

Please add 20% for UK postage or contact us for postage to other countries. UK Sterling cheques payable to *Third Age Press*, please.

 ... is a series (by Eric Midwinter) that focuses on the presentation of your unique life. These booklets seek to stimulate and guide your thoughts and words in what is acknowledged to be not only a process of value to future generations but also a personally beneficial exercise.

*A Voyage of Rediscovery: a guide to writing your life story*
   ... is a 'sea chart' to guide your reminiscence & provide practical advice about the business of writing or recording your story.
**36 pages        £4.50**

*Encore: a guide to planning a celebration of your life*
An unusual and useful booklet that encourages you to think about the ways you would like to be remembered, hopefully in the distant future.    **20 pages        £2.00**

*The Rhubarb People* ... Eric Midwinter's own witty and poignant story of growing up in Manchester in the 1930s. Also on tape including useful tips on writing or recording your story.
   **32 pages     £4.50     OR     audio cassette     £5.00**
         **OR all 3 booklets for only £10**

See our full publication list on www.thirdagepress.co.uk
         Send SAE for catalogue

# Defining Women
## ... on mature reflection

160 pages 248mm x 178mm £12.50
Edited by Dianne Norton
illustrated by Mig

The 'extraordinary ordinary women' invited to contribute to this anthology rose magnificently to the occasion, delving deep into their personal experiences and laying bare their innermost feelings as they met a variety of challenges. Gwen Parrish, U3A News

# How to be a Merry Widow
**life after death for the older lady**
by Mary Rogers   Illustrated by Mig

166 pages £12.50

• *If you are looking for a politically correct, objective view of how to cope with bereavement – do NOT buy this book!*

• *This is a book about coming to terms with widowhood after the shock of bereavement has begun to ease.*

• *Mary Rogers writes with candour and humour, in a deeply personal style. She manages to be funny, moving and at the same time, practical.*

*Our Grandmothers, Our Mothers, Ourselves*
*~ a century of women's lives* ... an anthology compiled by a U3A women's group  200 pages  £8.00

## On the Tip of Your Tongue: your memory in later life

by Dr H B Gibson . . . explores memory's history and examines what an 'ordinary' person can expect of their memory. He reveals the truth behind myths about memory and demonstrates how you can manage your large stock of memories and your life. Wittily illustrated by Rufus Segar.   **160 pages**   **£7.00**

### AND

## A Little of What You Fancy Does You Good: your health in later life

'Managing an older body is like running a very old car – as the years go by you get to know its tricks and how to get the best out of it, so that you may keep it running sweetly for years and years' . . . so says Dr H B Gibson in his sensible and practical book which respects your intelligence and, above all, appreciates the need to enjoy later life. It explains the whys, hows and wherefores of exercise, diet and sex ~ discusses 'You and your doctor' and deals with some of the pitfalls and disabilities of later life.  Illustrated by Rufus Segar.   **256 pages**   **£7.00**

**Buy both the above books
for the special price of only £10.00**

---

### Talking to My Gran About Dying   by Gina Levete

A book for young & old people ~ to stimulate discussion, share thoughts, ideas and anxieties to do with death.

**64 pages illustrated by Philip Jordan
£7.50 + postage**

## NOVEL APPROACHES: a guide to the popular classic novel   by Eric Midwinter

Oh for a good read and an un-putdownable book! Despite the lurid blandishments of television, there are still many of us who turn, quietly, pensively, to the novel in leisure moments.  This short text is aimed at such people whose interest has been kindled sufficiently to permit some extra contemplation and study.

***Novel Approaches*** takes 35 novels that have stood the test of time and embeds them in historical and literary commentary – a combination of social background giving scientific objectivity, and the author's artistic subjectivity.
**180 pages    £9.50**

---

*Two collections of one-act plays, written by third-agers, ideal for reading in groups, rehearsed readings or performance.  Their rich variety is certain to challenge and stimulate as well as provide entertainment.*

### The Play Reader:
### 7 dramas by thirdagers

1st published in 1995. Now available in A4 format, hole punched (binder not included ~ may be photocopied).
126 pages   £10.00

### The Play Reader2008:
### 7 more dramas by thirdagers

Available as an A4 hole-punched version (may be copied) - containing a PDF of 7 printable plays + CD to print from.
159 pages   £10.00

## Three enlightening & entertaining books
## by Eric Midwinter

### THE PEOPLE'S JESTERS
### Twentieth Century British Comedians

At one level, *The People's Jesters* is an absorbing exercise in nostalgia, with its perceptive and amusing profiles of scores of well-loved and well-remembered comics. Beyond that, it is an astute and definitive analysis of how comedians worked. With its combine of colourful content and shrewd comment, there are rich pickings here for all manner of readers.

**232 pages  248mm x 178mm  £12.50**

### BEST REMEMBERED: A hundred stars of yesteryear

. . . presents a galaxy of 100 stars from the days before television ruled our lives - an era rich in talent, innovation, humour and unforgettable melodies. These cultural icons achieved lasting fame through radio, cinema, stage, dance hall, theatre, variety hall and sporting fields. . Whether **Best Remembered** is used as a trigger for personal or group reminiscence or read as a rich but light scholarly text on our social and cultural history,  its lively style and fizzing illustrations cannot fail to please.

**168 pages  248mm x 178mm  £12.50**

### I SAY, I SAY, I SAY  The Double Act Story

Eric Midwinter cheerfully answers many questions about the rise and the fall of the double act and analyses the effects of television and other social dimensions on popular entertainment by way of explanation. Knowledgeable and readable, *I Say* is an attractively presented account of a significant element of popular entertainment over the last 100 years.

**154 pages  210mm x 148mm  £9.50**